The
MALA BEADS

Massachusetts

First Edition March 2024

10 9 8 7 6 5 4 3 2 1

ISBN: 978-1-7350592-0-4

This book is dedicated to Susi.
Everyone needs a friend who believes in miracles.

The MALA BEADS

A Novel of Hope and Discovery in a time of Chaos

Kathy Aspden

Why The MALA BEADS?

It was March of 2020 and the pandemic was in full swing. My retired respiratory therapist husband (a lovely, bearded, seventy-two-year-old man) had decided to dive back into hospital work to care for COVID-19 patients. His method of discussing this potentially life-ending decision was to send me a picture of his clean-shaven face (which I had not seen in years) explaining facial hair is a no-no when it comes to ensuring a tight fit for a respirator mask. Soon my entryway looked like a hazmat landing area. Laundry baskets for discarded hospital clothing, ultraviolet sanitizing box, ninety-nine-percent alcohol bottles everywhere—and me, virtually obliterating his third eye chakra with my incessant use of the infrared forehead thermometer.

I was already at the edge of my sanity when our daughter, Sara, contracted the virus. She was eight months pregnant with her second child. The breathing treatments, missed obstetric appointments, and torn rib cartilage from the coughing were difficult to watch from a distance. Not to mention the uncertainty of what this virus might be doing to her unborn baby. Sara tested positive right up until the day she delivered and was inconsolable when told she might not be able to take her daughter home with her after the birth.

Add to this, all the things every human on Earth was experiencing—deaths, riots, destruction, insecurity, societal chaos. It was too much. I wasn't eating or sleeping.

Enter the mala beads.

The mala bead necklace was a gift from my friend, Susi Bertini, who had brought them home from the Ekam Temple, in India, where they had been blessed by a holy man. One hundred and eight beads strung together and tied with a tassel, each bead used to count an intention—a prayer to the divine. Unlike Catholic rosary beads, there were no specific prayers to be recited so I began with a simple mantra (affirmation, wish), *I am happy. I am healthy. I am loved.* Whenever fear and doubt crept into my mind I found a quiet place, held my mala beads, and with a few deep breaths, chanted my mantra. The calming effects were immediate. I started focusing on the positive. The world around me became less of a fearful place, and I felt connected to something bigger than myself. My mantras varied over time, always positive and stated as if I had already received the blessings I was searching for. I began to imagine this gift for everyone and wrote a simple tale of need, which grew into *The Mala Beads*.

*

The Mala Beads is about human frailty and the enduring strength that can only come from a force greater than we know. I hope each character's journey will provide something meaningful to your own life's journey.

*

Researching a multicultural novel like *The Mala Beads* requires the help of many. I want to thank everyone who answered my questions by email, telephone, Zoom, or in person. Putting myself in the shoes of people from varied cultures, environments, and beliefs was both a challenge and my privilege. I pray I did justice to their stories and beg forgiveness for details that may have missed their mark. *The Mala Beads* was written with an open heart and the best of intentions. Thank you, also, to my family, friends, and beta readers. I couldn't have written this book without you.

India, 2019

THE BEADS

the beginning

After five years of contemplation, the sign came to him in the form of a brilliant morning sun whose rays were a startling shade of deep blue. In the center of his pineal gland, the third eye, an intense pain burst forth the words "yah ab hai." *It is now*. Without fanfare, the guru walked the short distance from the hillside into the sacred chamber of the cave. Needing nothing but the fire within his heart, he pulled the sandalwood mala beads from his robe and settled in lotus posture for prayer. Soon the unending chant, *om satyam narayanam*, echoed through the cavern's dark crevices in deep, melodic measure.

By the fifth day, he could feel sacred energy incarnating into the beads, creating a bond between himself, the wood, and the supreme consciousness of all that is. At midnight of the seventh day, a golden blue orb entered the cave—a signal that it was done. The guru stopped chanting and placed the beads in a lotus dish. Tomorrow he would prepare them for their journey to North America. For now, he would sleep.

United States, 2020

CHAPTER 1 ~ CLAIRE

Cape Cod, Massachusetts

Walking the rocky beach in the cold March wind was no longer her thing. At 58 years old, Claire was done being uncomfortable. "I'm going for a walk on the beach" had become code for "I'm taking a car nap at the beach parking lot." At the moment, reclined in her SUV's sunbaked driver's seat with a rolled sweater tucked under the small of her back, Claire felt *very* comfortable—until a loud rap on the driver's side window pulled her from sleep's edge to startled consciousness.

Her first thought was relief that the man was wearing a mask. She dreaded mask conversations but sure as hell wouldn't expose herself at this point. She began to roll down the window, chuckling about the absurd, circular, charades-like motion people still make for a push-button window—and then it registered that the roll-down-the-window gesture had been orchestrated using a handgun. Somehow her mind couldn't put a stamp on the moment. *Normal? Not normal?* She snapped to fully awake. This was not normal.

"Open the window." Although not a threatening shout, it was still a command. Claire pushed the button to raise her seat, then opened the window.

"Give me your purse." The gun barrel gestured toward the pocketbook lying unzipped on the passenger seat. Claire turned toward the purse. It was filled with crap, stuff she needed and stuff she didn't. She turned to look straight ahead at the beach. The ocean was calm, the wind had died down. A walk would have been nice.

"I have about eighty dollars—maybe a little more. I would love it if you would let me keep my bag and other stuff. I just got my license renewed and you know what a pain that is—especially now, with the pandemic and this whole extra level of identification …" Her words dwindled as her mind calmly went through what she had just said. *I would love it?* Claire couldn't make sense of her lack of fear. Maybe it was the gun. It looked antique, like a movie prop from the Wild West. She slowly turned her head to the left and took a good look at the gunman—the way they tell you not to.

The guy appeared to be in his thirties, her son Matty's age. His eyes were a striking mix of gold, green, and brown. His skin was beautiful, a slight gloss on his forehead. A month ago she would have worried he carried the virus. Not now. His was fear-sweating. Claire had done enough of it these last few weeks to know what it looked like. She could imagine the man's clamped jaw under his mask, microscopic fragments of tooth enamel being ground away by the clenching. She smiled to make him feel better. That's when she realized *her* face was naked.

"Oh hey, let me put on my mask. No sense my getting you sick." She pivoted to her purse.

"You better not have a gun in that bag!"

"No. I understand how this works. You have the gun, and I have some money—which I will happily give you if you'll let me." *Why did I use the word happily? Why not gladly?*

"Your mask is hanging on the rearview mirror," the man said, helpfully.

"That's my husband's. I guess at this point, what's the difference?" Claire flushed as she spoke, thinking about the DNA she and her husband, Joe, had finally swapped that morning. She put the mask on and adjusted the sidebands to fit her small face. Her own mask had been purchased in the children's department of Target. After a satisfied glance in the rearview mirror, she turned to look at him.

"Okay. So what do ya think? Can I just get the money out of my bag and give it to you?"

He seemed hesitant, as though he might run off. Where would he go? There were no other cars in the small parking lot. The seclusion was what Claire liked about this beach. It was technically public but rarely used. She decided he must have come through the path leading to the summer houses on Windy Beach Road. It was pointless for him to flee now. The damage was already done—her nap had been ruined.

"Either way I'm giving you the money," she continued. "Whether you let me rifle—*another bad word choice*—through this disgusting pocketbook of mine or you make me miserable by taking the whole thing, the money is yours. I, at least, want to take out the only picture I have of my great-grandmother. It was in a locket I gave to my daughter. I shoved the picture in my wallet, behind my license. It's really hard to get it out. Actually, my license is kind of impossible to pull outta that slot. I don't know why they make you take it out, anyway, it's sitting behind clear plastic—"

"How old is your daughter?"

"Why?"

"I hope she's old enough to take care of a gift like that—not lose it."

"She is. I'm older than I look."

"You look like you're in your late fifties," he said.

"Okay. Enough chit-chat. How are we doing this if I'm not gonna give up my purse?"

"How about if you hand me the bag, I'll go through it to get the money, then give it back?"

He looked earnest—like he was trying to work with her on this. Claire almost hated to let him down with the flaws in his plan.

"That won't work. If someone comes you'll take the purse and run. Besides, how are you going to search through it, hold your gun, and watch to make sure I don't call the police? I'm not gonna call the police."

"Where's your phone?"

Claire unplugged the iPhone from its charger and held it up.

"Throw it out the window," he ordered.

"Can't I just hand it to you? My phone case isn't that great—it's more for looks—and I didn't put that glass thingy on the front because I have a hard time texting as it is. Although my husband insists it doesn't really affect the performance—"

"Jesus. Just give it to me."

The masked robber took the phone from her and placed it on the bench behind him. Then he looked at her as if he were waiting for her to come up with their next move. So she did.

"How about if you come around to the other side of the car? I'll roll down the passenger window and dump my bag out on the seat. That way you can keep the gun on me while I go through everything"

"Okay. But don't do anything stupid."

"Oh, I'm pretty sure that ship has sailed," Claire replied, wondering if she meant on his part or hers.

The man walked around the front of the car, tripping on the cement curbing and momentarily falling from sight. She sat up taller to see if he was okay. In seconds he popped up and appeared at the passenger window, again making the archaic roll-down-the-window gesture. The hood of his canvas work coat had slipped back a bit to reveal a mass of dark hair, some of it in braids. He pulled the hood tighter while Claire pushed the button. The passenger window opened, causing a wind tunnel to surge through the car. In hurried panic, she tried to shut the driver's window and instead opened the window behind her. This was classic "Claire" and not behavior brought on by being held up at gunpoint. Then the left rear window went down.

"You're pressing the wrong buttons!" Master of the obvious, the purse-snatcher sounded like her husband.

"Don't you think I know that?" Claire retorted like a wife, then expertly hit the correct buttons to absolve herself of her flightiness. She took a deep breath, looked in the rearview mirror, and fixed her disheveled hair, suddenly hating that she had let her gray roots grow in. *No wonder he thinks I'm almost sixty.*

"We should hurry this up before anyone comes," the man said, again very husbandly.

"Right. Although these days no one gets close enough to see what's really going on in anyone's life." Claire wished she could take a minute to write that down. It was a rather profound thought. "You ready for this? It's pretty bad." She dumped the contents of her purse onto the passenger seat, then dug through all the zippered compartments and emptied those as well. She mentally made a plan to grab a grocery bag from the back of the SUV to organize the mess once this robbery was over.

Claire began compiling her money, first gathering the loose ones and fives thrown in most recently. She then went through the receipts, pulling out money that had been folded into them. Seeing the Job Lot receipt reminded her she wanted to buy birdseed later. The money was piling up, and she hadn't yet opened her wallet.

"I seriously need to be more organized. I've had a lot going on these last couple months. My husband was in the hospital with Covid." She felt her accoster back away. "Oh don't worry. He's not positive now. And I've been tested again recently. You're safe." Assuring the safety of everyone around her had become a daily thing. She finally got to the wallet. There was fifty-eight dollars in the compartment where all the money should have been.

"Ma'am, you don't need to count it. Just give it to me."

"It'll just take a second." Claire continued to count the stash without looking up. "One-hundred-and-eight dollars. Wait! I haven't checked my tuckies! I always have emergency money in a hidden slot in my wallet." Claire dug her fingers into the tight pocket attached to the billfold and pulled out two one-hundred-dollar bills. "You're in luck!" She unfolded the bills and put them on the pile, then surveyed the disaster that was her pocketbook. So many receipts—she didn't remember going to that many stores. And used napkins, hand sanitizer, her child-size mask, and a week's worth of mail. There was a book she meant to give to her mother, along with her inhaler, the checkbook with the overdue cable bill sticking out of it, a half-eaten bag of Oreo cookies—and the magic mala beads!

The mala bead necklace was in the same gauze drawstring bag as when Susi gave it to her the day her husband was admitted to the hospital, the printed instructions rolled tube-like inside. It was time to part with it. She picked up the little satchel and placed it on top of the money in her hand.

"Three hundred and eight dollars. I will give it all to you, no questions asked, if you take these mala beads and promise to use them. Follow the instructions inside the bag. Do it *exactly* as it says."

"Lady, you're crazy. I have a gun. You don't have a choice."

"Everyone has a choice. I choose to believe you won't shoot me and that you'll honor my wishes. In exchange, I won't contact the police." Claire stuffed the money and the mala beads into a crumpled bank envelope and handed it through the window to the gunman.

"Namaste," she said softly, as she rolled up the window. The man fled down the beach path. Claire finished her nap.

March 26, 2020

CHAPTER 2 ~ NATE

Hyannis, Massachusetts

Nate ran up the stairs at a gallop. By the time he reached the apartment, he was a mess. He had just robbed a woman at gunpoint. He took a couple of deep breaths to slow his heart, then put the key in the lock and turned it. The door swung open before he had a chance to pull it.

"Hey. Glad you're back. I was just gonna wake the baby up to go to the laundromat. Now I don't have to."

His wife, Kelly, looked like a vision. This second pregnancy had only enhanced the natural beauty Nate had fallen in love with. At eight months along, she was still a ball of energy—probably from running after their two-year-old son.

"Nate? You look horrible. Babe, you okay?" She backed away as she spoke. Nate pulled a lie from the air like a guy embracing a newfound skill.

"I'm so out of shape. I'm never taking the elevator again—just ran the stairs for exercise." His wife touched his cheek in a loving gesture, though they both knew it was a temperature check.

"Well, that's a weird resolution considering the elevator's been broken the whole time we've lived here. So, you good if I go to the laundromat?"

No. I'm not good. I'll never be good again. "Sure. I'm gonna run to the bathroom, then I'll bring the laundry down to the car."

"Sounds like a plan."

His wife moved aside so he could pass. He felt the gun handle brush across her pregnant stomach through their clothes. "I'll only be a sec." He sprinted for the bathroom.

*

Nate sat on the toilet, his head cradled in his hands. The gun rested on the laminate sink-edge, right beside the spot where a previous tenant's burning cigarette had lingered too long. He felt a complex mixture of fully revved and paralyzingly weak. His legs were tingling, with numbness in his hands and feet. He stood part way up and pulled the two bullets from his pants pocket. *Two bullets.* For what he had planned, one would have been sufficient.

Suicide wasn't his first choice. His first choice was to support his family, have a second baby, and buy a house of their own. On Cape Cod, you could make good money tending bar and playing in a band. They were two careers that fed each other. The band made you notorious, which elevated your bartending status—which elevated your tips. Customers would follow you from club to club to hear you play and be part of the glory of it all. After six years, Nate had quite a following. Winters were always hard, but between his jobs and Kelly's waitressing, they made it work. He had already begun the class for The Wampanoag Tribe's first-time homebuyer down payment program. It was a solid plan. A pandemic shutdown wasn't anywhere on it. *Neither is the shame of a criminal record.*

Nate pulled his cell phone from the pocket of his Carhartt jacket lying on the floor at his feet. Eleven-forty-five. Not even lunchtime and he had managed to find his grandfather's gun, talk himself into pawning it, fall into an abyss of depression, and consider suicide. *What an asshole*. He was already half-past rational when he got to the beach. Just one car in the lot—a car he thought was empty. He could get the job of killing himself done before its owner returned. Two bullets. As though if you missed the vital part of your brain with the first bullet you could use the second one as a backup. *What an asshole*. Then he saw the open purse sitting on the seat with money scattered on top like an invitation. It would have been so easy if the car door hadn't been locked. Grab the bag and run …

"I'm gonna drag the laundry down myself!" Kelly's voice broke through the bathroom door and his thoughts.

"No," he replied in a surprisingly normal voice. "I'll be out in a minute. I need to talk to you about something before you go." Silence. Nate got up, flushed the toilet for effect, and ran water while he put the gun and bullets on the top shelf of the bathroom closet. He reached into the back pocket of his pants and pulled out the bank envelope. The lady's little gauze bag was visible on top of the money. Nate stuffed it into his front pocket—where the gun had been—and headed out of the bathroom. Kelly met him at the end of the hall, lugging two big laundry bags.

"Is that the bathroom water running? What's going on with you?" She squeezed past him and shut off the tap. He pushed the envelope at her.

"I borrowed some money."

"From who?" she asked, as she opened the envelope and began counting.

"A customer—from the bar."

"Nate, that's not a good idea. We can't start owing money to everyone."

"It's okay. We don't have to pay it back any time soon—he actually said we don't have to pay it back at all, but I said of course we do …"

"This is three-hundred-and-eight dollars!"

"Yeah. He gave me everything he had on him. That's how well off he is, he didn't even know how much money was in his pocket. Don't use it toward the rent. They can't evict us during a pandemic. Buy groceries—and a couple tubs of formula in case the breastfeeding thing doesn't work out."

Kelly grabbed him by the shirt and pulled him tightly against her—their baby not a weighty obstacle.

"I love you, Nate. You've always got our back."

Nate kissed her head and held her until she signaled the hug was over. He was usually the first to end a hug. Not today. He could have held on to her for the rest of his life. He grabbed the bags of laundry and headed for the three flights of stairs and the long walk to the residential parking lot, thinking about how close he had come to losing it all. *What an asshole.*

*

The paper was yellowed and crinkled, with what looked like a spaghetti sauce stain across the top. The edges had that fuzzy quality that paper gets when handled a lot. Nate let it curl back up while he checked out the beaded necklace.

The beads were made of polished wooden balls strung together with twine like the kind a baker uses to tie up a cake box, except it was red. There was a red tassel secured to the necklace with another wooden bead, and knots tied between each bead like on a good string of pearls. Nate had seen these before. Sometimes the summer girls who came to the gigs had them wrapped around their wrists or worn as necklaces. Hippie jewelry. He unrolled the paper again, smoothed it flat, and read:

This japa mala holds ancient and powerful Sanskrit energy used to manifest miracles.

To manifest your miracle you must follow these instructions precisely while keeping an open heart.

Sit in a meditative posture with your eyes closed.

Breathe in deeply, exhale slowly. Do this seven times while envisioning your intention.

Say your intention aloud, then begin the mantra.

You will chant OM SATYAM NARAYANAM 108 times using the mala beads to count—one bead for each incantation.

When you have completed this mantra, your miracle will come. Be patient.

Once your intention has been realized you will pass this sacred energy to the next person in need.

~Namaste

Nate read it twice. "This is freaking nuts," he muttered to himself. But he had robbed the woman at gunpoint—granted, the chamber of the gun had been empty, but she didn't know that. This was the least he owed her. The *very* least.

Om satyam narayanam. How the hell am I gonna remember that? He wrote the words, separated by syllables, on the back of a medical bill, making a mental note to send the hospital another five-dollar payment to keep the bill from going to collections. He looked at the clock on the kitchen stove—twelve thirty-five. How long would Taylor stay asleep? How long does it take to chant a Sanskrit mantra one hundred and eight times? *How long before we get kicked out of this apartment?* Nate went to the living room and pushed the coffee table aside so he could sit on the rug and lean against the couch. He crossed his legs in front of him, noticing the beach sand still clinging to his jeans.

With the paper in his lap, he practiced the words a couple of times for pronunciation. He just wanted to get this done without messing up. Then he picked up the beads and held them loosely with both hands the way he had seen Kelly's grandmother hold her black rosary beads, touching the bead to the left of the tassel. He took seven slow, deep breaths. Without having to analyze it, Nate stated his intention: "Just let me support my family." He began the chant. Before long, the words sounded natural. They rolled off his tongue and vibrated through his lips like the lyrics to an old Beatles song. Eventually, he closed his eyes and let the mantra fill his mind. The beads felt smooth and familiar, comforting, his left hand readying each bead for the right to count ...

*

Nate opened his eyes. He could see the microwave clock from where he was seated and was surprised that only fifteen minutes had passed. He sat with what he had just done, feeling calmer than at any point in the last month. His ringing cell phone jolted him back to reality.

The number wasn't familiar. An immediate stomach pit formed at the thought of the woman somehow tracking him down, or worse—the police. He didn't have to answer, but he did.

"Hello?"

"Is this Nate Silver?" the voice on the other end asked.

"Yes," Nate answered, certain he was about to pay for this morning's crime.

"This is Eddie Marco. I don't know if you remember me, your band opened for us a couple of years ago at the Melody Tent."

"Yeah! Of course I remember you, man. That night was amazing." Relief flooded Nate's body.

"I know it's last minute, but we're scheduled to record an album next month in Boston, and our sax player, Ben, had to go to Florida to take care of his dad. I remembered how good you are, and you got the right vibe. It's a lot—you'd have to learn a dozen songs in less than a month. The money's not great—three thousand up front—but you'd get a piece of the profit if things go well."

For a brief second Nate thought about Kelly, ready to deliver in a few weeks, and the logistics of taking care of Taylor when she did. Then his mind flashed to the gun, and his laugh was loud and spontaneous. "Will I need a lawyer to figure out the royalty stuff?"

"Up to you," Eddie responded, no offense in his voice. "We plan to just throw your name into the contract instead of Ben's—plus you'll get the extra three thousand."

"I'm in."

"Great! Our manager will call you tonight. Thanks, Nate. You're saving our ass." Eddie hung up before Nate could say another word, which was perfect since he was on his knees crying into both hands—the one holding his phone, and the other still clutching the mala beads.

*

A toddler's cry broke through the swirling thoughts in Nate's head. *What just happened?* His mind shot through the day's events at warp speed. He couldn't wait to tell Kelly about the miracle, but how? *"I got these beads from a lady I was robbing at the beach when I went down there to kill myself with the gun I initially planned to pawn ... "* Maybe a story for another day. For now, he put the scroll and the beads back in the gauze satchel and tucked it into a gift bag left over from his son's second birthday.

Taylor was winding up, ready to be freed from his crib. Nate bolted toward his cries. It wasn't that his son needed immediate attention—he would have eventually busied himself with the fish stickers on his ceiling—it was that his room abutted the apartment next door and the walls were thin. No sense riling anybody up, especially *those* neighbors. The couple, Lori and Duane, had seemed okay when they moved in. Months later, their apartment noises told a different story. The guy clearly had a quick fuse that his wife was getting the short end of. Nate thought about the necklace. Maybe he could give it to her. It would have to be anonymous. There was no sense further connecting himself to the robbery or his neighbor's troubles.

Nate opened his son's bedroom door. Taylor's outstretched arms and wide, drooly smile pushed away every thought but one, *What an asshole. I almost lost it all.*

*

The following morning, after he heard the husband leave for work, Nate tip-toed down the hall and hung the birthday bag over the couple's doorknob, giving their door three quick raps. "Good luck," he whispered, then scurried back to his apartment where he would play with his son and wait for FedEx to drop off a packet of songs for him to learn. *Namaste, beach lady.*

March 27, 2020

CHAPTER 3 ~ LORI

Hyannis, Massachusetts

Washing dishes was calming—the warm water, the suds. Sometimes Lori closed her eyes and imagined she was in her childhood home. Her mother always bought the same kind of sponges. They started out hard yellow and eventually became squishy mush, able to glide like silk over the surface of a plate or squeeze into the smallest opening of a glass or canning jar. Instead of the windowless wall of the apartment, Lori pretended she was looking through her mother's kitchen window at the scruffy backyard filled with old finds, a result of having two parents who embraced the notion that somebody else's trash was their treasure. Old worn benches and yard statues created the texture. Birdhouses, hanging lanterns, and wind chimes adorned the limbs of every tree. In her remembered vision, Lori saw the beauty she had been unable to see while living there. Back then, all she wanted was to get herself to a perfect house with a manicured front lawn. That's what Duane had promised her—a perfect little life.

Even without the benefit of a good therapist, Lori now saw the warning signs she had intentionally ignored. Duane was controlling—she had twisted that trait to mean he only wanted what was best for her. He separated her from friends and family—it was flattering to know he needed her all to himself. He was exciting, adventurous, and risky in the bedroom …

His latest go-to move—choke her until she was lifeless, then slap her into consciousness—was the thing that scared her the most. What started as sexual play was no longer playful. Lori was terrified of her husband.

Today was Friday, the most terrifying day of the week. Duane hated his job. By the time the weekend came, he was a mix of foul mood and reckless glee at the prospect of two days off. The pandemic had worked in her husband's favor. The Friday night wooing-dinner-out was no longer necessary. Wooing in general was no longer necessary. He now came home to a cooked meal, a timid wife, and a twelve-pack of beer. Lori squeezed her eyes tighter to block out what always followed.

The knock on the door made her jump. She dried her hands and quickly searched the apartment for something Duane might have left behind so she could meet him at the door with it in hand, but spotted nothing. *It must be a delivery* she decided, still fearful it might be him. She wasn't allowed out of the apartment. "For your own protection," he had said. She went to the door and looked through the peephole. The hallway was empty. She cautiously opened the door. Nothing. Then she heard something rustle against the knob as she swung it closed. She reached around and felt a bag which she quickly unhooked and brought into the apartment, locking the door behind her.

*

The bag sat on the table for six hours while Lori cleaned everything from the cabinet under the sink, to the vegetable drawer in the refrigerator. The whole time, she debated the wisdom of opening it. It was not her birthday. Duane sometimes set traps, like ordering something online addressed in her name and then punishing her for opening the box. This could be a setup. Or it could be something he wants her to wear for him tonight—*or something I have to do for him.* There was never a clear path to what would please him. It was four-thirty. Dinner was in the oven. He would be home in an hour. She looked around the room one more time for a hidden camera—he seemed to know things he shouldn't know. She opened the bag.

Mala beads were the last thing Lori expected. She once had some just like these, purchased at a county fair when she was a teenager. "Om mani padme hum," she had chanted as a lark, without knowing the meaning. She read the rolled paper, easily committing the mantra to memory. A scene flashed through her mind of a movie where the spy eats the secret message to destroy the evidence. This would be no joke if Duane found out someone suspected she was in trouble. Lori knew what her intention would be. *Find a way out of this mess.* With a burst of *I have nothing left to lose*, she took the beads into the bedroom, sat cross-legged on a bed that had become her hell, and followed the directions to the letter.

*

It was half past six. Duane was an hour late. The calm Lori had experienced after one-hundred-and-eight mantra repetitions had vanished. She sat at the kitchen table in a puddle of anxiety, now certain the mala beads were part of some twisted game of false hope Duane had concocted to further torture her. He would demand to know what she had wished for. She couldn't think straight enough to come up with a lie. *I'll say I wished for a house of our own.* As the solution appeared, it disappeared, envisioning his punishment for her wanting more than he provided.

Knock. Knock. Knock.

Lori froze in terror. Duane—adding more layers to the game.

"Ma'am, please open the door. I'm with the Barnstable Police Department."

She made herself go to the door and open it.

"Are you Lori Waldon?"

She nodded her head.

"Ma'am, I'm sorry to tell you this, but your husband was in a motor vehicle accident at approximately 5:05 pm. His injuries were substantial. He didn't make it to the hospital—"

Mama's kitchen window was Lori's last thought, as she collapsed into the officer's arms and everything went black.

March 30, 2020

CHAPTER 4 ~ DEBBIE

Santa Claus, Indiana

Everyone was understanding, but you can't *never* return to your job just because your mother unexpectedly died of a stroke. It's not like you suddenly stop needing money just because you can't muster the will to get out of bed in the morning. Debbie knew she would have to go back to work eventually. Today was that day.

She opened her iPhone and looked at her schedule, gauging how difficult it would be to get through the day based on the clients her boss had given her. They were all regulars, which was going to be a problem. Santa Claus, Indiana is a small town where everyone knows everything. They would know she did CPR for fifteen minutes before trying to call 911. They would know she couldn't find her cell phone in the mess of her kitchen table and had to run a mile to the nearest neighbor to call for an ambulance. As nice as her customers would act, their knowing wouldn't allow her to just get through the day. She'd have to be polite, eventually consoling the sorrow her tragedy would provoke in them. Her mother had been right. Debbie's disorganized ways were going to get her in trouble someday. Of course, her mother was referring to lost paperwork as the mess that would be her daughter's undoing, not the loss of her own life.

In the end, the coroner said it didn't matter. Her mother would have died even if Debbie had found her phone. What did matter, was the shoebox filled with every card, note, and letter her mother had ever written to her. Debbie couldn't find that either—and now her misery was fixated on those missing words.

*

"If you're up for it, I'm gonna add one more color and cut at the end of your day," Debbie's boss, Debbie, said. By her tone, Debbie knew it was already a done deal. At this point, she didn't care.

"Sure. Who is it?"

"She said she's a friend of yours—Lori Waldon?"

Okay, now I care. Lori was a school friend who had managed to marry well and get out of Santa Claus shortly after hairdressing school. Debbie was not up for a mirror image of what her own life could have looked like, had she been more blond, more thin, more pretty—less of a mess in general. Tears stung her eyes.

"Oh, honey. Your momma's right up there watching over you," Mrs. Linnell said sweetly, patting Debbie's arm.

"You shouldn't touch my arm while I'm trying to cut your bangs, Mrs. Linnell." The end of this day was nowhere in sight.

*

Lori looked awful—dark circles under her eyes, no makeup, five-inch roots attached to ten inches of limp, unhealthy hair. *Maybe she's pregnant*, Debbie thought to herself.

"So, I heard you and Duane live in Massachusetts, on Cape Cod," Debbie's ice-breaker felt awkward. For twenty minutes they had discussed nothing outside of Lori's hair—their mandatory masks hiding their expressions.

"Not anymore," Lori replied. "Duane is dead, and I'm never leaving Santa Claus again."

"What?" Debbie blurted. "Oh, my God! Lori, I am so sorry!"

"Don't be. He was a horrible man. I was lucky to get out of it alive. You're the first person I've told."

Debbie waited while Lori shut her eyes and steadied her breath before continuing.

"I took a bus from the airport and I was gonna go straight to my parent's house when I realized how bad I look. I won't tell them what he did to me—at least not right away. It'll be easier to keep it from them if I don't look … like this."

Debbie placed her hands on Lori's shoulders and met her eyes in the reflection of the mirror. "After we do your hair, let's grab some makeup from the esthetician's cabinet—she'll never know."

*

There was nothing uncomfortable about watching Lori cry through her appointment. Whether from joy or sorrow, tears were shed every day in the salon. People spilled all kinds of feelings while sitting in her chair. She and Lori bonded more in those two hours than they had in fifteen hundred hours of cosmetology school. And her hair came out perfect—just the right amount of blended color. Debbie was proud to be known for her excellent Balayage technique. After a little makeup, Lori looked like a well-cared-for woman who had experienced the tragedy of her husband's death—her hair beautifully styled, but her gaunt, dark circles barely covered by the layer of base makeup Debbie had applied.

"This is amazing, Debbie. I feel almost normal." Lori's gratitude soothed like a balm over Debbie's own wounds.

"How are you getting to your parent's house? I'm done after you and I can drive you there." As she was offering, Debbie thought about how messy her car was and hoped Lori would decline.

"That would be great. I know once I see my mama I'm gonna fall apart. It's probably better if I don't have them pick me up here."

"Perfect," Debbie faked. "Just give me ten minutes to clean up and I'll be ready to go."

*

The car was where *Debbie* fell apart. She had been holding it together for nine hours, but clearing the messy passenger seat after struggling to make room for Lori's suitcase in a trunk still filled with summer stuff at the end of winter was too much. She sat behind the steering wheel of her dirty car and sobbed. Her nose ran, and her face became blotchy and red. She couldn't even cry without being messy.

"I'm the reason my mother died!" she blurted. "I'm such a slob I couldn't find my cell phone to call nine-one-one! I can't even clean out my mother's apartment because my own place is filled with so much crap! And I think I threw away all the cards and letters she wrote me inside a box of old sneakers!" She let Lori hug her and pat her back, feeling guilty about being consoled by someone who had been through such hell.

"I'm good at cleaning. Duane always flipped out if our apartment wasn't perfect. I can help you get organized, and you can catch me up on the latest hair color techniques. We can help each other."

Debbie sniffled assent, pulled it together, and started the car. She drove the ten minutes to Lori's parents' house in silence. When she pulled into their long driveway she was surprised by the eclectic little bungalow, expecting something more grand.

"This house is adorable!"

"I know," Lori replied. "It's my mama's pride and joy.

Debbie got out to help retrieve the suitcase while Lori ran to her mother, who was standing in the front doorway. Lori's dad appeared out of nowhere to take the suitcase.

"Thank you for giving our girl a ride," he said formally. Debbie stood awkwardly, wondering if she should go to the steps to say goodbye. It was too much, watching Lori with a full set of parents. She turned to go. A second later she was pulled into a hug. Lori thrust something into her hand.

"We're both gonna be okay. I'll call you in a few days, by then I'll need a project to keep my mind busy. This—you—made things so much easier. Thank you." Debbie watched Lori run back to her parents, then she drove home to her empty apartment.

*

Of all the things she could have asked for, *I want to feel better* seemed kind of stupid. But that's what Debbie said aloud when she used the mala beads Lori had given her. It had been two days. She didn't feel any better and had stopped expecting she would.

Time was coming down to the wire with her mother's apartment. The landlord already had it rented and wanted to paint it before the new tenants moved in. Debbie considered calling a charity to take everything away and be done with it. *Then I can really hate myself.* Instead, she loaded some boxes into her dirty car and headed over to start packing as much as she could before Lori came over to help.

*

The apartment was immaculate—as if her mother had known to tidy up before she died. Emptying the place would be relatively simple, even for an only child. Debbie began in the bedroom, where she planned to put her mother's clothes into the trash bags she knew she would find under the kitchen sink. The contents in the very first drawer she opened nearly knocked her over. It was her letters! Bundled together with twine, organized in little stacks. Debbie untied the first packet, noticing an unfamiliar letter on top. She sat on her mother's military-tightly-made bed and began to read:

My Dearest Baby Girl,

I hope you're not angry at me for taking these letters from your closet. I found them when you sent me to grab a pair of your old sneakers that day we took a walk. I saw how important they were to you—hanging on to them all these years—and I decided to hang onto them for safekeeping. I knew you would find them when you needed to.

I want you to know how proud I am of you. You've gone so much farther than I ever could have. My life was simple, take care of you and your father—and the house. It's all I had. I didn't even finish high school—ha-ha, now you know my big secret! So keeping a nice house was the one feather in my cap. I always envied how you never let chores get in the way of real life. If a friend needed you or wanted you there to do something fun, you would just drop everything and seize the moment! The way you juggled work and hairdressing school, what an adventure your life has been! I wish I could have said yes to having more fun or taking a risk like going back to school. I'm just not that way.

I hope you know that I got all my joy from watching you, and that forever will not be long enough to look at your beautiful, happy face! I love you with all my heart.

Love,

Mom

Debbie read the letter over and over again, feeling the burden of her guilt and sorrow lift away with each word. For the first time since the terrible day of her mother's death, Debbie felt better. *Thank you, Lori. Namaste.*

April 1, 2020

CHAPTER 5 ~ TONY

Santa Claus, Indiana

Tony got the beads from his hairdresser, along with a rambling story about some letters her mother had written. He hadn't been listening. His paranoia level was at DEFCON TEN. This pandemic scared the shit out of him. Why he had chosen to risk a trip to the hair salon was anyone's guess. He was a middle-aged, overweight diabetic with a blood pressure problem and the occasional arrhythmia. A run-in with Covid-19 would surely kill him. When he got home from the salon—without stopping to buy the groceries he needed—Tony pulled the strange little bag from his pocket, flung it on the counter, and sprayed it down with Lysol. Then he went to his liquor cabinet and poured himself a small glass of Jack Daniels Honey —and then a larger one.

It was no surprise that the alcohol wasn't helping things. It never had. He was working from home, and living alone. His two grown children had moved out of state, and his wife of twenty-six years was now his ex-wife of one year. Zoom chats were suffered through. He found he had very little interest in his new grandson, Antonio the Third. All he could think about was the coronavirus. His job as a statistician didn't help. For eight hours a day, he compiled numbers on each hospital admission diagnosis, length of stay, co-morbidity, and outcome for the state health department. His work had tripled overnight. Every situation now looked dangerous—getting the mail, receiving a casserole from a well-meaning neighbor, driving to the drug store to get his prescriptions. It was all suicide as far as Tony was concerned. Taking a bag of beads from a woman whose job it was to touch people to make them look pretty was the height of stupidity. *What was I thinking?* He had tried to beg off, but Debbie, his hairdresser, wouldn't take no for an answer. She also made him promise to do this chanting thing. *It won't be the first promise I've broken.* He sat down in his recliner and fell asleep.

*

Tony's mind burst into consciousness with one thought—*Not again!* His heart was racing, and the top of his head hurt so much it wouldn't have surprised him to find his new haircut in flames. Both arms ached, and his legs were cramped up from toe to waist. He tried to exert enough force to lower the footrest of the recliner but jack-knifed in spasmodic pain with the effort. An aspirin, some magnesium, two glasses of water, and a cool shower sometimes did the trick to lower his raging blood pressure. He had forgotten to take his evening meds. Too late now. He rolled off the recliner, half-crashing to the floor. He was big. His downstairs neighbors would enquire about this two a.m. fall. Tony hoisted himself up and staggered to the kitchen. On the counter was the Jack Daniels. It was tempting—sometimes it reversed the curse. The bag of beads was lying right beside the bottle. He grabbed it in a fist, planning to hurl it across the room. Whether it was Debbie's earnestness or his guilt over another unfulfilled promise, something broke inside Tony. He felt a stab of heart pain and an overwhelming surge of emotion. He was suddenly gasping for breath through gut-wrenching, animal-like howls. His head, his heart, and his body had had enough. As he slid to the floor he imagined the relief of dying from a heart attack, now, rather than COVID-19 later.

*

By morning, Tony had wept, prayed, vomited, and eventually chanted the manifestation mantra one hundred and eight times before falling asleep just as he should have been logging onto his computer. When he woke up—still on the kitchen floor—he called in sick to work, took his morning medication, and crawled into bed. Each time he awoke, shivering from alcohol withdrawal or COVID-19—at this point, he didn't know or care which—he grabbed the mala beads and said one-hundred-and-eight prayers. Sometimes they were a chant, sometimes just a few words, *Thy will be done*, sometimes the *Our Father* from his youth. This continued for three days, occasionally drinking water and choking down a handful of Cheese-Its. On the fourth morning, he woke up, took a shower, and made himself a scrambled egg and black coffee. After eating, he cleaned the kitchen, dumped the rest of his whiskey down the drain, and went on Amazon to order himself some mala beads. As difficult as it would be to give them up, he knew the ones he had been clutching for four straight days were not his to keep. "Namaste," Tony whispered to himself, as he completed his purchase, and began his new life.

April 7, 2020

CHAPTER 6 ~ JAIMIE

Memphis, Tennessee

Lately, the hospital where Jaimie worked was more like a police station than a medical facility. Voted the second most dangerous city to live in, with more than half the violent crime tagged as domestic abuse, Memphis, Tennessee was a tough place to be an ER nurse—even before a deadly virus. When the mayor proclaimed the pandemic lockdown a "safer at home" executive order, Jaimie was nauseated by the irony. *How safe are these people gonna be at home?* The question nagged at her throughout her day.

"Worry about the patient in front of you," was what Debare would have told her. Debare had focus. Jaimie had *pretend* focus. Her shtick was to look calm and centered while mentally multitasking every situation in the room. It was one reason she knew she wouldn't work in the emergency department forever—too much simultaneous trauma. *Debare was the other reason.* She almost couldn't think of him. The pain it caused was physical, like a gut punch or a collapsed lung. Jaimie spent every shift trying not to think about what Dr. Debare Sunday would have said *or would have done*. Debare had been everyone's favorite, but only Jaimie's lover.

Their relationship began the moment she laid eyes on him. He was soft-spoken and commanding, a combination that made people slow down to listen to what he had to say—his precise Nigerian accent a distinct contrast to her Memphis drawl. His skin was perfect and liquid, like a river at night. She gave him shit about how beautiful he was—too beautiful to touch, too beautiful to rake her nails across his back. She had amused herself once by meticulously going over every inch of his flesh, looking for scars or blemishes of any kind. His laugh was deep and genuine when she touched the places that tickled him. "What do you use on your skin?" Jaimie had asked him. Her own skin looked ashy and dry compared to his. Up until she met him, the skin she envied was pastel white, like her mother's. Jaimie had lamented inheriting her father's dark, broad features and uncontrollable hair. Now, she could never be Black enough, or shiny enough. She wished she could run her hand across her own body and feel Debare's skin beneath her fingers.

His departure had been sudden. With travel restrictions widening by the day, the government wasn't taking time to scrutinize visas. Intelligence rumors of Boko Haram terrorists infiltrating the U.S. gave Homeland Security the red light to deport Nigerians based on flaws in their paperwork. "When in doubt, throw dem out," Debare had said, rather philosophically. He gave Jaimie the key to his apartment. "The money is paid for the year. It was in my mind to ask you to be with me—give up your flat. I'm *sori*, Jammie. I should have asked sooner. *Mo ni fe re*."

I love you too, Debare.

In the four weeks since his deportation, Jaimie had heard from him twice. "*No napa*—no power," he explained, having easily fallen back into Nigerian Pidgin English. She couldn't bring herself to change his sheets, let alone move the contents of her apartment to his. So each night she picked up a change of clothes from her efficiency and 'visited' his place—as if he would be there when she walked in. The first night she convinced herself he hadn't left. His clothes were still there, books on the shelf—his zither leaning against the bottom of the bookcase. She picked it up and plucked a few notes, thinking about how he had played *The Sounds of Silence* for her the first night they made love. In the bathroom his shaving gear was gone, but on the counter was the glass tub of the magic oil that made his skin glow. It was his mother's secret recipe. Jaimie was certain his mother had no idea how much of it Debare used for their mutual pleasure—*or maybe she did.*

"What's in it?" Jaimie had asked, trying to identify the smells.

"I could relate it," he replied with a sly smile. "Oh, and then I'd have to full-ground quench you."

"Well, that sounds like something I might like."

"Jammie, quench is to end your life—full-ground kill you. *Sori, geh, no vex.*" She loved it when he spoke Pidgin English.

Jaimie used the oil to summon his ghost. The night's darkness turned her hands into his. Debare's dream visits allowed her to survive the chaos of her days. But lately, no amount of wrapping herself in his smell could conjure him. Her dreams had become restless struggles. She awoke with lingering bits and pieces of the worst parts of her life—the loss of her mother, her brother's death from an overdose, the despair of being alone. Jaimie wasn't sure how long she could keep it together. Only the possibility of seeing Debare again kept her functioning.

*

Jaimie's phone rang as she finished her shift. Safely removing a NASA-like protective suit wasn't something you could hurry. She stuffed everything in the sanitation bin and pulled her sandwich-bag-enclosed cellphone from the pocket of her scrubs. Too late. *What if it was him?* It rang again.

"Hello?"

"Jaimie? It's your Uncle Tony. I'm in the hospital parking lot." She hadn't heard a word from her uncle since her mother's funeral, four years ago.

"Uncle Tony? I can't believe it's you. Is everything okay?" *He must need money.* Jaimie began mentally tallying her bank account, wishing she had already given notice to her landlord. She would owe him at least one more month's rent.

"Do you have a break soon? Maybe we can meet somewhere? I picked up a couple of sandwiches and some coffee at Front Street Deli." Her uncle sounded uncomfortable.

"Sure. Give me ten minutes and I'll come out the entrance by the main lobby," she replied.

*

Uncle Tony looked good. Jaimie couldn't remember ever seeing him anything but red-eyed and drunk. He moved in for a hug. She put her hand out. "Uncle Tony, I need to keep my distance. I go from shift to shower. We all do. Work has been …" The sentence evaporated for lack of an appropriate word.

"Hell," he filled in.

"Yes," she answered. "Are you here for a job at this hospital?"

"I'm here to see you. I drove out this morning."

"That's a six-hour drive! Is everything okay?"

"Yeah, no. Everything's good. I'm good, your cousins and Aunty Kate are all good. There's a baby in the family now. A boy …" It was Tony's turn to trail off.

"That's great news. I still don't get why you're here?"

"Jaimie, I've been a bad uncle. Your mother—she was everything to me growing up. I just came out here to say you can count on me. If you need anything—money, a person in your corner, whatever—I'm here for you." Jaimie was shocked at the sight of her uncle's eyes welling up.

"Uncle. I don't know what to say. This means so much—it's been hard, all of it."

"Well, that's what I came to tell you. We can't eat in the car together, so take this bag of sandwiches." He held the bag out to her.

"There's something special in there for you. It changed everything for me, so I want you to have it. Okay," he said as he opened his car door and got in. "Jaimie, call me any time. I hate texting, so just call me." And then he left.

*

The sandwiches were good. Jaimie ate both of them after showering, oiling, and putting on Debare's dress shirt and boxers. While she ate, she played with the mala beads and practiced the mantra. It was only eight-thirty and she couldn't wait to go to bed. She would use her intention to manifest Debare back into her dreams. She lit a candle and sat cross-legged on the floor. After taking seven long, deep breaths while envisioning her lover coming to her in her sleep, Jaimie said, "Bring my Debare back to me," then began to chant, "*Om satyam narayanam, om satyam narayanam, om satyam narayanam…*" When she was finished, she blew out the candle and climbed into Debare's California King bed, whose dimensions, he once told her, were referred to as a 'six-by-six' in Nigeria. She fell into a deep sleep.

*

He came to her immediately, his silky skin covering every inch of her body, filling her. When their lovemaking was over, she was consumed by dread—determined to never wake up. She began to cry.

"*No lele*, Jammie, my love. It's all sorted. Do not cry. I caught a med flight out of Port Harcourt yesterday. Now I must quarantine for two weeks. You must as well. We will stay right here—in 'dis six by six." Jaimie felt her body relax for the first time in weeks, wrapped in the safety of Debare's embrace.

"Namaste, Uncle Tony" she whispered, as awakening overtook her consciousness.

April 22, 2020

CHAPTER 7 ~ ANGEL

South Memphis, Tennessee

Angel celebrated twenty years as a hospital employee in January of 2020, just one month before working in healthcare made you a hero in the eyes of the world. She had been cleaning patients' rooms for most of that time, after a brief stint as a tray girl in the kitchen. The hospital was where she met her husband, George, gave birth to her three sons, and made many good friends. Over the years, she and George's income had steadily grown, allowing them to purchase a house and set aside a few dollars toward a college fund for the boys. It was a good job. It was a good life—until her co-worker and best friend, Mae, died of the virus. Now Angel was terrified to the point of wanting to quit work, even if it meant losing everything.

She was a short, overweight, middle-aged African-American woman, with high cholesterol and acid reflux—all things that Mae had been. She and Mae used to revel in their size. "We're just big, beautiful women!" they would exclaim to each other whenever the subject of dieting came up. Both were great, competitive cooks. Mae had recently one-upped her by creating a cheddar cheese waffle and fried chicken strip sandwich with a tangy muenster cheese sauce. But no one made better beans than Angel's Famous Smoky Barbecue Baked Beans—she had the awards framed on her kitchen wall to prove it. Now Mae was dead, and Angel vacillated between crying and anxiety attacks for most of the day. She had already looked into unemployment, but the hospital didn't approve her temporary leave request. There were people worse off than her coming to work every day. George told her to just quit, he could take extra shifts in the maintenance department. She couldn't do that to him. He was no spring chicken, ten years older than her with a couple of cardiac stents. But the anxiety was getting bad. Twice this week, she had to pull to the side of the road to vomit on her way to work. Her aunt had given her an expired prescription of Ativan, which she cut in half and only took at night when she couldn't turn the direction of her thoughts.

*

She had barely made it to the employee bathroom. Anxiety gave her loose bowels, the icing on the cake when she was already struggling. After she polluted the room, Angel flushed the toilet and exited the stall. That's when she saw one of the nurses, Jaimie, washing her hands at the sink. The idea of making such a stink in front of Dr. Sunday's new fiancé was finally above what she could handle. Angel began babbling an apology.

"You don't owe me a thing, Miss Angel. We all jus' hangin' on by a thread."

The sympathy was a diuretic. Water poured from Angel's eyes, and words of despair flowed from her mouth, ending with, "I'm too scared to be here! I don't want this virus to be the end of my life—like my friend Mae. I got boys to finish rearing! I'm not goin' to my grave fo' emptying somebody's trash can or moppin' out their john." She suddenly felt foolish, complaining to a nurse who worked the front line. Her embarrassment caused more crying, causing more embarrassment.

"I wish I could give you a hug right now, but no one wants a hug from someone working in the ER." The nurse continued. "I don't know what you believe about this world, but I have something you might need." Angel looked up from her tears and saw Jaimie pull a small bag from her pocket and place it on the sink. "I didn't know who the next person would be, but it is surely for you, Miss Angel."

Who the next person would be? This girl was making no sense. Before Angel could ask what she meant, the nurse was gone, leaving behind the gauze bag. Angel washed and dried her hands, using her damp paper towel to wipe away the tears and sweat from her face. Then she picked up the bag and stuffed it into her pocket. *Time to get back to work.*

*

It was late when Angel finally sat down at the kitchen table to examine what the nurse had given her. With three teenagers privacy was at a premium, especially now with remote school. George had just finished doing an oil change on her Honda and was in the shower with a plan to go straight to bed. She told him she was staying up to pay bills. George was trusting by nature. She could have been having sex on this kitchen table for all he knew. But she had never given him reason to think twice, so he didn't. She pulled open the drawstring of the gauze bag and dumped it out on the table.

Everything about the contents of the bag looked risky—anti-Jesus kind of risky. For all Angel knew, the words on the paper could be a message from the devil, or some plot sent over from Nigeria, or wherever the heck Dr. Sunday was from. *Choose yo'self somebody else, lady!* She stuffed the necklace and paper back into the sack, then got up to put on tea water—she might as well take advantage of this rare alone time. Her phone was by the stove. She picked it up and searched the words *mala beads*.

"Mala beads, commonly known as a japa mala or simply a mala, are a type of prayer beads. Prayer beads have been used for centuries by a range of religions, from Hinduism to Catholicism. … They traditionally include 108 beads in addition to a guru bead, which is larger than the rest of the beads and often has a tassel."

Angel was Baptist, but she wasn't ignorant. She had seen rosary beads before, and these mala necklaces. She painstakingly typed the mantra into the search engine of her phone and hit enter.

"The soul of this mantra is reality. Reality is God. God is reality. So long as we've got a TRUE cause for what we need and there's reality in our targets, our expectations, our actions and karma, we will manifest all that we need."~ DHYAAN GURU DR. NIPUN AGGARWAL

"Well, that don't sound like the devil."

The kettle's whistle made her jump. Her nerves were frayed. She shut off the stove, returned to the table, and pulled out the mala beads. They felt good in her hands. *Jaimie is a nice girl, and everyone loves Dr. Sunday* she reassured herself. She practiced the mantra a few times and decided it was a go. She was done being anxious and scared.

*

Angel woke to the sound of her boys fighting over the bathroom. When she looked at the clock, she was surprised to see she had overslept. She calculated her remaining time and decided she could lay in bed for five more minutes. Maybe the bathroom would be free by then. She stretched while trying to remember if she had taken her clean uniform out of the dryer. Then she got up, went to the now-empty bathroom, peed, brushed her teeth, and ran a pick through her hair. Angel liked this new routine of showering after work. It gave her more time in the morning.

*

The coffee tasted good. George made a better pot than she did. *Maybe I should sleep late every morning, let that man work his magic with them coffee beans,* she mused, trying to remember when her husband last worked his magic on *her*. It was a sunny day. She could hear the birds singing outside the kitchen window. *I hope that fool car runs better* she thought to herself, thankful George knew how to do those kinds of things. George being handy had saved them a lot of money over the years. Mae's husband—

Mae! She waited for the breath-robbing crush of pain that accompanied any thought of her dear friend. Nothing. Just a gentle sadness, surrounded by calm. Angel shut her eyes, and Mae's face immediately appeared. She was wearing her Kentucky Derby hat—the one they made together for a party. It was a foot high, overloaded with ribbons and flowers. They had wet their pants that day, posing and pretending they were socialites. Mae sure knew how to have fun. Angel smiled at the memory, grateful to have had such a wonderful friend. "Namaste, my sweet Mae," she whispered, eyeing the mala bead bag on the table. She picked it up and held it to her heart for a minute. Then she put the bag in her purse, knowing someone was going to need it as much as she had.

I better pick up the pace, she reminded herself. *Don't want to be late for work ...*

April 24, 2020

CHAPTER 8 ~ KHAN

Memphis, Tennessee

Khan loaded the paper into the lottery machine for what felt like the one-millionth time. It seemed everyone needed a chance at winning a million dollars. Lottery tickets, liquor, and cigarettes were the only things selling these days. And toilet paper. According to those four items, business was booming. On top of the regulars, the store had become a daily drop-in for a host of new faces. At first, Khan tried to make sense of it. Why would more people suddenly stop at this convenience store? It wasn't as if the big grocery stores were closed. He eventually concluded they were simply in pandemic lockdown, and their homes were closer to his store than their jobs had been. *His store.* Most people thought that was the case—he sure worked enough hours to justify ownership. It was Yazid Syed's store. Yazid had six stores, a happy wife, four children, and a very busy life. Khan had no stores, but he did have a wife and five children—all living in Pakistan.

When he came to America eleven years ago to set up an American life, he was told it would be a simple thing to bring over the rest of his family. That simple thing turned into work visas, renewals, hold-ups from lost paperwork, an eventual Green Card, and finally a date for his wife, Habiba, and four of the five children—the youngest of which Khan had never met—to come to the States. Habiba said no. She would not leave until the visa for their oldest child, Samama, was in order. Sam was twenty-two. As an adult, he was subject to different visa requirements than his siblings. That was six months ago. With the pandemic, it was becoming even less likely Khan would soon see his family. Still, he prayed and did what he could from his end. The house he rented was big—three bedrooms, one and a half baths, and a little backyard. He had been slowly setting things up. With the help of an older woman from the Sunni Islamic church, Habiba's kitchen was finished. Heavy steel pots and pans for making rice and meat dishes (Khan's mouth watered thinking of his wife's Biryani and Nihari), every manner of utensil, and a tawa to make her Chapati were tucked into the cabinets—along with some more modern things like a Ninja Bullet for making sauces.

"She can just buy Naan at the store," he had told the church woman. "She does not need to work so hard when she gets here."

"Do not say that!" the woman admonished. "Habiba will need to feel at home! That is what this kitchen is for!"

Americanized woman, Khan thought to himself, although her dominance reminded him of his mother. He thought about how his life was going to change. *Not much*, he lied. He had been in limbo for so long, faithful to his family, and living for the day they would be reunited. Khan had painted every room in the house, including the basement. He planned to set up a bedroom down there for his eldest son until they could secure his college admission. Sam wanted to be a scientist. He was strong in biology. Everything Khan knew about his children was facilitated through his weekly phone calls. He was a strict parent. Habiba left most of the disciplining up to him and he was kept very well informed of their progress. His children were fluent in English. They worked hard at teaching their mother, who struggled to understand even his most slowly said English sentences. She will learn when she gets here. *When she gets here.* He was losing faith it would ever happen.

*

"As-Salaam-Alaikum." *Peace be with you.* The shop door opened and in walked a regular customer, Miss Angel, from down the street. She was not a lottery player, but her husband was, and her boys came in regularly to buy junk food or pick up bread and milk for their mother. They were friendly faces, even when masked. Miss Angel had dropped off a few surgical masks for him when this whole mess started.

"Wa-Alaikum-Salaam, Miss Angel," *And onto you, Peace.* "How are you, today?"

"I couldn't be better, my friend. I'm finished with work and the sun's still shining. How are you doing?"

"I am well," Khan responded, as she walked past him toward the milk case.

"What's the word on your wife and kids?" Few customers had any idea about his family in Pakistan, but once Miss Angel learned of their existence she never hesitated to ask about their welfare. Over the years he had told her many stories. Today, there was nothing to tell. Their arrival was stalled. Today, he was depressed.

"It is hopeless," he answered. "They are making more restrictions. It will take a miracle."

Miss Angel swung her milk onto the counter. "I'll take two of those lottery tickets my husband thinks he's hiding from me. That way he won't have to find an excuse to run out later." He got her two Tennessee Cash quick picks and waited as she opened her purse, wearing a pair of neoprene gloves. She paid her money, said her goodbyes, and was walking toward the door when he saw her turn around.

"I might just have a miracle for you, Khan." He watched her pull a little satchel from her purse. She handed it to him under the plexiglass germ guard. "I know it's crazy, but it worked for me. Good luck!"

*

The mantra was familiar to Khan. He executed it with devotion and ease. Sunni Islamic religion embraced the concept of angels and messengers. Miss Angel had been both. Within days, Khan received word from his immigration attorney that a date for his family's arrival had been set. He decided to give the japa mala beads to the next person who asked about his family's well-being. Surprisingly, it didn't take long.

April 27, 2020

CHAPTER 9 ~ DANI

Memphis, Tennessee

As a unique mix of extrovert and self-proclaimed hermit, Dani was having no trouble functioning in a pandemic lockdown. She had her books, her podcasts, her Zoom classes, and her remote job. She was an experience junkie, not the kind who had to jump out of a plane every five minutes (although skydiving was a box already checked), but the kind who needed to know a little bit about everything. One month it was hydroponic gardening, the next it was Judaism. After high school, she began taking classes at the local community college, signing up for any course that interested her. She initially did it for the cheap student health insurance. A few years later, she found herself accidentally graduating from community college—*an associate degree in God knows what*. Now Dani worked for a company that did insurance billing for doctors' offices. It wasn't a job holding her over until the right one came along—it was the job she wanted. The money was decent, the hours flexible, and it allowed her the freedom to pursue the things that mattered to her. To her mother's dismay, the idea of a life partner was only a theory since she couldn't imagine giving up any of her interests for a man.

For the sake of her mental health, Dani tried to stay away from news and current events. She had read once that a person's global information access should be no larger than the distance they could run in a day's time. *Keep it local, keep it meaningful*. There was no point in her knowing about a horror story halfway across the world. Dani worked at impacting the people in her daily life. *Be pleasant to everyone and help where you can* was her motto.

The Shelby County food bank was her current charity. Giving boxes out to those in need was very satisfying. At the end of each week, they gave Dani an enormous box of meats, vegetables, and dairy. It was ten times more food than she could eat, so she looked up recipes that included whatever ingredients were in the box and made soups, stews, ethnic dishes, and power drinks. She shared them with her neighbors, carting them in an old, red, Radio Flyer wagon.

*

Dani had two frozen containers of root vegetable chicken thigh stew left in her wagon when she stopped at the corner store to pick up toilet paper. "Hey there, Khan! How's it all going?" She smiled behind her homemade mask. "I brought you some stew. Feel free to spice it up a little. I know it's no substitute for your wife's home cook—"

"She is coming! Habiba and my children are coming!" The convenience store clerk exclaimed. "I will pick them up at the airport next week!"

Dani put both hands over her heart, knowing it would be inappropriate to hug him. "I am so happy for you! I can't wait to meet them." Khan then told her about the laptop computers he had just ordered for remote school, and how he hoped he hadn't made his daughter's room too babyish. He had no idea about what a thirteen-year-old girl likes. Dani was overwhelmed by his joy. "If there is anything I can do," she said, "please ask me. I live right down the street and I'm home all day." *Like the rest of the world.*

"Thank you, Dani. You are always kind to me. My wife will need a friend like you." As he spoke, his eyes filled with tears and he pulled a small bag from under the counter. "I have something for you …"

*

"A miracle wish," he had said when he told her the story. Dani had a lot of experience with angels and messengers, just about everything she needed or wanted came by way of The Divine. Her prayers were always answered, even if the answer was no. She had been practicing yoga and chakra clearing for years, working on being grounded to the earth, while communicating with the stars. She had her own mala beads, made from rosewood—a wood known for its feminine spiritual energy and healing. These beads looked to be sandalwood.

After holding the gifted beads for an hour, Dani realized there was nothing she wanted. She already prayed daily for the health of the planet and the people on it, her Amazon Alexa reminding her to stop what she was doing and "say a prayer" every day at eleven-eleven. At two o'clock each afternoon, her artificial intelligence friend was also set to say, "This is a reminder: Be happy." No. There was nothing she needed for herself. She decided to hold off on the miracle mantra, knowing something would point her in the right direction. It always did.

*

Kahn's little family was set to land at Memphis International Airport on Tuesday. Dani spent the weekend making welcome gifts. For Habiba, she gathered plantings from her vast supply of indoor plants and put them together in a bright ceramic pot. For Khan's only daughter, Dani went through her Christmas box, picking out twinkling fairy lights strung on copper wire, and adding a set of sheer beaded curtains she no longer used. Finding gifts for the four sons was tricky. They ranged from her age, twenty-two, down to eleven. Dani wasn't a fan of junk food, but she knew it was the way to a boy's heart. So she compromised by making homemade energy bars from sunflower seed butter, oatmeal, and chocolate chips. For good measure, she added chia seeds and crushed hazelnuts. Then she wrapped everything in brown paper and tied them with twine. For a finishing touch, she created a heart-shaped stamp out of some packing foam and stamped red hearts onto each package. Satisfied with her work, Dani loaded the gifts into her cart and set off for the corner store.

*

The owner, Yazid Syed, didn't acknowledge Dani as she pushed through the doorway. *Khan must be busy making preparations,* was Dani's immediate thought at not seeing him behind the counter. She wheeled her wagon up to Mr. Syed, who did not look up from his paperwork.

"Excuse me. I have something for Khan," she said.

"He is not here," the owner said, still focused on his numbers.

"I can see that. Can you tell me when he will be back?" Dani glossed over her irritation at being ignored.

"I do not know."

"Khan is a friend of mine," a slight exaggeration. "I have gifts for his wife and children. Can you call him and let him know I've left something?"

"Khan is in the hospital. He got sick from eating bad chicken stew. Someone from the church is getting his family tomorrow. I will give it to them."

Sick from eating her stew? Oh my God! "What kind of sick?" Dani asked, guilt washing her face red.

"The kind where I have to cover his shifts." Mr. Syed gestured to the lottery stand beside the counter. "Leave everything there."

Dani pulled the planter and the bag of presents from her red cart and left them where he had directed, doubting the wisdom of leaving another gift of food. She rushed back to her apartment in a state of mental chaos. Everyone else had eaten the stew and been fine. *Maybe*

Khan has a food allergy, she decided, and set to work readying her meditation area to say a very powerful manifestation mantra: *Restore Khan to total health.*

*

Three days passed before Dani got the nerve to go back to the store. During that time, she alternated between faith that the mantra had done its job and terror that Khan was dead.

The little bell rang when she pushed open the door. Her fear of learning Khan's fate almost made her turn around and leave. Then she saw the man behind the counter. He was the image of Khan, only younger. Dark hair, golden brown skin, and striking green eyes like his father.

"Dani?" The young man asked.

"Yes," she replied, certain he was on the lookout for her because of what she had done.

"Alhamdulillah! I was going to search for you after work."

"Is your father …? Please tell me I didn't kill him with my stew."

"No! You have saved his life!" Khan's son replied.

"I don't understand," she stammered.

"He left your stew here by mistake and foolishly ate it the next day, hoping it would still be good. It was not. When he went to the hospital with the pain they noticed something was wrong with his heart. They had to do a procedure—an angioplasty. If they had not found this, my father would have died from a heart attack. The artery was completely blocked and now it is restored! You have saved his life!"

Dani began to weep with relief.

"Please do not cry. When it is safe, you must come and meet my family. My mother wants to thank you for your gifts—and she would like the recipe for your candy bars …"

May 4, 2020

CHAPTER 10 ~ BARBARA

Memphis, Tennessee

At eighty-two years old, Barbara thought she had seen it all—but apparently not. This pandemic was the topper. The media covered the event in a way that seemed futuristic as if the virus had been either manufactured in a lab or dropped onto the Earth from outer space. Barbara knew better. Her mother was a toddler in 1918 when the previous pandemic, the Spanish Flu, was in full swing. It had picked up speed and volume during Philadelphia's Liberty Loan parade on September 28, 1918, then marched its way across the state of Pennsylvania, up the Monongahela River, and into her mother's little town of Turtle Creek. Many times, Barbara heard the story of how her grandfather had single-handedly nursed his wife and eight children back to health, then gone on to help the Westinghouse Electric workers build an emergency hospital right in Turtle Creek. Her mother had spared no detail when it came to the gruesome, hemorrhagic way in which the flu victims died. Pennsylvania, alone, lost sixty-thousand people to the avian-inspired virus. *And now, here I am, finishing my life the same way my mother began hers—in a deadly pandemic. Holy hell.*

Other than the daily death count, it was the logistics of living in a pandemic that bothered Barbara. She was old and lived alone. Her daughter and son didn't return to Tennessee after college (her one piece of free advice: Don't let your kids go to out-of-state schools). Lately, the topic of "Mother's future living situation" was brought up with more frequency. Each time, she told them she was fine. She wasn't leaving her home. To do so was a slippery slope that would begin with selling her house and moving in with her daughter, and end with a nursing home. It was the writing on every old person's wall. *Nope. I'm not leaving this house*. She had her little circle of sustaining friends and hobbies—well, just one hobby. She went to Qigong on Thursday mornings. Even with her very limited interests, Barbara's life had been full. A run to TJ Maxx for a new pair of tennis shoes could take up a morning. She'd hit Kroger's or Cash Savers once a week for groceries. Barbara was not unhappy with how her life turned out—up until now.

*

She hadn't left her house in weeks. She wasn't afraid of dying, *everyone does it,* she was afraid of all the moments leading up to dying. With more than a touch of COPD from an old smoking habit, Barbara had already experienced the alarming terror of being unable to catch her breath. She imagined this coronavirus to be that awful, times one hundred. So she stayed home and managed to make do. It was getting more difficult as the weeks passed. Her daughter, Lea, had set her up on Stop & Shop's grocery delivery. All she had to do was log onto her computer, *a feat by itself*, and put in the items she wished to buy. That worked for exactly one grocery delivery, but then she messed up the password and had to call her daughter to reset it. Now the login was screwed up again, and she was locked out of her account. Lea had thinly disguised impatience with her, each call ending with, "Mom, you really shouldn't be living that far away by yourself." It took Barbara everything to stop from screaming, "You're not the boss of me, little girl! And *you're* the one who lives so far away!" Now she was out of coffee, and down to canned goods—mostly salty canned goods. The last thing she needed was a trip to the hospital for her blood pressure. The girl next door came by every so often to look in on her, and usually brought a frozen meal or two. The chicken stew she dropped off, last week, fed Barbara for three days. Waiting for a charity drop-off after a lifetime of fending for herself made her angry. She had done her part—sensibly managing her limited income, keeping herself in good physical condition through diet and exercise—she didn't deserve for things to end like this. *What old woman does?*

*

Barbara was sitting at the kitchen table, wrestling with two bad choices—call Lea or take a chance on a grocery store run—when she heard a knock at the door.

"Miss Barbara? You in there?" It was Dani, from next door. Barbara grabbed her mask and went to the door, opening it a few inches.

"Well, hello!" Barbara said, with the happy affect she saved for company. She tried not to look behind the girl to see what was in her cart.

"Today I made squash soup! And I brought you an extra little something." The girl held up a bunch of beets by their leafy tops. "I want to like beets—I truly do. They're so high in fiber and vitamin C, but I just can't get past the taste. It's like eating dirt, if you ask me. If you don't want them, I'll sure as likely find somebody who does."

Dani's generosity caused Barbara's happy mask to crack. She didn't cry, though everything in her wanted to. She could feel her face redden above the one KN95 mask she got at the Dollar General when this thing began.

"Miss Barbara, are you okay?"

"I'm just overwhelmed, Dani. I have thyroid medication to pick up, my roots need coloring, and the storm knocked a big tree onto my deck last night. I just feel so damn unsure of everything." Embarrassment took over. "And now I'm babbling like an old woman."

"I could do a few things if you need me to," her neighbor helpfully responded.

Barbara was tempted. "No. You do enough for me." She took the beets from Dani. "I love beets. I eat them raw, just shred them right into my salad." *When was the last time I had a salad?*

"Miss Barbara, I have something else for you. You have to promise me you'll do it—give it a try." Dani pulled a small bag from the colorful patchwork satchel she had slung across her chest. Barbara hoped it had nothing to do with figuring out the internet. The girl continued talking as she passed the soup and the little mystery item through the partially opened door. "If you need help with it, you can just call me. In fact, you can call me any time you need help." With a smile and a nod, she was gone—Barbara's only link to the outside world.

*

The writing was small, even with her reading glasses. Barbara hadn't increased her eyeglass prescription strength in twenty years after seeing an article that said the higher you go, the more you'll need them. Instead, she grabbed her dome-shaped magnifying lens—a present from her friend, Jon, who pulls the lenses out of old car headlights. She carefully placed it over the worn paper that came with the necklace. The directions made no sense. It was all Greek to her. She left it on the table and heated up some of the squash soup, adding what was left of her saltine crackers. It was delicious.

*

It was evening when she sat down to the beads again. She wrote out the mantra on a piece of paper and said it a few times under her breath. There was nothing reverent about her utterings. Barbara was frustrated. *One more goddamn thing for me to learn* was the thought in tandem with the words on her lips. She had arthritis. She wasn't going to sit on the floor like some crazy yogi. She folded her hands in prayer, trying to remember the last time she had prayed in earnest, and began the chant. Then she realized she was doing it wrong. She had forgotten the beads, the intention, the breathing. "Screw this," she said aloud to no one. The urge to have a cigarette swept over her in a way it hadn't for years. *The good old days.* "Well, they're gone. You better get used to it," she admonished herself. She grabbed the directions and decided to give it one more try. Holding the beads, she shut her eyes and took seven, long, deep, frustrated breaths—ending in a coughing jag. Barbara pushed through. "Send me some goddamn help." One hundred and eight times she read the foreign words, eyes wide open like she was reciting schoolwork. *There. I'm done.*

*

The phone on her nightstand rang just as she closed her eyes.

"Hello?"

"Nanny?" Lea's daughter, Kalie, was the only one of her three grandchildren who called her that.

"Hey, baby girl, everything okay?" Her family knew not to call past nine unless it was an emergency.

"I got laid off from my job. I can't make next month's rent." Barbara immediately began listing the reasons why she couldn't help financially. "No, Nanny. I don't need money. I'm gonna give up my apartment. I just can't—" Her granddaughter began to cry. Barbara waited.

"I don't wanna go back home. Mom and I … she's so bossy, and I don't need her running my life. I just need somewhere to live till this pandemic's over. Can I move in with you?"

A strange head-to-toe tingling overtook Barbara's body. Her prayer had been answered.

"Of course you can, baby girl. I would love it."

May 14, 2020

CHAPTER 11 ~ KALIE

Memphis, Tennessee

It killed Kalie to give up an apartment so close to the South Carolina coast, but it had come down to that or lose her car to the bank. Soon her unemployment would kick in, and she could start giving her grandmother some rent. She had forgotten how cute Nanny's place was. Sure, it was small—two tiny bedrooms, a living room, a kitchen, and a bath—but the outside was amazing. She had almond trees! Their glorious, sweet-smelling flowers were in full bloom, already attracting every bee in the neighborhood. *Maybe we could get our own bees!* Kalie began mentally rearranging the backyard to make room for a box of bees. She had seen a YouTube video about converting an old dresser into a beehive and was already fantasizing about how she would paint it. Kalie loved to paint. At Savannah College of Art and Design, she had explored every facet of art, from fabric making to historical building restoration. At her mother's insistence, she had settled on graphic design because of the steady income. "They don't call them starving artists for nothing," her mother had said more than once. Slowly Kalie stopped painting altogether, focusing all her hours in front of a computer screen. Graphic design had turned out to be mostly boring. When she got let go from her job as a medical illustrator for a textbook company, it was a relief. Being in Memphis with Nanny was a relief.

*

"Where are your art supplies, Nanny?" Kalie asked as they lugged the last of a fallen tree off the deck and toward the road's edge.

She planned to put a social media post up for free wood. If they didn't get any takers in a day or two, she would call a landscape company to haul it away.

"Oh, I don't paint anymore. I threw it all away—most of it was like me, old and dried up," her grandmother answered.

"What about your paintings?"

"Donated them to Goodwill. By now, they're probably painted over by some other wannabe artist."

Kalie's heart sank at the thought of someday parting with her own paintings after realizing her dream of being an artist had gone nowhere.

*

With the ad for the firewood up and running on the web marketplace, Kalie indulged herself by scrolling through the free listings. Within seconds, she saw a decent wooden five-drawer chest. *A beehive!* She googled the address. It was less than five miles away. After a few back-and-forth messages about contact-free pickup, Kalie was on her way to get her treasure.

*

The beehive turned out to be more work than she expected, but Kalie was extremely pleased with the results. Instead of the original, simple dresser-hive design, she had opted to use a mason jar system, with the jar lid rings wedged upside-down into the perfectly cut holes she created with a used jigsaw she bought for cheap on the web. The inverted jars were then screwed to the lids, where the bees would build their golden honeycomb palaces. At least that was the plan. The drawers came out so well that Kalie kept opening them to admire the perfect rows of honey jars she had created.

Painting the dresser was like finding a long-lost love. She used her graphic computer skills to lay out a colorful Victorian pattern with a mix of architectural peaks, windows, doors, and flower boxes—all painted with miniature, three-dimensional precision. Once the paint was cured, she would spray the whole thing with a low VOC polyurethane to protect her artwork. The project took a week. By that point, Kalie's research had led her to the conclusion that it was too late in the season to get bees. *No problem*, she decided. *I'll just wait till next year.* Next year? What was she thinking? She wouldn't even be staying with Nanny by next year. Her mother had already sent a dozen job listings located in places she didn't want to live. Each time, Kalie accepted the information as though she were truly considering taking the job. Her mother was a hard woman to say no to.

*

"What's the matter, baby girl?" Nanny had crept up on her as she sat slumped on the front steps.

"Mom called this morning. She wants to know how my interview went," Kalie responded glumly.

"What interview?"

"Exactly. I lied to her to get her off my back."

"I know how that goes," her grandmother said without a smile. "Your mother's like a dog with a bone. What do *you* want to do?" Nanny sat down on the steps beside her.

"I want to stay here for a while, figure things out. I think I hate graphic design."

Nanny got up, quickly went into the house, and was just as quickly back at her side. She handed Kalie a little bag. "You can stay here forever as far as I'm concerned, it's about what *you* want. These are mala beads. They answered *my* prayers." Nanny gave her a hug.

"Figure out what you want and make it happen." Then she left and went back to doing whatever it was she did all day in her little house.

Kalie got up and walked to the backyard, reading the curled instructions as she walked. Then she sat on the ground, crossed her legs, and leaned her back against the trunk of the largest almond tree. *Let art be my life* was her plea to the universe, and she began haltingly to chant, "Om satyam narayanam …"

*

The low-odor polyurethane still smelled so strong that Kalie finally appreciated her face mask. She used a handcart to drag the beehive box to the end of the driveway where the smell wouldn't creep into Nanny's open windows. After spraying it down with two coats, she opened all the drawers as far as they'd go to let the whole thing air out while it dried. Then she stood back, so in awe of the masterpiece she had created that she barely noticed the dark car driving slowly past the driveway and turning to stop in front of her. The man rolled down the window and startled her when he spoke.

"Hey there. Is that one of those backyard beehives?"

"It is."

"My wife's been talking non-stop about getting one of these. The ones she keeps showing me are nothing like that one," he continued.

"It's a one-of-a-kind," Kalie responded and went on to tell him how the drawer/jar system worked.

"Her birthday's this weekend. How much do you want for it?" The question took her by surprise. So did her answer.

"Eight-hundred-and-fifty dollars."

"Sold," he said. "Will two hundred hold it until I come back with the rest? In fact, can I pay for it and pick it up on Saturday morning?" She nodded her head, still stunned by what just happened. He got out of the car and handed her two one-hundred dollar bills along with his business card. As he was leaving, the man winked and said, “You better start making more of those. My wife’s friends are gonna be so jealous—and I’m gonna be a hero.” He drove off. Kalie grinned from ear to ear. She had just sold her first piece of artwork. *I love you, Nanny. Namaste.*

May 19, 2020

CHAPTER 12 ~ AARON

Charleston, South Carolina

There was a time when Aaron thought his co-worker, Kalie, had a thing for him. In his mind, he envisioned her confessing her love, and him responding, "Is now the time to tell you I have loved you since the day we met?" *And then they lived happily ever after*. The truth was, it was he who had the crush, and Kalie who let him down in a way that allowed them to remain friends. That was a year ago, and Aaron was no longer looking for happily ever after. He was just looking to stay alive. He needed a kidney.

When Aaron began peritoneal dialysis six months ago, his doctors assured him he would be getting a kidney in no time. Not only was he young and healthy, he was in what he referred to as 'The Swap a Kidney' program. It was really called The Paired Exchange Program. His sister, Denise, wasn't a match for him, but she had a kidney and was willing to exchange hers for one that *was* a match for her brother. With this option available, Aaron's chances of getting a kidney more than doubled. Instead of just the cadaver waiting list, he would be paired with registered live-donor exchanges all over the country. Then the coronavirus shut most of the swap program down. Anyone who could wait, did. As much as Aaron hated dialysis, he was now considered a person who could wait—which in his mind was bullshit.

Three times a day, Aaron had to insert two quarts of dialysate through a catheter and into his peritoneal cavity, where it stayed for four or five hours before draining back into the bag and being thrown away. At night, he sometimes had to use a machine called a cycler to help the dialysate do its job. When he found out that the dialysate was just a sterile electrolyte solution, Aaron joked to his friends that he was simply inserting some very expensive Gatorade and was currently into the Frost Glacier Cherry flavor. But it was no joke. He was depressed and angry. The propaganda paperwork about dialysis was very different from the reality of dialysis. He had already gotten a pretty bad infection at the catheter site and was in a Zoom support group for all the other problems that accompanied peritoneal dialysis—like bloated-belly-distorted body image dysphoria, weight gain from the glucose in the solution, and general depression about being a twenty-eight-year-old man with a life-threatening illness. It was a lot to unpack in a one-hour Zoom session. Never leaving the house wasn't helping.

*

Kalie's package arrived just as Aaron was emptying his third bag of used dialysate of the day. The FedEx guy had wrung the bell, knocked, and was leaving without delivery by the time Aaron put the finishing touches on his catheter (he was not risking another infection). He ran out the door.

"Hey! Don't go! I'm right here!" He hollered, wildly waving his arms at the leaving vehicle. It was at that moment he realized how starved he was for *anything*—a package he wasn't expecting, a friend, a date, a kidney. The FedEx guy must have sensed this. He abruptly turned his van around, jumped from the seat, and handed him the package.

"Just need a signature," he said and pushed the DIAD and attached electronic pen toward Aaron with his gloved hand.

"Sorry, man," Aaron said, as he signed. "I'm not an anti-masker. I just forgot to grab one in my rush to get this. The driver nodded his head in seeming neutrality and took his DIAD back, wiping it and the pen with a sterile wipe he had produced from nowhere. Aaron watched with envy as the man jumped back into the van and sped away. It didn't look like a bad job. It looked like freedom.

*

Aaron was reading the note Kalie sent when he realized he hadn't sprayed down the box with disinfectant or washed his hands. Having an active infection of any kind could squelch a transplant deal if one ever came along. *Screw it.* He continued to read:

Dear Aaron,

I hope this finds you doing great. I think a lot about our fun times at work. You were the lifeline to my sanity! But even if they call me, I'm not coming back to that company. In fact, I won't be doing graphic design for any company in the future! I'm pursuing my art and my painting. I've already sold my first piece! It was actually a repurposed piece of furniture—but it's a start.

I know things weren't easy for you even before this crazy pandemic, which is why I'm sending you this special gift. It's not a scam. It works. Read the instructions and do what they say. It's kind of like a chain letter—after your miracle comes true you pass it along to the next person.

Aaron this is your miracle, I know it in my heart.

Love, Kalie

He was crying before he finished reading the instructions sent with the mala beads. Kalie had been his lifeline too. She was the thing he looked forward to each day at work—the bright spot in his life since the Glomerulonephritis he had acquired from an untreated childhood strep throat finally took over his kidneys. Despite all he had been through, Aaron wasn't a pessimist—but what if this wasn't his miracle? What if Kalie's good intentions turned out to be one more disappointment? It would be more than he could bear. Worse, his failure could dissolve her belief in the magic she had sent. He decided he would put every ounce of intention into the mantra—for Kalie.

*

Aaron's cell phone vibrated in his pocket when he was almost done with the mantra. He pushed through to the end, certain the interruption had ruined everything. *Maybe I should do it again,* he thought while answering the persistent buzz.

"Aaron? It's Jayne from Dr. Steinman's office. How soon can you get to University Hospital? We have a kidney for you!"

I love you, Kalie.

"I can be there in eighteen minutes."

May 19, 2020

CHAPTER 13 ~ JOHN

Marshfield, Massachusetts

Being uselessly on-call was draining for John. He liked action, but organ transports had lately been few and far between. People staying home from work meant fewer car accidents, barely compensated for by the do-it-yourselfers who fell from ladders while cleaning their gutters or those who electrocuted themselves while changing their own light fixtures. It was like that old movie *Death Takes A Holiday*. Except death wasn't taking a holiday, only viable transplant deaths were on vacation since COVID-19 organs didn't qualify for transplant. Finally, after weeks of nothing, John got a call from Jen at the New England Organ Bank.

*

Rita F was a twenty-nine-year-old pregnant woman who had been strangled to brain death by her husband. For months her body was kept alive by machines, waiting for the day her fetus was mature enough to survive. That day came yesterday when doctors delivered a healthy five-pound, eight-ounce baby girl with curly dark hair like her mother. Today, a team of doctors would perform another type of delivery. They planned to harvest two healthy kidneys, one liver, a heart, two lungs, a pancreas, intestines, multiple tissues, and two corneas. Rita F had taken excellent care of her body, and the results of her diligence would help up to eighty separate individuals. It was one perfect kidney that John was here to collect and transport to a patient at University Hospital in South Carolina—and he was thrilled to do it.

*

The pickup, the flight, and the delivery all went without a hitch. As John stood at the operating room desk trading signatures on the required paperwork, a nurse ran up to him.

"Oh, hey! I'm glad you're still here!" She went to hand him a small white bag. "This is from the patient. He said to give it to you."

John was caught off guard. "I can't take anything meant for the donor's family. You'll have to contact New England Organ Bank, they can—"

"It's not for them. It's for you. The patient said, 'Give this to the guy that brings my kidney.' That would be you." She handed him the bag. "Have a good flight back."

*

Hello. My name is Aaron. Thank you for bringing me a new kidney. You were summoned to this task by powers greater than you know—greater than any of us knows. To show my gratitude, I am passing along this miracle to you. Use it to manifest what you need most at this moment. ~ Namaste, Aaron

"Well this is not what I expected," John said aloud, as he went through the rest of the bag. A miracle mantra—mala beads. *How crazy is this?* However, he did have a situation that could use a miracle.

*

John and his wife, Sheila, had been married ten minutes when his grandfather died—literally ten minutes. Instead of a honeymoon, they went to a funeral. John was devastated, not just to have his grandfather die at his wedding, but as the only child of an only child, John was Grandpa's favorite. The family land his grandfather willed to him was supposed to be his wedding present—Grampa just hadn't gotten around to doing the paperwork. So John waited a year for the probate to be finished. During that time, he picked out a house plan, settled on a builder, and got all his ducks in a row. He and Sheila had been living with her parents in a retirement-sized condo to save money for the build. They were beyond ready to officially begin their own life. Then, the town building department told him the lot wasn't buildable. Ironically, the wording they used to break John's heart was, "Your land doesn't meet the requirements for a buildable lot—no right-of-way access. It turns out it was never *grandfathered* into the deed." The inspector's advice was to hire a lawyer. Sheila wanted to just sell the land and buy a house. John refused. It was a mixed blessing to live with in-laws—your marital disagreements remained quietly civil. He wasn't sure for how long.

John had a two-hour flight and a pressing dilemma. He did the mantra.

*

Logan Airport was understandably empty. John retrieved his truck from the short-term parking lot and threw his duffle bag in the back. There was no rush-hour traffic with schools closed and so many people hunkered down from the pandemic, so he'd be back in Marshfield in time for dinner. He wondered what his mother-in-law was making. She wasn't a fan of people messing around in her kitchen, so he hadn't tasted his own wife's cooking in ages. *Did Sheila even like to cook?* He couldn't remember. He toyed with the idea of telling her about the mala beads and suddenly felt foolish about having used them. The guy in the seat beside him probably thought he was terrified of flying, praying like that. John pulled into the fifty-five-plus gated community and parked in the guest lot. He took the mala bead bag from his coat pocket and locked it in the glove box. He was starved—maybe his mother-in-law had made lasagna.

*

"I think we should just sell it—make enough for a down payment on a house."

As if I don't know what you think. "No one's gonna buy a lot they can't build on," John answered for the hundredth time.

"But John, the whole lot is filled with Christmas trees. That's got to be worth something. And it probably *is* buildable. Let someone else fight the town—someone with deeper pockets. We can't spend everything we've saved on a lawyer." His wife was pleading her case on a loop. He couldn't do it anymore. He rolled over and put his back to her. The headboard of their bed shared a wall with his in-law's headboard. Fighting in private wasn't an option.

"Sheila, let's just go to sleep. It's been a long day." He didn't feel bad when she didn't answer. *Relief.*

*

It had been a couple of days. Sometimes he called the organ transplant coordinator to see how the patient had fared. Most times he didn't. He hoped this guy had gotten his miracle—*even if I haven't*. After a Zoom consultation with a land court lawyer, John had gone straight to a realtor. When he got home he would tell Sheila the price he was quoted. Maybe they would have quiet sex to celebrate him giving in. The thought didn't cheer him.

John pulled into the complex, stopping to grab the mail from the mail center, dozens of identical, gold cubicle boxes. *Who would ever live in a retirement community?* In the mailbox, along with ads for hearing aids and CPAP equipment, was a card addressed to him, forwarded from Grandpa's nursing home. He tore it open and read the enclosed condolence card, then the note folded inside.

Dear John,

I'm sorry to hear about your grandfather. He was a wonderful man. My father was very fond of him. You probably don't remember us, but we owned the lot in front of your grandfather's Christmas tree lot. Please call me. I have a story to share.

Trevor Schaeffer 413-555-1639

John got back in his truck and drove to the guest lot. He hated calling strangers, especially those who had something personal to say. He opened the glove box to throw the card inside so Sheila couldn't force him to respond. The mala beads stared back at him. The words *make the call* went through his head. John reread the card, pulled out his phone, and dialed the number.

*

"I can't believe you never heard this story," Trevor continued. "I mean, your grandfather was a hero! There my dad was, lying in the snow with his leg split open from the chainsaw, his prized tree splayed out on top of him. And your grandfather comes into the woods—on the very same day—at almost the exact same time—to cut down his own Christmas tree! He ends up using his belt for a tourniquet and carries my dad all the way back to the road where his truck was parked. By then Dad was unconscious from loss of blood. Another ten minutes in the woods and he would have been dead."

"This is crazy! I can't believe Grandpa didn't tell us. But that's how he was—not a guy to brag about stuff. I miss him so much." John was shocked to hear himself say this intimate thing to a person he never met.

"I'll bet," Trevor answered. "So I heard you're gonna build on the lot. That's great!"

"We can't," John responded. "It's landlocked." And he went on to tell Trevor about the town's decision. After a pause, Trevor replied.

"I'll tell you what. What if I deed you a twenty-foot wide strip that connects your property to the main road? You'll have to pay for the lot survey and attorney transfer fees."

"That would be amazing!" John was stunned. "How much do you want for it?"

"How about, in honor of my Dad and your grandfather, we write something in the deed that says we have the right to one Christmas tree a year, but you have to cut it down for us. That sound good?"

"It sure does!" *It sounds like a miracle*.

May 22, 2020

CHAPTER 14 ~ CHARLOTTE

Marshfield, Massachusetts

As much as Charlotte loved having her daughter and son-in-law live with them, it was difficult to watch young love in bloom while she was busy performing CPR on her own marriage. Charlie was a good guy. *Charlie and Charlie for life*, her wedding invitations had said. Life is a long time, especially with someone who barely talks.

In the early days of their marriage, action compensated for a lack of conversation. Their time was spent socializing in groups, where Charlie's quietness wasn't as noticeable. And there was the physical piece—hiking, playing golf, doing yard work together, *having sex*. Before she knew it, their busy life made conversation more of a business transaction. "Can you pick Sheila up from softball?" or "I have a school committee meeting tonight," with yes or no answers sufficient. Until they retired, Charlotte hadn't realized how little Charlie spoke. Some days it was limited to two or three sentences. The question "Are you going to answer me?" largely went unanswered. Charlotte had tried everything—matching him silence for silence, giving him engaging easy-answer questions, pretending it didn't matter, and finally, screaming her disappointment at his blank, controlled face. Marriage counseling compounded her frustration since talking is part of therapy. Moving to a retirement community was Charlotte's last-ditch effort at getting a fuller life. Then the pandemic shut down that option before it had a chance to start. Now, as excited as she was for Sheila and John to move ahead with their construction plan, she was dreading being alone with Charlie.

*

One night at dinner, Charlotte's son-in-law told this amazing story about a mala bead necklace that was given to him by a patient in South Carolina. It was so unlike John to share something like that. Slightly embarrassed, he relayed how he had said the mantra as a solution to their land problem. Sheila looked miffed to be hearing this for the first time, but Charlotte felt weirdly electrified by the story.

"So, who are you planning on passing the beads to next?" she asked, when he was done with his tale, and showing them the contents of the intriguing little bag.

"Charlotte, you've been so good to us, letting us live here for free, putting up with the house-building delay. There must be something you want badly enough to say a really hard sentence a hundred and eight times. Just don't wish for us to be outta here any time soon!"

Charlotte's laughter covered her excitement. She wanted to grab the gauze bag from his hand. "Thanks, John. I love having you guys live with us. I'm sure I'll think of the perfect thing to ask for."

*

"Charlie, you staying up to watch the news?" A head nod was her answer. "Okay. I'm going to bed," Charlotte said, knowing he would fall asleep in the recliner, giving her hours alone to perform the mantra. She headed with gleeful anticipation to their bedroom and turned on the white noise machine she had purchased on Amazon when she realized only a thin wall stood between the newlyweds' headboard and her own. "No sense being a voyeur" Charlotte had told her silent husband, though she was more concerned with her daughter noticing the *lack* of exciting noise on her and Charlie's side of the sheetrock. After stacking two pillows on the floor beside the bed, Charlotte settled herself in a traditional cross-legged yoga pose, mala beads in hand. She had already spent some time practicing the mantra in the bathroom after dinner, so she was ready to begin. Seven deep breaths, and then, "I want to save my marriage. Om satyam narayanam …"

*

Charlotte felt too excited to sleep. *Maybe I should make myself a cup of tea.* As quickly as the thought entered her mind, it was replaced by an overwhelming exhaustion. She fell into a deep sleep.

*

The dream was like watching an old movie, the edges of the scenes slightly blurred with low-definition fade. She easily recognized her mother-in-law's kitchen, the daisy-covered wallpaper, the avocado appliances. At the table sat Charlie, his appearance unchanged, though she knew he was five years old. Tears ran down his cheeks. Her father-in-law, a man Charlotte had never warmed to, stood over the boy.

"B-but …" Charlie-the-boy sputtered. His father's hand was fast across his cheek.

"I told you, boy. Don't say another word unless you can say it right!" The punishing man said through his clenched teeth, his hand raised and ready to backhand his son again. "Did you get your chores done?" The father baited.

"I … I …" The hand came back down, knocking Charlie from the chair.

Where was his mother? As soon as Charlotte's mind asked the question, she felt herself in the scene, becoming Charlie's mother. "Please, Charles! Stop! He can't help it—"

"Stay out of this! You keep treating him like a baby and he's never gonna talk right!"

She watched Charlie cower on the kitchen floor while his father continued to ask questions he could not answer. For a brief moment, she became the father, then she was Charlie. It was unbearable. It finally ended with her as witness and Charlie's father telling him to "Get the hell out of my sight, and don't say another word in this house until you can say it without sounding like a dummy!"

The dream ended. Charlotte slept soundly till dawn.

*

"I didn't hear you come to bed last night," Charlotte said to Charlie as she entered the kitchen. He was reading the morning paper at the table. He smiled at her. "You fell asleep in your chair, again." He nodded.

Suddenly, the light streaming into the kitchen caused Charlotte to experience an optical illusion. A dark old kitchen and their bright new one shifted back and forth before her eyes, fusing the two realities. She stumbled from the disorientation it created. Her husband leaped from the table and caught her before she fell. "You okay?" he asked, his face so close to hers. She felt his worried eyes connect to her confused ones, causing her legs to give out again. He gently helped her into a chair.

"Did you stutter as a child?" She whispered the question.

"Yes." He answered.

Charlotte bent over and put her head between her knees to stop herself from fainting. Charlie crouched in front of her.

"Should I call nine-one-one?" he asked. She shook her head no and raised her eyes to meet his, for the first time seeing him for who he truly was—a kind and wonderful man. Then she held both sides of his face and her body flooded with understanding and compassion. She thought her heart would burst from the warmth of the emotion she felt.

"I love you, Charlie."

Her husband laid his head in her lap. "I know."

Charlotte's tears of gratitude fell onto him. *Namaste.*

May 25. 2020

CHAPTER 15 ~ MARIANNE

Seattle, Washington

Being a twin wasn't what it was cracked up to be for Marianne. Rather than the mystical connection of feeling her twin's pain, more often than not she was the cause of it—and vice versa. Everything was a competition between Marianne and Charlotte, and had been for as long as Marianne could remember. It wasn't their fault. People naturally made comparisons the moment they saw the blond, blue-eyed, identical twins, and that habit grew until it became the worst of rivalries. The two sisters fought about looks, grades, boys, and popularity—then later, the accomplishments of their husbands and children.

As luck would have it, each had a child who was recently married, and each child had a house being built. Marianne and Charlotte now compared lot sizes, locations, square footage, and, of course, progress. With the building permit held up on her niece's end, Marianne's son, Michael, and daughter-in-law, Sandy, were way ahead in a competition they didn't know they had entered. Then Michael fell through a second-story chimney opening while having a discussion with the builder about the size of the dream-suite master bedroom he was creating for his wife. His paralysis was nearly total. Game over. Nothing would ever be a win again as far as Marianne was concerned, unless it was the misery contest—her first round nailed when she became a widow a few years ago.

Charlotte could not have been more wonderful to her. She flew right in the moment she heard and stayed with Marianne through the worst of it. Or what Marianne thought was the worst of it. It was the day-to-day knowledge that her son would never be the same that killed her as a mother. Your dreams, his dreams, his wife's dreams—all dead. Every morning, Marianne woke up with the same heavy heart. She sleep-walked through the day, at first with hopeful ups and downs, now with only downs. She barely noticed when the pandemic began—other than how it related to Michael's appointments and therapies. Through it all, her daughter-in-law was a rock. That was a competition Marianne had easily won—the in-law category. Sandy was a keeper. She was smart, funny, loving, and treated Marianne like a woman to be thanked every day for creating the most wonderful husband in the world. "They say if you're looking for a happy marriage, look no further than how well a son treats his mother," Sandy had said to Marianne when they announced their engagement. She had included Marianne in all the wedding plans, asked her advice, and was the one to tell her the big news, "We bought land right in the same town as you!" Other mothers might have to worry about some girl stealing their son away. Not Marianne.

*

Charlotte's call with the news about Sheila and John finally getting started on their house was in no way a boast. Her sister said it apologetically, as though it were information she was obliged to tell but didn't want to. Hearing Charlotte's voice made Marianne wish Seattle and Marshfield weren't on opposite coasts, a thing she had never felt before.

"I sent you something overnight through FedEx. You'll need to sign for it," Charlotte said to her in closing.

"What is it?" Marianne had asked.

"You'll see," Charlotte replied, cryptically. "When you get it, just try to keep an open mind. It does what it says it does."

It does what it says it does? Marianne wracked her brain seeking possibilities for this mysterious item, then she let it fall from her mind like everything did these days. Nothing was important enough to merit a second thought while her son's life was ruined. "Thanks, Charlie. I'll keep my eye out for it."

*

At first, she thought it was a joke. Who would give a woman with a paralyzed son a lucky charm or a fake genie's lamp? Charlotte's note said it had fixed the land problem and saved her marriage. *The power of wishful thinking maybe?* If that were possible, Michael would be walking in the door for Sunday dinner right now. For eight months, Marianne had already said every form of prayer and made every bargain that was hers to offer. She couldn't bring herself to ask for one more miracle cure for her son. Her heart couldn't take the disappointment. She decided to ask for something else almost as important. She would ask for her daughter-in-law's happiness. Sandy had been everything to her son before she became everything to his care. Marianne knew the life her daughter-in-law was living bore no resemblance to the one she signed on for. "In sickness, and in health," Sandy had said when Marianne had her first serious talk with her about the future. All well and good to be in it for the long haul, but everyone needs a piece of happiness to sustain them through a burdensome life.

Marianne got out her yoga mat and sat on the kitchen floor beside the gas fireplace. She had a crazy desire to toss the bag of beads, with its complicated directions, into the flames. Thank heavens there was a sealed glass door in front of the gas log. *Talk about bad juju.* She reread the directions one more time, practiced the mantra aloud, and then began. *Give my daughter-in-law the happiness she deserves ...*

*

Each week Marianne cooked meals and divided them into seal-a-meal boiling bags. It was the least she could do to help. Sandy was back to her marketing job, working from home. Because Michael's former position as a business banking lender included full disability insurance, money wasn't an issue. To Marianne's surprise, the couple decided to keep the house despite Michael almost losing his life in it. The plan for a working fireplace was scrapped, and in its place, an elevator was installed. Michael and Sandy's huge circle of friends had contributed toward the handicapped modifications through a variety of online fund-raisers. Everyone was doing what they could to ease the trauma of the wonderful couple.

This week Marianne made her son's favorite, chicken and dumplings. She didn't have a clue if the dumplings would be anything but mush once they were thawed and reheated. It wouldn't matter either way since Michael's food had to be cut small and mashed to avoid choking. As she put the batches into freezer bags, she thought about the mala beads and a block of solid cold fear engulfed her. *Oh my God! Why did I ask for Sandy's happiness? What if her happiness doesn't include my son?* It would kill Michael to lose the love of his life after losing everything else. Marianne counted back, eight days had passed since she did the magic mantra. Was it too late to reverse her intention? What could she possibly say? *I don't want my daughter-in-law to be happy?* With shaking hands, she finished loading the bags and put everything in a cooler to bring to Sandy and Michael's freezer.

*

The initial sight of her son hadn't eased with time. Each visit Marianne would plant a smile on her face before opening the door, then loudly announce her presence—as if she might somehow catch the two lovebirds having sex—then head straight to wherever her son's motorized wheelchair was parked. With the partial use of one hand, Michael had gotten pretty good at navigating through most obstacles. "This is my revenge for you not letting me play video games when I was a kid," he joked, not guessing the pain his joke caused her. Today he was all smiles when he greeted her at the door.

"Let me take that cooler for you, Mom."

"Ha-ha," she replied.

"Seriously, put it on my lap and I'll wheel it into the kitchen. I helped Sandy bring in the groceries the other day. Now that she knows I can do it, there'll be no rest!" Michael had always been a character. It was good to see him in wise-guy mode. Marianne used to give it right back to him. Maybe she could practice that along with her happy face. Sandy came swooping into the room.

"Give me that!" She kissed Marianne's cheek and grabbed the cooler in one graceful motion. Marianne started to follow her. "Mom, stay with Michael. I'm just gonna throw this on the counter. We can put it away later. We have something to tell you." Michael zoomed toward the living room. Marianne followed, feeling confused by their conspiratorial joy.

"Sit," her son ordered. She did as she was told. Michael performed a three-point turn and backed into the space beside the sofa across from her. Sandy joined them, sitting beside her husband and leaning in to take hold of his hand.

"Do you want to tell her?" Sandy said to Michael.

"No," Michael replied. "You tell her."

"Well, she's your mother. You should tell her," Sandy insisted.

"Will somebody please tell me what's going on!" Marianne didn't mask her aggravation.

"Okay," Sandy began. "Through the magic of science …"

Oh my God, thought Marianne, *my son is going to walk again!*

"We are having a baby!" she finished. "You're going to be a grandmother!"

"What? How?" Marianne sputtered, having already mourned the possibility of this news.

"She told you, Mom—the miracle of science," her son answered, sporting a huge grin. "Trust me. You don't want to know the details." Marianne looked from one to the other.

"Please tell me this isn't a joke."

"Nope! We found out eight days ago! We were waiting until the bloodwork came back to tell you. Of course, it's early. But everything looks perfect!" Sandy's face was an explosion of happiness. Michael didn't take his gaze off her as she spoke. Marianne jumped up to kiss them.

"How are you feeling?" she asked, as she hugged her beautiful daughter-in-law.

Sandy's gaze went straight to her husband, nothing but love in her eyes. "It's a miracle. I feel like the luckiest woman in the world."

Marianne's heart filled with happiness.

Thank you, dear Charlotte, for your part in my family's miracle. Namaste.

May 28, 2020

CHAPTER 16 ~ SANURA

Seattle, Washington

Whenever someone told Sanura that her yoga class had saved them, she took the compliment with an indulgent smile. Sure, it probably centered their frayed nerves or kept their body from rusting for lack of use, but did it really save them? Sanura doubted it. She knew what it was to be saved. Yoga had truly saved her life.

*

The Egypt of Sanura's childhood was a full cornucopia of demographics—cities packed with museums and history, deserts full of ancient artifacts, and some of the most beautiful beaches in the world. Tuition-free higher education, freedom of religion, and growing gender equality were ideals touted by the Egyptian government. Sanura's father owned a cotton gin in Kum Ombu, north of the Aswan High Dam on the River Nile. Though their income fluctuated with the price of cotton, it never dipped below what it took to provide well for a family of eight. Sanura began her life in a world of comfort and possibilities, never imagining that her path was as narrow as the belief system of the generations of women who had gone before her.

*

Both Sanura and Mesi had heard the rumors. The sisters knew exactly what their mother and grandmother were fighting over. At eight and nine years of age, they were a brain trust when it came to shared information. What one didn't know, the other provided. Taller and leggier, Sanura was constantly mistaken as the older of the two instead of the youngest child in a family that included four sons. Had it not been for her bold and curious personality, Sanura could easily have been overlooked. She spent much of her life wishing she had been.

*

"They are too young!" their mother, *Mut,* stated, with mock authority to their grandmother, though Sanura knew her *Teta* was the real boss of the family.

"Will you have them wait until they are shamed?" Teta replied, just as fiercely. "No husband will have them!"

"They are babies, yet! We will discuss this in a year!" Mut replied. The girls watched their mother turn her back to signal the end of the conversation, albeit prematurely. Teta had the last word.

"It is done. Tomorrow they will be cut. Your husband has agreed."

Sanura and Mesi scrambled to their bedroom to combine everything they knew about 'the cut.' It was not much, but enough to justify the terror they felt. They considered running away. By morning it was too late. Six village women, along with their mother and grandmother, paraded into the girls' bedroom before the sun had risen or their eyes had opened. It marked the last normal day of Sanura's life.

*

The surgeries were performed simultaneously in one room. The girls were held down by the village women, their legs spread wide, arms held in a clasped vice grip above their heads. Sanura could see Teta lying across Mesi's struggling body, and her precious Mut was heavy across her own chest. There was no anesthesia. Sanura's screams blended with her sister's until Mesi fell into unconsciousness and the only screams left were her own. The clitoris and pubis were removed, as well as the inner and outer labia. The two cut sides were then pulled tightly together over the vulva and stitched, leaving a small hole toward the bottom for urine and menstrual blood to escape. After the procedure, a band of rope was wrapped around their upper thighs to prevent them from ripping the sutures. The girls were carried home and put to bed in their little girl beds, adorned with the soft cotton quilts of their father's legacy and their mother's handiwork. Ten days later, Mesi died of sepsis and Sanura became mute, since there would never be words to describe her trauma.

In her silence, Sanura was finally the afterthought her formerly gregarious personality hadn't allowed her to be. She dutifully performed her school work and chores, then retreated to her room where she had taken to wearing her sister's clothing and sleeping in her bed. When the day came that Sanura no longer fit into Mesi's school uniform, she sank deeper into the endless well of her depression. In an attempt to make her suitable for marriage, her father enlisted teachers of various talents, hoping something would jar her back into the world of the living. Sanura remained emotionally detached, despite her mastery of the various skills. She became less and less a part of the world around her, hoping to someday disappear altogether. Then she met an American yoga teacher named Renee.

*

Renee had traveled from America to Egypt to study Kemetic yoga. The course was expensive. Between tuition and accommodations, she had used her entire savings. It was worth it. Kemetic yoga was sometimes called Black yoga in the States. It was an ancient Egyptian method based on seeking wellness and enlightenment within each individual. As a Southern Black woman,

Renee's desire to connect the two things most important to her, yoga and her Black heritage, was fulfilled with this trip to Egypt. She was in the final days of her studies when her yoga instructor sent her to the home of a wealthy cotton merchant. Renee's assumption that it would be a class for bored wives looking to fill their day could not have been further from the truth. As she was led into an empty courtyard, carrying her mats and a shoulder bag containing her portable CD sound system and meditation chimes, a beautiful young girl entered the room with her mother.

"This is my daughter, Sanura. She does not speak," the woman said. With no explanation or fanfare, the mother left the girl standing alone.

Renee laid a mat on the stone floor, and gestured to it, not knowing if the child had hearing. The girl sat, her legs crossed, her back erect—a natural yogi. Renee laid her own mat in front of the girl. She lit a candle and pressed play to start her meditation music. She would simply begin her practice and assume the girl would mimic her. In the lotus position, Padmasana, with legs crossed, each ankle resting on the opposite thigh and her hands resting palms up on her knees, Renee touched each pointer finger to thumb in Gyan Mudra. It was a basic but powerful pose designed to increase the air element, improve mind power, and assist in spiritual enlightenment. Renee closed her eyes and let her body relax. A Kemetic proverb floated through her mind. *"The purpose of all human life is to achieve a state of consciousness apart from bodily concerns."* She set her practice intention, *I ask for the highest and best good for the young girl who sits before me, as well as for myself.* She began with "Om…"

*

For the first time since Mesi's death, Sanura's body was at peace. With her eyes closed and the deep, resonating, bell-like sounds of the music, there was nothing to do, or be—just exist. The words *i am* mingled with the sound of *om*. When the session was finished, her crying began. The instructor came to her and sat on the mat behind her, circling Sanura's body with her own—letting her spend her emotion without comment or judgment. A safety and wholeness enveloped her. Even Sanura's tears felt right. All was as it should be. The absence of her beloved sister was suddenly bearable. Their relationship had survived death. Mesi was right here in this room. Sanura did not want this knowing to end.

"How can I feel this way forever?" she whispered to the woman still wrapped around her and holding her hands in a prayer pose in front of her.

"I will teach you."

*

So the journey to connect Sanura's scarred body to her spiritual wholeness began, eventually leading her to move to Seattle, Washington, where Sanura would learn the details of her circumcision from an American gynecologist provided to her by a humanitarian group against FGM, female genital mutilation. He would show her a diagram of normal female genitalia, and explain to her what was missing about her own. They would discuss her frequent bladder and kidney infections, and the doctor would emphasize the need for at least minimal reconstruction to reopen the area to allow normal function of the urethra and vagina. Sanura would agree to think about it, all the time knowing she would never consider a surgery of any kind. *No one will ever cut me there again.*

*

Barry came into Sanura's life shortly after she opened her yoga studio. He was everything a woman could want. At thirty-three (four years her junior) Barry had already made his mark on the world, having graduated from Penn State University with a Master of Science in Electronic Engineering, and then walking straight into his daddy's telecommunications company. Together, Barry and his father pioneered into practicality most of the current 4G technology. His life was fast-paced—filled with innovation, ideas, and long hours. Yoga was Barry's saving grace. "You're my saving grace, Sanura." She told him she didn't date students, *or anyone.* Keeping him at arm's length turned out to be impossible. Soon he was taking three classes a week. At the close of each class, he handed her a business card with his private number scrawled across it in red sharpie. With thirty-three business cards tucked into a green lotus dish on her dresser, Sanura finally gave in to seeing him. On their first date, he told her he loved her. She had been in love with him from the first touch, a gentle assist during a difficult yoga pose.

In a rare bout of magical thinking, Sanura let the dating continue as though intimacy were a possibility. Barry's kiss was breath of life. She couldn't even look at his hands without losing herself. As many times as he told her he loved her, she refused to reciprocate. To do so would make it harder to break up with him when she came to her senses.

One night after dinner, she gave him a pamphlet on female genital mutilation. "This will explain why we must not see each other again. You will find another yoga class."

The next day, Barry was waiting for her as she descended the steps from her apartment to the back entrance of her yoga studio on the ground floor below.

"This explains nothing, Sanura," he said, waving the pamphlet in his hand. "You've been hurt. I can help make it better."

"There is nothing to make better. This is who I am," she replied, her back to him, key in the lock. Then she slid through the studio doorway and locked the full-glass door behind her without looking back at him. *It is done.*

*

"I won't touch you. I'll sleep on the floor. Jesus, Sanura! I'll sleep in your fucking bathroom! That's it! You can lock me in your bathroom at night! Let's stop having this conversation. I know you love me." Sanura had caved into seeing him, again. Their relationship was now past the breakup point. The pandemic had forced her to close the studio and go into lockdown. Barry wanted her to move in with him. Her refusal only made him beg to move in with her.

"You cannot live in my apartment. It is too small. And you need your computers, and your … I do not know what—your things that you do for work." She wasn't going to be budged.

"That's right, but I need you more. I have two bedrooms. You and your cat will have plenty of room. How 'bout if I buy the place right next to mine?"

"Don't be ridiculous."

The bargain they struck was to continue living separately but meet at the studio three times a week where he would film her for live Zoom yoga classes.

*

Everything had become a challenge. Black Lives Matter protests over the death of George Floyd permeated all corners of the city, including Sanura's neighborhood. Of the many yoga studios in and around Seattle, few were owned by people of color. Sanura was shocked to see that hers was the one with the broken glass window.

"Do they not know I am Black?"

"Babe, I'm sure it's nothing personal. Consider it doing your part for the cause." Barry screwed another sheet of plywood into place while Sanura held it. After securing the window, they went back inside to clean the shattered glass. An hour later, they had done what they could.

"Grab some clothes and that damn cat, and we'll stop at the grocery store on the way to my place."

"Barry—"

"I'm not leaving you here."

Sanura scanned the studio, deciding two yoga mats were all she would take. Then she remembered the little shopping bag she had found hanging over the doorknob, undisturbed despite the vandalism. "Someone left this for me," she said to Barry, taking the bag from the chair where she had thrown it. He reached for it.

"I'll check it for explosives." She smirked, but the mention of explosives jarred her nerves. She would go with him without a fight.

*

The cat settled in surprisingly quickly, as though he knew his owner would insist on leaving had he behaved otherwise. *Traitor* she thought, watching him curled up in Barry's lap.

"I am done with this day. I need sleep." Sanura kissed Barry's head. He reached for her hand and brought it to his lips.

"Everything's gonna be fine, Sanura. I'll toss this ball of fur into your room before I go to bed."

"Keep him. He likes you better."

*

The energy in Barry's guest bedroom felt light. Sanura had her sage and candles with her but saw no reason to clear the space. She could feel the day's tension ease from her neck as she put her few belongings in place. She hadn't brought much, knowing she would not be here long. Once finished, she picked up the mysterious doorknob bag and sat on her folded yoga mat to examine its contents. Inside was a small muslin bag and a card that read:

Dear Sanura,

My heart is breaking for every person of color. Like many white people, I am examining my flaws. What can one white woman do? Not much, it seems, except reach out to her Black friends. You are important to me. Coming to your classes saved me from an avalanche of despair when my son became paralyzed. I hope you know how much you mean to so many.

These mala beads have magical powers. They granted me a wish that I didn't know was possible. I hope they do the same for you.

With love,

Your faithful yoga student, Marianne.

When Sanura lifted the beads from their gauze bag, she knew it was true. She was in the presence of powerful magic. She held them close, savoring their aura. Her mind went to her first yoga experience and she was filled with hopeful anticipation. A miracle was about to happen. *What should I ask for? I will ask only for that which is in my highest and best good.*

*

The flash of pain happened halfway through the japahoma. It split between Sanura's eyes and through to the top of her head. Behind the pain, a scene was forming …

She and Barry were climbing a hill. They were dressed like hikers, smiling in the glare of the sunshine, shielding their eyes to gaze at the top of the hill. Sanura felt a presence behind them. Barry turned around to look down the trail they had just walked.

"Come on, Mesi! Your mother and I are going to win!" Sanura turned to see the image of her sister—laughing, joyous, alive—bounding past them toward the top of the hill. Barry laughed and took Sanura's hand. They ran to catch up with their daughter. The vision ended in the blaze of the sun.

Sanura looked down at her shaking hands. She was on the last bead. "Om satyam narayanam."

*

She found the card in her wallet:

Raymond D. Briggs, M.D., FACS, ASPS, ASAPS

Specializing in FGM reconstructive surgery

Sanura tucked the card back in its place. Tomorrow she would call their office to schedule surgery. She could hear Barry talking to the cat. "What do ya think? You ready to go to bed, little guy?" Sanura wanted to go to him and profess her love, but she wasn't ready to share the luscious feeling of knowing they would be together. Knowing they would have a daughter. Knowing she would live a full life. She wanted to sit a while longer with the bliss of knowing. *Thank you, Marianne. Namaste.*

May 29, 2020

CHAPTER 17 ~ BARRY

Seattle, Washington

The world was going to hell at 5G speed, and Barry felt guilty he couldn't immerse himself in the misery of it. The pandemic was raging, America was raging—politically and racially, *were they the same thing?*—and he had never been happier. World circumstances had forced Sanura to move in with him. He would have thrown that rock through her studio window himself if he had known that was all it would take to get her here. Barry even liked her silly cat. Now, if he could just figure out a way to keep her from leaving. Sanura was tricky. She could flip the switch before Barry even knew what topic they were on. She was a puzzle. He liked puzzles. He wanted to get to the bottom of *this* puzzle.

Over the last weeks, Barry had read everything he could get his hands on about female genital mutilation. The whole thing boggled his mind. The literature ranged from almost normal circumcision-like cutting—the kind they do to boys all the time—to horrific disfigurement. He had no idea what category Sanura fell into. Other than handing him the pamphlet, they had never discussed it. He sure as hell wasn't going to bring it up now. They had their version of sex. She satisfied him without intercourse. The truth was, she satisfied him by just being in the room. He loved her. His parents wanted to meet "this older Egyptian woman yoga instructor." *Four years older is not an older woman.*

Barry had been light-years ahead (or behind) his peers. While they were all drinking at the abandoned warehouse, he was reading his father's back issues of *Popular Electronics Magazine*. As a tall, well-built Black man, every sports coach he met tried to recruit him. Little did they know he didn't even watch sports, let alone play. It was just not his thing. Technology was his thing. He was a maker in the grandest sense. Since joining his father's company, he had acquired three US patents under his name. Technology was his thing, and now love was, too. Barry had always imagined that at the perfect time the perfect woman would find her way into his life, and they would create the perfect family. Two out of three isn't bad. If Sanura's genital issues made having children impossible, so be it. He just wouldn't tell his parents until he had to. *Look at me, already talking family. I would settle for getting her to stay one more night.* Sanura wasn't a high-maintenance woman, yet Barry couldn't *maintain* her. She didn't require anything of him—zero. Whatever he said or did was fine with her as if she were indifferent to him. He wanted desperately to matter to her.

*

Sanura was already up and dressed when Barry and the cat rolled out of bed at 7 a.m. She looked ready to flee.

"I'm going to the farm market I saw on the way here. Can I take your car?" she asked, the first words of the new day.

"How did you sleep?" he replied.

"Good. Very good. Can I take your car?" she repeated.

"I can get dressed and go with you?" Barry suggested.

"No. I just need your car."

"Sure. Of course." She was gone before he poured his first cup of coffee.

*

"Let's get your litter box out of Mama's room." Sanura had insisted she didn't want to inconvenience his bathroom with cat smells. Barry, like most men, wasn't known for his keen sense of smell. He walked into her room—in perfect order, yet already filled with her essence. It was as though she had an emergency bag full of magic at the ready. On the window sill were crystals and candles. The bare spot on the bookshelf now contained Tibetan bells and a small statue of a lotus-sitting Buddha. A mandala tapestry covered the bed. Nothing of his had been moved, yet he had been effectively erased from the room's narrative. *How does she do this?* On the desk was a gauze bag. Barry couldn't stop himself from going to it. Sanura's mala beads. He read the manifestation message and mantra, deciding this was where she got her magic. Barry didn't analyze his desire for science and magic to exist in the same realm. He knew he needed a supernatural influence to keep her. *What would be the harm?*

They were her beads, he couldn't ask for his own selfish wish. He decided he would ask for Sanura's happiness and take whatever consequence that wish produced. He performed the magical mantra.

*

Barry heard the car pull into the driveway, so he scooted the cat into his bedroom and closed the door to keep him from escaping while they brought in the groceries. Sanura walked in carrying one huge sack of overflowing produce. Barry rushed to take it from her.

"Is there more in the car?"

"This is it," she responded, tossing her purse onto the breakfast bar. He started to unpack the bag.

"I will do that. I have a system." He backed away, trying to read her mood. She had one mood for everything—unpredictable. He had the sinking feeling that his mantra had backfired. She pulled the Italian parsley from the top of the bag and put it in the sink. He watched, unsure if he still factored into his own house. Sanura turned to look at him—a beautiful smile on her face.

"I would like to stay here. I love you. The rest is unimportant. We will figure it out together."

Like a scientist who had proven the existence of the realm beyond the veil, Barry's face ranged from elation to disbelief.

"It worked," he said in awe.

"The mala beads?" Her question was low and direct.

"Yes," he whispered, an admission that could strike the end of their beginning.

"What did you wish for?" Sanura asked, her face unreadable.

"Your happiness," he answered.

"Then, yes. It has worked."

May 30, 2020

CHAPTER 18 ~ ROBERT

Seattle, Washington

It took Robert ages to embrace yoga. He was inflexible in all the ways a retired man can be—stiff joints, stiff back, an inability to bend to another person's ideas. Yoga helped him stretch out his body and his mind. Robert had initially signed up for the class to find a woman to take care of him. After a lifetime as a single man, he suddenly found himself in a panic about his future. What if he broke a hip or came down with cancer? Who would be there to take care of him? He had no children and couldn't rely on his nephew, whom he hadn't seen for years. It wasn't as though he had a ton of money to dangle under someone's nose to entice them to take care of him. He had some, just not dangling amounts. So a year ago, Robert decided he needed a wife. An AARP magazine story about ways to meet women gave him the yoga idea. The article listed all kinds of options, from joining Habitat for Humanity (he was terrible with tools) to frequenting spas (he worried he would be more likely to meet a gay man than a woman). After a brief try at ballroom dancing (definitely not for him), Robert settled on beginner's yoga. That was where he met Marianne.

Marianne was everything Robert wanted—petite, blonde, attractive, with a history as a devoted caretaker to a husband who died from colon cancer. She was perfect. It took a couple of weeks for Robert to get the nerve to approach her after class. He was surprised to find she began yoga at the same time he had. *She must be looking for a new spouse too*, thought Robert, after their first conversation. He soon found out she was searching for a way to control the anxiety she felt after her son became paralyzed. The idea of a woman with anxiety threw him a bit, but not enough to stop him from pursuing her. Her misery sparked his 'knight in shining armor' gene, which Robert hadn't known he possessed. Chatting after class turned into weekly coffee at the nearby coffee house. Apparently designer coffee was another thing missing in Robert's life. Little by little, he added more missing pieces. Marianne would mention a series she had watched, and he would get right on it just to have one more connection with her. She suggested sushi one afternoon—he liked it. They took walks by the nearby lake. Robert, who had never before walked solely for the pleasure of it, began taking walks on his own. Marianne was opening a whole new world to him. He was waiting for the other shoe to drop, but there was nothing about being with her that bothered him. He finally decided to officially ask her out.

*

"I still can't believe you've never had a scone," Marianne chided, as they finished their post-yoga breakfast.

"Me neither," Robert replied. "These things are amazing—crack cocaine amazing. The inside is soft, the outside a little hard and crunchie. What's not to like?"

"Women always introduce guys to new things. Didn't you ever date?"

"I wasn't a breakfast dater," he said, thinking how convenient of her to bring up the topic of dating. "And I sure wasn't a yoga guy. I worked, golfed—had some romances. They just didn't spill into my everyday life—like you have."

Robert saw Marianne's face go red. *Is that a good sign?* He wanted to add more to what he had said, though he had been pretty obvious. The ball was in her court. She finally spoke.

"Robert. You know this isn't a date, right?"

"It could be. We get along, enjoy each other's company—"

“No. We won’t be dating. I have enough on my plate, my son … my daughter-in-law is going to need help. Dating is—not what I can do.

Why did I open my mouth? He tried to hide his disappointment, make it a joke. “Marianne, I get it. I’m a lot for any woman’s plate. It was a dumb idea, I don’t want to mess up a perfectly good friendship.”

That was the last time he saw her. Marianne didn’t show up for yoga the next week, and shortly afterward the country was in a pandemic. In-person yoga classes were canceled. Robert had her number and could have called her, he just didn’t see the point. Now, it was Zoom yoga and no Marianne—definitely not the same.

*

“So you’re still into the yoga thing.” As the only other male in their class, Barry always gave Robert shit about his loyal participation. Barry was a loyalist, too. He had a good excuse. He was dating the yoga instructor, Sanura. They were both tall and strong—her so beautiful, him so dark—making Robert occasionally fantasize about their sex life. Barry also knew about Robert’s thing for Marianne. “Where’s your girlfriend?” he asked the first couple of times Marianne didn’t show up to class. “You scare her away, man?” *Yes, I did.* It was no longer funny.

One day Barry messaged him in the Zoom chat box during the yoga class, which was being filmed from an unfamiliar location. *Meet me outside the studio in 30 minutes. I have something for you.* Robert rarely went out these days, just nature walks and grocery store runs. He couldn’t guess what Barry had for him. He hoped it wasn’t some crazy hallucinogenic mushroom or something. Yoga people were a little ‘out there’ sometimes. He threw on his sweatpants, grabbed a mask, and headed out the door.

*

Robert got there first and was surprised to see the yoga studio boarded up. He stayed nervously in his car until Barry showed up and tapped on the window.

"I've got something special for you," Barry said, slipping something through Robert's partially opened window.

"What is it?" Robert asked.

"You'll see. The bag will tell you everything."

"You must have a ton of friends, why give this to me?" Robert asked Barry, holding the strange little bag.

"I like you. You're an okay guy." Barry answered.

This dude is smoking something. "There better not be anything illegal in here, my friend." Robert tried to sound kidding, but he sounded like what he was—a sixty-seven-year-old man with a slight paranoia problem.

"Nothing like that," Barry said, humor in his eyes. "*Your* girlfriend gave it to *my* girlfriend, who gave it to me, and I'm giving it to you.

Robert lit up. *It's from Marianne!* Maybe there was a note inside.

"Thanks, man, for … whatever this is."

*

Why would Marianne give this to me? Robert had gone through the possibilities and narrowed it down to *she still likes me*. It was the only explanation that made any sense—and that didn't make sense either. Was this like giving a daisy chain to a girl, he wondered? *And why give it to me through Barry?* With more questions than answers, Robert sought help from the internet. He looked up mala beads, mantras, and manifestation rituals, and eventually found himself on YouTube watching one mantra after another. He had no idea mantras were such a thing. Sure, he had done a bunch of chanting in yoga class, but he didn't think to do it on a daily basis. He took out the little scroll and read the instructions again. What if this is real? It would be nothing to mess around with. Robert thought about what he wanted, or more to the point, what he wanted from Marianne. Her friendship. It was as simple as that. He just missed her. He practiced the mantra a couple of times, unrolled his yoga mat, and began to breathe, setting his intention. At the last moment, he realized Barry could be just screwing with him. "Fuck you, Barry, if you are." Then he resumed his breathwork, stating, "I want my friend, Marianne, back." And began counting his repetitions of "Om satyam narayanam."

*

Robert didn't know what he was expecting, he felt no different. He got up, rolled his mat, and went into the kitchen to scrounge up some dinner. The cupboard was pretty bare. He opened a can of baked beans and ate them with crushed saltine crackers. *A sodium bomb dinner*, which was why it tasted so good.

It was 10 p.m. and Robert was suffering through the nightly gloom and doom report on television. The news had never bothered him before he retired. Now he worried about his meager IRA dwindling down to nothing and whether the kid next door was a drug addict who owned a gun. His cell phone rang. His only calls were telemarketers, partly because he never gave out his number and partly because he had no friends. "M. YOGA" flashed on the screen.

"Hello?"

"Hi, Robert? I know it's late to call. I hope you weren't sleeping. It's Marianne."

"No. I was just sitting here—watching the news."

"Well that's brave of you," Marianne answered, an attempt at humor in the response.

"What's up?" He tried to sound casual over the pounding of his heart.

"Remember how you said we could be friends? Well, I could use a friend right about now." Marianne stopped speaking. Robert couldn't think of a response, so he waited for her to continue. "Six weeks ago I was diagnosed with breast cancer. I was so depressed about my son's accident that I decided to refuse treatment. I stopped coming to yoga. I stopped doing anything."

"Marianne. I'm so sorry to hear this."

"Everything changed last week. Michael and Sandy are having a baby. I don't want to die, but I don't want to go through treatment by myself. I know it's a lot to ask—could you be my person through this? I need someone who won't hold me to the woman I've pretended to be—strong. It's an act. I'm terrified. I need to be able to fall apart a little, lean on someone. If it's—"

"It would be my honor to be there for you," Robert interjected without hesitation. "That's what friends are for. Do you already have a plan for treatment? I have a nephew who's an oncologist if you need a second opinion ..."

June 1, 2020

CHAPTER 19 ~ VANESSA

Seattle, Washington

Vanessa wasn't sure how much longer she could hold her urine. Her appointment was at eleven. It was only ten-forty-five. *Why do they make you drink so much water before an ultrasound?* She understood the concept of using her bladder as a window to her uterus. At twenty-four weeks pregnant, she was sure her bladder was already looking like a picture window smashed up against her baby girl. *Or boy?*

"Vanessa G," the nurse called from the glass behind her station. Vanessa waddled up to the window, holding her insurance card and ID in her hand.

"Vanessa, your appointment is at one o'clock, today," the nurse said.

"I thought it was eleven?"

"It's one. If we had room, I'd squeeze you in, but as you can see…" the nurse gestured to the full, socially distanced, waiting area.

"I gotta pee," was Vanessa's frantic response.

"The bathroom is through that doorway, down the hall, to the right," the nurse called after her as she rushed out.

Vanessa didn't make it to the bathroom.

*

She had worn her light blue yoga pants for two reasons—they were stretchy enough to easily lower for the ultrasound, and they went well with her favorite sweater, a navy blue, V-neck pullover that used to be her mother's. The dark urine stain went from seat to ankles, with no masking what had happened. Jeff had just dropped her off on his way to work since significant others weren't allowed in the ultrasound because of the pandemic. So here she sat on a metal bench outside the hospital, alone and unable to stop crying. To top it off, she would have to drink the thirty-two ounces of water all over again.

Venessa wrestled with the idea of calling Jeff. They hadn't spoken more than a few words to each other since the call from her obstetrician last week. As if a pandemic pregnancy wasn't joyless enough, now there was this problem with the baby. She was working unsuccessfully on not blaming all of this on her husband. If Jeff had told her he was using testosterone gel she could have researched it. He didn't tell her. Or talk to a doctor. Or have a prescription. *Or a clue*. To be fair, he started using it because he thought it would elevate his sperm count and help her get pregnant. Who knew pregnant women shouldn't come in contact with testosterone? Who knew it could cause ambiguous genitalia? Who knew any of this—until they knew? And then they couldn't un-know it. "Hermaphrodite" was the term her doctor threw out there when he made the call. "Your labs are way off. Have you been exposed to testosterone?" he had asked. "No," she answered confidently. Vanessa wished she could erase the conversation she and Jeff had when she told him about her doctor's strange call. She had said horrible, marriage-ending words.

*

"Did your water break? Do you need a doctor?" Vanessa hadn't noticed the man's approach.

"No. I—I peed myself." *There. Be out with it*. "I was waiting for a test." *Go away! This is hard enough!*

"I'll be right back," the man said, reassuringly. *Right back why?* she wondered, wishing her face mask covered her entire tear-streaked face.

Within minutes the man was back. He handed her a pair of scrub pants and a rolled-up pair of disposable hospital underwear. "They said there's a bathroom you can use in the lobby."

"Thank you," was all she managed to say. The man remained standing in front of her. Was she supposed to pay him? He reached into his pocket.

"I have something else for you."

Oh God, please! I can't handle another thing. Vanessa waited for him to hand her a bible or brochure. He pulled out a little bag.

"These are mala beads. A friend gave them to me and I used them to create a miracle last week. I'm supposed to pass them along. I think you should take them."

"Okay?" She took the little bag. "Thank you?" The man left, and Vanessa walked into the hospital with as much dignity as her urine-soaked clothing would allow.

*

The hospital Chapel was empty. In an hour Vanessa would be back in the radiology department with a technician who would know the fate of her baby before she did. *What do I need to manifest?* She went through the list. *I need this baby to be normal. I need my husband to forgive me. I need my mother.* Vanessa knew she could cross her mother off the list—not just because she was dead, but because her mother was always with her. She felt her in the largest of ways during the smallest of moments, like now. Getting Jeff to forgive her was also within her power. Sure, it was the worst fight they ever had, but they loved each other. No matter which way this went, she would apologize to him tonight. She patted her stomach. "That leaves you, little girl."

A sign saying 'Interfaith Meditation Room' had been added below the word 'Chapel' on the door, so her chances of being struck down by lightning for sacrilege seemed remote. It didn't matter. She would sell her soul for this baby. In that instant she understood motherhood. Vanessa sat in the first pew, directly in front of Jesus' cross, and began what might be a pagan ritual. Seven deep breaths. "I ask that my baby girl be normal and healthy…"

*

"How was your shift?" the friendly Uber driver asked.

"Good." Vanessa didn't explain the scrubs.

"Things getting better?" he continued.

"Time will tell," she answered. Then she pulled her phone from her purse and occupied herself with a text to Jeff saying she was on her way home. She pictured every healthcare worker with their heads down, texting to avoid questions about the horror of their day.

*

Jeff greeted her at the door and took the bag of soiled clothes. "Did they hire you at the hospital?"

"I peed my pants," Vanessa sobbed, unable to hold back another minute. Jeff pulled her into him, rubbing her back and kissing her head. She let him console her.

"Ness, you should have called me. I would have left work and brought you clothes."

"Because you're a good person!" she wailed.

"No. Because *you're* a good person, and you're my wife, and I love you," Jeff replied, still hugging her tightly.

"I'm sorry I was so mean."

"I'm sorry I was so stupid. How's our baby?"

"I don't know. The tech wouldn't tell me anything. She wouldn't even let me see the screen!"

"Bitch." Jeff said with a conviction that made them teammates again.

"Want me to order us a pizza?" he asked.

"Yes. A bad one, like meat lovers with extra cheese. I'm gonna go take a shower."

"You got it, girl." Jeff kissed her head and pulled out his phone to make the call.

*

The water was a soothing elixir over her body. It washed away her dried tears and urine. With soapy hands, she caressed her baby bump while she thought about the man who gave her the beads. He was unassuming—khakis, a short-sleeved golf shirt, glasses. He could have been a chiropractor or a dentist. He didn't look like the spiritual type. The baby moved. Vanessa was beginning to feel it more and more in the last few days. *Swimming in the shower*. "Whoever you are, your mommy and daddy plan on being obnoxious about how much we love you," she said as she dried off and pulled on the clean clothes Jeff had tossed into the bathroom. *Jeff.* She thought about the wisdom journal she had been writing for her daughter. She had a new entry: *Don't ever beat up your best friend.*

*

She knew from the doorbell's buzz that there was pizza waiting for her. Vanessa couldn't wait to dive into it—she hadn't eaten since breakfast and was pass-out kind of hungry.

She entered the kitchen and saw her purse on the counter, its contents half dumped out and rummaged through. Jeff was standing at the table holding her cell phone. The mala beads had fallen to the floor and were resting on the toe of his work boot.

"That was the doctor. The labs and ultrasound came back." His face told her everything she needed to know, she wanted to hear him say it. "Congratulations, Mama! We're having a perfect baby girl!" Vanessa rushed to his arms. *Thank you, Jesus!*

June 5, 2020

CHAPTER 20 ~ KATRINA

Sacramento, California

If Katrina had to listen to her social worker say "It's all about choices" one more time, she was going to commit murder. *Sure, lady. I'll bet your list of choices looks a little different than mine.* Katrina's current choice had come down to two bad options—go to rehab, or lose custody of her kids. The judge had only agreed to outpatient therapy because there weren't any beds available. The whole thing was a complete waste of time, but she wasn't letting anyone take away her kids.

Being an alcoholic had perks similar to riding an ocean wave. There was an excitement to it. One minute you were on top of the wave, letting the momentum pull you into its exhilarating spin—and the next minute you were being tugged below the surface into the undertow, barely able to stop from drowning. Katrina couldn't decide where on the wave she currently was—somewhere near drowning. Her ex-husband, Mark, and his stupid wife, Jennifer, had ambushed her with a child-endangerment complaint, triggering a review, which triggered a drinking bout, which triggered a DUI. There were a lot of triggers in Katrina's life and not many choices, but she wasn't letting anyone take away her kids.

Cole was five, blond, fair-skinned, and unusually responsible for a boy his age. Her little *Colie*, always so sweet to his mommy and never any trouble. Tommy was another story. He was a busy kid from the moment he was born. An early walker and talker—Tommy was a dark-haired, three-year-old wrecking ball. He was funny and smart and had a way of tugging at Katrina's heart no matter what kind of trouble he made. She and Mark had been sharing custody since their divorce, six months after Tommy's birth. Everything was going along fine until he married that Barbie doll look-alike. It wasn't Katrina's fault that Mark had rushed to get a vasectomy before Tommy was even born. It was *his* choice, not hers. She would have had more babies, maybe tried for a girl. Now Mark was married to "the love of his life," despite not being able to give the woman a child of her own. *Well, you can't have my kids, bitch! You're lucky you get them on weekends!* Everything about Jennifer bugged Katrina—her perfect hair, her job as a preschool teacher, the fact that she sent Katrina a million pictures of the boys every time she had them. It was all a farce designed to undermine her bond with her children. It wasn't going to work. Her babies knew who loved them more. "How much does Mommy love you, little Colie?" "To infinity and beyond!" he would answer, Toy Story was his favorite movie. And Tommy was a snuggler—once she cornered him on the couch and put on the right cartoons. Everything would have been perfect if Mark hadn't decided he no longer loved her. *Again, not my choice.* He had dragged her from Seattle to California and knocked her up twice before deciding she wasn't "the one." She couldn't move back to Seattle without a court order. And now she couldn't even raise her children without some whiny know-it-all from the state interfering. *Thanks, Mark. None of this was my choice.*

*

Today was especially aggravating. The rain hadn't stopped for days. Her house was a mess and she wasn't up for any of it. She sat on the couch and tried to catch up on a television series on her iPhone, while the TV blared with Mickey Mouse Clubhouse, and the kids pulled out every toy they owned. *Oh my god, it's so loud in here!* It was no use. She couldn't care less about the program she was watching. Clearly, the characters at the fake fire station weren't making "good life choices." She thought about calling her sister, Vanessa, but couldn't stomach another word about Vanessa's perfect life. Jeff was a one-in-a-million, their life was amazing, they were having a baby. As true as it was, Katrina still couldn't handle hearing about it. As if on cue, the phone rang.

"Hey. How's it going?" her sister's upbeat voice was barely audible with the noise.

"Cole, turn that TV down!" Katrina yelled, louder than she needed to.

"That good?" her sister remarked.

"What do you expect? It's raining. We're cooped up in this apartment. How's it going with you?"

"Good. We're having a girl."

Of course you are, Katrina's mind responded, while her mouth said, "That's great! I'm so excited for you guys. You're gonna love being parents!"

"Kat, I thought I'd hear from you yesterday. Did you get what I sent you in the mail?" her sister asked.

"I didn't get the mail, yesterday." *Or the day before.* "It's such a pain in the ass getting the kids dressed and walking to the post office. There's usually nothing good in the mail anyway." Katrina tried to make that last bit sound like a joke.

"Well this will be worth the effort," Vanessa replied. "And Katrina, call me if you have any problems figuring out what you have to do. It sounds a little spooky, but it really can change your life."

"Oh, dear God! Please don't tell me you sent a self-help book. I am at the end of my fucking rope with people telling me my life is my own damn fault!"

Silence.

"Sorry. It's just the rain," Katrina excused.

"Are you sure you're okay?" Vanessa sounded sincere. "I know it's been tough since Mom died, just the idea that she can't come out there to give you a hand—"

"I don't need a hand. I need a break. I need something to go right for a change."

*

The little bag of voodoo beads wasn't worth wrestling Tommy to the ground to get his shoes on. Katrina barely read Vanessa's letter, wondering how her sister could be so gullible. *Miracle manifestation my ass.* "Come on Colie. Grab your brother's hand before he gets hit by a car and killed."

*

Mac 'n cheese was the quickest fix for dinner. When the day started, Katrina had taken a pound of ground beef from the freezer, planning to make meatloaf and mashed potatoes. That was three glasses of wine ago. She made a game of getting the kids to bed as quickly as possible. "Whoever brushes their teeth first gets an extra handful of Skittles!" Tommy was the winner. She ended the night by having the kids take turns holding the dustpan while she swept Legos, crayons, and Pepperidge Farm Goldfish into it, then dumped it all in the toy box. Five scoops for each kid. "Go to bed!" she screamed when Cole got up to get Tommy some water.

*

"Screw you and your perfect life, Vanessa." Katrina was seconds from pulling the mala bead necklace hard enough to scatter the beads. "Mark, screw you and your perfect wife, too." She put the beads down and poured a little more wine. The mantra was a tongue-twister. Like the kind the cop had used when he made her get out of the car and walk a straight line. "Say any little puddle soaks your toes." She told the judge it was impossible to say, even sober. The officer assured the judge he was just trying to get her to move out of the puddle.

"Om satyam narayanam. See, Vanessa? I'm not a drunk." The words were surprisingly easy to say. Most of the time she couldn't even say her sister's name when she was drinking. "Om satyam narayanam." Katrina got up from the couch and grabbed another bottle of Pinot Noir. She fumbled with the corkscrew and finally managed—bits of cork floated on the top of her wine. Using substantial effort, Katrina brought the bottle, wine glass, and mala beads to the dining table. With a sweep of her arm, she shoved all the boys' coloring books and masterpieces to the floor. "I'll show those fuckers I'm not a drunk." She unrolled the little paper. By then she was seeing double. "Om satyam narayanam." She didn't need the directions. Seven deep breaths. "I can't lose my kids." Katrina did the mantra.

*

Someone was slapping her across the face. She put her arm up in defense. "Wha the fuck?" she slurred.

"Ma'am! Is he allergic to anything? Medication? Food?" Katrina struggled to open her eyes. The fireman was right on top of her. She tried to look around him, see what was happening. Cole was screaming. "Is your son allergic to anything?" She could see Tommy on the stretcher, an oxygen mask over his face. She tried to struggle away from the man holding her down.

"What's happening! What's the mather with my son?" Her tongue was thick.

"His blood sugar's over four hundred. Did he take his insulin today?"

"He doesn't have diabetes!" she responded, now fully alert. "He was fine when I put him to bed! Cole! What happened to your brother!"

"He was shaking! I told you he needed water!" A female EMT took Cole into her embrace.

"Your son couldn't wake you," she said. "He called 911 and stayed on the phone till we got here."

"I can't lose my kids!" Katrina screamed. "I can't lose my baby! Tell me what's happening to him!"

I can't lose my kids ... I can't lose my kids ... What was she trying to remember? *The mantra!* A moment of clarity surfaced through the confusion. *I need help.*

"Where's my phone?" The EMT handed her the phone her son had used to call for help. Unintelligible dispatch voices projected from the speaker on her shoulder.

Katrina pressed the Siri button, unable to focus on her contacts list. "Call The Asshole," she said into the phone. Mark picked up on the first ring.

"What's up?"

"Something's wrong with Tommy. They're taking him to—" She looked up at the paramedic.

"Mercy General."

"Mercy General," she repeated. "Can Jennifer come pick up Cole? He's—not good—traumatized. And you need to meet Tommy at the hospital. I've been drinking. Mark, call me every five minutes!"

"I will." Mark hung up. Katrina got up and went to the stretcher. They were snaking an IV line under the shirt she had dressed Tommy in, three days ago.

"You're gonna go see Daddy," she whispered. A warm blanket was tucked around him, Cole stood silently watching as they finished setting the bag of fluids.

"Ma'am, we're taking him in now." They pushed past her. Cole began screaming Tommy's name.

*

Katrina thought Jennifer would have bolted to Cole, asleep on the couch. Jennifer rushed to embrace her, instead.

"Oh my God Katrina! You must be terrified! Are you okay?"

"Cole saved Tommy's life. I was black-out drunk on the couch," she said evenly, a cup of coffee in her hand, and calmer with Mark's call saying Tommy was doing better. "Jennifer, I can't lose my kids and I almost lost one tonight. Can you and Mark take them? I don't know for how long, I have to check myself in somewhere. I need help. I can't lose my kids."

"Oh my god! Of course." Katrina let Jennifer hug her while she sobbed. "You'll get through this. Mark and I will do everything we can to help. You have two beautiful reasons to get sober. Your boys love you so much."

Katrina pulled herself together. "I'll pack their stuff." She went down the hall and stopped, unable to enter their bedroom. *What if they never come back?* She pushed the thought from her mind. Her boys would be safe with Mark and Jennifer. They have to be, *I can't lose my kids.*

With bags in hand, she walked back to the living room where Jennifer was sitting on the couch holding Cole. Katrina stood still, experiencing an unfamiliar emotion. *Gratitude.* It was gratitude that touched every fiber of her being as she watched her ex-husband's wife kiss the top of her son's head.

Thank you, God, for this second chance to be a good mother. I won't waste it.

June 6, 2020

CHAPTER 21 ~ JUAN

Vacaville, California

The order to evacuate came as Juan was beginning his 7 a.m. shift. He immediately called his wife, Rosa.

"I can't talk!" she yelled, on pick up. "I'm waiting to see if Randy can get his hands on another trailer." Juan could tell she was in the barn. The horses sounded as riled up as she did.

"I'm gonna clock out and come home. Can you see the fire from where you are, or is it still just smoke?"

"Just smoke," Rosa replied. "Don't come. By the time you get here, we'll be gone. We shoulda left yesterday—like Randy said." Juan tried not to bristle at the sound of Randy's name.

"I'll meet you. Are you going down to Buckertown? Like we talked about?"

"Juan. I gotta go. Randy just pulled in with another trailer. I'll call and let you know where we end up." His wife hung up. *Fucking Randy, a smart-ass, wannabe cowboy from Montana.*

Juan took a deep breath. He should have called in sick today. Rosa Ranch wasn't big, but it was everything to his wife. The Quail fire was eating up acreage just northeast of the ranch at a rapid pace—*spreading like wildfire,* a consequential phrase ruined by people using it for everything from crabgrass to a diaper rash. *I should be there right now—not him.*

When money got tight last year, Juan went back to his job as an intake nurse at a rehab clinic. Then the ranch proved too much for one person so they hired Randy, giving him room and board as part of his pay—and putting Juan out of the loop. It was like going to work knowing that your kid's daycare was costing half your paycheck, and you weren't even sure what was happening while you were gone all day. Not that anything was happening between Rosa and Randy. *Rosa and Randy.* He hated to say their names in the same sentence. *Of course nothing was happening.*

Juan and Rosa had a tight marriage. They also had their heritage. They were both descendants of the Muwekma Ohlone People. They met as kids at a cultural camp for the Muwekma Ohlone Tribe of the San Francisco Bay Area. He was from Santa Clara and she was from Winters. It was exactly one hundred miles from his house to hers—a distance that got shorter as they got older. Eventually, they both ended up at Feather River College, Rosa taking equine studies, and Juan getting his vocational nursing degree. Rosa's dream of owning a horse ranch eventually became Juan's dream. After fifteen years of knowing they would get married, they finally did—on the newly acquired Rosa Ranch, surrounded by an entire Tribe of friends and family. Their ceremony was spoken in Chochenyo, the language of The People, and filled with Indigenous foods—hazelnut chia pudding, and black oak acorn bread. Though they were both raised Catholic, their ceremony also gave thanks to the animal gods of their native culture—the Coyote, the Eagle, and the Hummingbird. Embracing a synergy of old and new, innovative and traditional, Juan and Rosa had carved their own path with the blessings of the land and The People. It was a beautiful life that could be burned to the ground in the change of the winds.

*

The entrance buzzer at his desk went off. Juan looked up to see a woman at the door with a duffle bag. He pushed the intercom button. "Can I help you?" he asked.

"I'm here to check in. My name is Katrina Sylvester," she answered, with the weird mix of enthusiasm and resignation clients often displayed when they were voluntarily checking themselves into rehabilitation. It was different from the patients who were being forced into a program by the courts, admissions that sometimes required security and sedatives.

Give me a willing victim any day was Juan's thought, *especially today*. He had already told his supervisor he was signing out after this admission, he needed things to go smoothly. The computer showed the insurance and referrals had already been processed. *Good.* He texted the female matron on duty and buzzed the new patient in, coming around to the other side of the glass partition to meet her at the intake table. "Welcome aboard. You can put your bag on the table, and empty whatever's in your pocketbook into this container. We'll inventory it and place your valuables in the safe." Juan watched her as she removed everything from the small shoulder bag—a clutch wallet, sunglasses, sanitary protection, pictures of her kids in little glass frames, her cell phone, and a small gauze bag of jewelry. "Can you hand me your purse?" he asked. She did. Juan checked the lining for any signs of contraband, looking for new stitching or bulkiness. He handed it back to her. "You can put everything back in it. Most of it will be given back to you after you're checked into your room."

"I need the pictures of my boys now," she responded. This was Juan's soft spot—patients being separated from their kids, too much of it in the news these days.

"If you remove the pictures from the frames, you can take them now," he told her. She quickly complied, then picked up the gauze bag.

"I need this too." She opened it for him, showing him it was a wooden bead necklace and a scroll of paper.

"They'll let you have it back after the psych eval. We need to make sure you're not a danger to yourself." The woman stared him straight in the eyes—unusual in itself.

"Do you have a problem?" she asked.

Oh god, he thought, *please don't be a lunatic.* "With you? No. I don't have a problem. I'm just trying to do my job."

"No. I mean do you have a problem that you need to solve?"

Where are you goin' with this, lady? "I'm good," he answered.

"These are special magic. They saved my kid's life. I'm supposed to pass them along. You're the first person who's seen them since they took my son to the hospital." She was getting agitated. "I'm supposed to pass them along! What if he gets sick again because I didn't do it right?"

Lola, the female attendant, walked up behind him. "Everything good?" she asked.

"All good," Juan answered. "This is Katrina. Her room is one-oh-nine, and it's ready when she is."

"I just need to pass this magic necklace along," the woman said, again, with rising agitation. "It's part of the directions. I'm giving them to him." she pointed her finger at Juan.

"Katrina, we can't take presents here," Lola said.

"I'll sign something. They're not mine. You just use them one time for what you need and then give them away." She frantically unrolled the paper and began reading out loud. "Once your intention has been realized you will pass this sacred energy to the next person in need." She looked up at them with desperation. "I don't want to screw this up. I can't lose my kids."

Lola looked at Juan. "Sounds pretty clear to me. Do we have a form for this?"

"Not for gifts. We have a disposal form—for things the client wants to throw away. I'll grab one."

Juan went to the reception file drawer and took out the last form in the file, then scanned it into the printer to make more copies. *Losing more precious time.* He called Rosa. It went right to voicemail. Juan watched through the protective glass as Lola checked out every possession in the patient's duffle bag. Copies finished, he rushed back and planted the form on the table. Lola filled it out with both caption and description listed as "string of wooden beads." She then made an additional notation that it was being taken by Juan Gaudiosa and had them both sign. Juan didn't think it was overkill to ask Lola to take a picture of Katrina Sylvester handing him the bag. People get let go for a lot less—especially his people, The People.

"You can't throw it away," she said one more time. "You have to read the directions and do what it says."

"I will," he promised, to hasten things along.

*

Still no answer on Rosa's phone. Juan called Buckertown Ranch. The kid that picked up sounded like he was ten. "Hello."

"Can you tell me if Rosa Gaudiosa has gotten to your ranch? This is her husband, Juan."

"I don't know. My dad's out there with someone who just got here," the boy responded.

"How big is their trailer?"

"Two horses."

Two horses. It's not her. Rosa would never leave the other two behind. "Do you have a paper and pen? I'm gonna give you my cellphone number. Give it to your Dad and ask him to call me."

Juan stood watching the live fire report on the admission's computer while he waited for the call. The Quail fire looked stalled for now. Looks could be deceiving. He opened the traffic app on his phone. The roadways from their ranch were green or orange, relatively clear no matter which way they went. Juan had about one more minute of patience in him before he took off in search of her. The only thing keeping him there was good cellphone service and the computer. It was one hundred percent old school once he hopped into his '97 Nissan Frontier. No fancy GPS—for that matter, it didn't have AC or a working passenger window, but its diesel engine never gave up no matter how hard he pushed it. He just needed a definitive direction to push it in. The phone rang.

"Juan Gaudiosa."

"Juan, it's Mandy from Buckertown. Davy said you thought your wife was heading our way? That's news to me. I haven't heard from her, but the service is sketchy, so you never know. If I hear anything I'll call you. You do the same."

"Thanks. I will." Then he left the building at a run. In his arms were towels, a couple gallons of water, and some extra N95 masks he stole from the locked storeroom. *There. That'll give you good reason to fire me,* he thought, knowing they wouldn't, hoping they would. Juan dumped everything into the Nissan and checked the glovebox for his cigarette-lighter-adapter phone charger. Then he spent more precious time pulling the broken window into place, there was no sense driving into a fire with your passenger window open. The roller was off-track, its cog teeth ground away from overuse. He finally took off.

*

The closer Juan came to the ranch, the more certain he was that Rosa wouldn't be there. The smoke was getting thick. The roads were empty. Every few minutes he checked his phone for a message or a ping on the locator app. Nothing. He pulled through the wide unlocked gates, with their overhead cattle-stamp sign—double back-to-back R's encircled by a rose. She wasn't there. The Ford truck was gone, her two-horse trailer sitting by the barn, half-ready to go. Randy must have found them a four-horse trailer. Juan sat in the Nissan and went through his options. Get out of here was number one. He called their two closest neighbors to see what they knew. No answer on the first. Frank, an old, widowed rancher with a property too big and too empty, answered on one ring. The noise in the background made it impossible to hear him.

"Frank, where are you?" Juan yelled into the phone.

"Vacaville. The shelter at 3 Oaks Community Center."

"Have you seen Rosa?" Juan asked loudly.

"No. Just that jack-ass cowboy you hired. If you're on the wrong side of fifty and living in somebody's stable room, it's because what you *don't* know is bigger than what you *say* you know," Frank replied with painstaking slowness.

"I get it, Frank. Where'd you see him? Did he say where they were going?"

"He came to see if I had a trailer—as if I'd have one when I got no horses." Another long pause with Juan straining to hear. "Dumb-ass talked about Winter's Meadow—somebody he knew there."

Winter's Meadow? Why would he go northeast instead of south? They'd be heading straight for the fire—even if they tried to circle around, it would be too close to the action.

"How sure are you that's what he said?"

"Damn sure," Frank replied with old-man conviction. Juan hung up, sped off the ranch, and headed north onto Pleasants Valley Road—right toward the fire.

*

Ten minutes in, the smoke was too thick to see. Juan pulled to the side of the road and put a second mask over the first. He checked his phone through tear-soaked, irritated eyes. Nothing. He tried Rosa's number again—a busy circuit signal. He wished he hadn't been so insistent on not putting Randy's number in his phone. *Pride cometh before the fall.* If Rosa was dead, he would stay here and die too. He tried to remember everything he knew about ritual fire purification. It calmed his mind.

"I need a miracle," he said, aloud.

You have a miracle, his mind answered.

"I need a miracle," he said, again.

You have a miracle, his mind volleyed back. *The wooden beads.*

Juan pulled the sack from his pocket and read the directions. He was going to have to do the abridged version, just his intention and the words. He didn't ask to live. He didn't even ask for Rosa to be alive. "Lead me to my wife, whether she's in this world or the next." Juan began the chant. Somewhere along the way, he passed out from smoke inhalation. The pinging phone locator woke him. Rosa was just west of him, about two miles away. Juan threw the Nissan into gear and headed off-road—a straight line his quickest route. A mile out he lost the signal but gained a little visibility. He looked at the compass on the rearview mirror—the one extra feature on the truck that actually worked—and continued to drive west, eventually finding a dirt road.

*

The surprise of seeing her almost caused him to bottom out in a ditch. Rosa was getting the horses out of the trailer, preparing to set them free. She was alone.

"Rosa Gaudiosa," he hollered, two names meant to be together for eternity. She spun around at the sound of her name.

"Juan! Oh my God! How did you find me?" She sobbed and flung herself onto him. He pulled his outer mask off and put it on her, then held her tightly while she regrouped. Over her shoulder, he saw both tires blown on the right side of the oldest, most decrepit horse trailer he had ever seen.

"Nice trailer. Where's Randy?"

"Probably halfway to Montana by now. He left two hours ago to get help."

"So, what's our plan?"

"One side is blown, the other side too low to make a difference. I guess we let the horses go, and get ourselves to safety," she answered, clearly despondent.

The smoke was getting thicker with the change of the wind. Juan eyed the Nissan's 6 by 5.5 bolt pattern on the tire rims. After two-hundred-and-eighty-thousand miles and twenty years of repairs, Juan knew his vehicle's stats. It was the same bolt pattern as the trailer rims.

"We're taking the wheels off the Nissan and putting them on the trailer. If it doesn't work—or we run out of time—we'll unhook the trailer, let the horses go, and take the Ford. We're not leaving here in separate trucks."

*

Twice they almost gave up, once with a rusted bolt, and the second time in a threatening black wind. An hour later, they were ready to go. Juan took everything out of his trusty Nissan, then pried the rearview mirror from the windshield so they'd have a compass. When he reached below his seat for his emergency supply box, he saw the wooden beads on the floor. The miracle of it hit him like a clap of thunder. He searched for the rest of it, the gauze bag and the little paper, and found them between the driver's seat and the center console. Juan stuffed everything into his pocket, slammed shut the door of the only truck he had ever owned, and ran toward the only woman he would ever love.

"Makkin Mak Muwekma Wolwoolum, 'Akkoy Mak-Warep,

Manne Mak Hiswi!

We Are Muwekma Ohlone, Welcome To Our Land,

Where We Are Born!"

June 7, 2020

CHAPTER 22 ~ FRANK

Vacaville, California

There was nothing Frank hated more than uselessness. So now he hated himself. Knowing when to throw in the towel used to be a source of pride for him. Is that cow giving her last pint of milk? One more repair for the tractor, or buy a new one? *Has my wife seen enough suffering and it's time to let her go?* In the past, his innate sense of timing had saved him from uselessly spinning his wheels. Yet now, in his old age and growing stubbornness, Frank had stayed on his ranch until both it and he were useless. No horses, no cattle, no crops—not even a dog to worry about. He spent his days in the least productive way possible—watching the weather channel and listening to talk radio. Every day was a miserable waste of time. Why he hadn't found the courage to slit his own throat was beyond him.

Looking back, his progression from productive to useless began with his wife's death. A few depressing months, an offer from Juan and Rosa to purchase his last two horses, a kitchen door that needed replacing—Frank began taking the easy path. It was a path he hadn't known existed. "Do the right thing, not the easy thing," his father always said. "Do the right thing, not the easy thing," Frank had said to his only son. Apparently, the right thing for his son was an environmental engineering degree and a job in British Columbia. With no one to care about things except himself, Frank was surprised to find he didn't care at all. Dishes sat in the sink, he secured the kitchen door by bracing a board beneath it at night. It especially didn't matter this year. *What a shit show.* A Pandemic, fires everywhere, shootings, protests, a political gunfight at the doorstep—Frank couldn't find one good reason to give a damn about anything. He surprised himself by going to the shelter during the Quail fire. He didn't go because he was afraid of dying, he went because after years of smoking filter-less cigarettes, *thanks for nothing, Marlboro Man,* he couldn't take a deep breath without coughing, let alone hang in there until a fire killed him. And now, after a good lunch and a buffet dinner at the community center, along with a surprisingly comfortable night on a cot, Frank wasn't in any hurry to go back to his empty ranch. He had been kind of hoping the whole place would burn to the ground, but it looked like CAL FIRE had things under control. It was time to go home.

*

Frank had taken no precautions when he left his farmhouse. He hadn't even shut the windows. Other than the smell of smoke—and like every old man his olfactory powers weren't anything to brag about—there was no evidence that the fire had gotten close to his property. He threw his bag on the kitchen table, pulled a beer from the refrigerator, and turned on his radio. Two boring hours later, he heard tires roll up his driveway. A glance out the window told him it was Juan and Rosa.

*

"You found your wife. Good for you," Frank said, acting like Rosa's safety was no big deal. The tight embrace he gave her spoke otherwise.

"Thanks to you," Juan replied, clapping him on the back.

"Where's that brainless idiot you hired?"

"Don't know. Don't care," Rosa replied. "It's embarrassing that I let him talk me into his exit plan."

Frank watched Juan's face. Love, relief. Devotion.

"We have something for you," Juan said, handing him a small bag. "It's spirit magic, an answer to a prayer."

"I don't need no thank you," Frank flushed with awkwardness. He didn't like presents.

"It's not a thank you. You'd be doing me a favor. After you use it, you're supposed to pass it along. I got too much work to do to find someone else to pass it to."

"How'd you make out at your place?" Frank asked.

"Not bad. A lot of acreage charred, but the house and barn are still standing. The biggest casualty was Papaw's truck. Burnt to a crisp on a dirt road northwest of Pleasants Valley." Juan looked at his wife. "Its last good day was spent saving our horses."

"Sounds like your papaw was watching over you," Frank said, in an unusual moment of sentimentality. Again, embarrassment overtook him. He pocketed the gift and shrugged his shoulders, suggesting he was done with this conversation. They took the hint, made their farewells, and drove off. Frank wiped at his eye. It was hard to watch a couple at the beginning of life while he was at the end. He went back inside to his radio.

*

A few days passed with nothing new happening. Frank went to Aldi's to pick up groceries and beer. He ran into a friend of his wife's who he never really liked. After their initial hello, he had to see her in every aisle. He finally skipped a few aisles to avoid her—sadly they were the ones with the peanut butter and tuna—and went straight for the beer. He had been in a bad mood for such a long time that he couldn't tell if seeing her had furthered his foulness. He skipped the drugstore and went home. What he was rushing back for was anyone's guess.

By the time the sun set, Frank was jumping out of his skin. He was too miserable to eat, not miserable enough to kill himself. Purposeless. He sat at the kitchen table and pulled a deck of cards from the little drawer that, back in the day, had held silverware. He and his wife used to play cards every night after dinner. He was cheating at his second game of solitaire when he thought about Juan's present and got up to retrieve it from the kitchen cupboard. He pushed the cards aside and opened the bag. After examining the beads and seeing absolutely nothing special about them, Frank read the paper:

This japa mala holds ancient and powerful Sanskrit energy used to manifest miracles.

To manifest your miracle you must follow these instructions precisely while keeping an open heart.

Sit in a meditative posture with your eyes closed.

Breathe in deeply, exhale slowly. Do this seven times while envisioning your intention.

Say your intention aloud, then begin the mantra.

You will chant OM SATYAM NARAYANAM 108 times using the mala beads to count—one bead for each incantation.

When you have completed this mantra, your miracle will come. Be patient.

Once your intention has been realized you will pass this sacred energy to the next person in need.

~Namaste

"Why the hell would they give me this?" he said aloud. "Mumbo jumbo bullshit." He almost picked up the phone and called Juan to ask him if it was a joke. Then he remembered Juan's face, the grateful look of it. He wondered if satyam had to do with Satan. *What the hell does keeping an open heart look like?* "Probably the opposite of mine," he decided. Rosa and Juan were good kids, from god-fearing families. He and his wife went to their wedding—there was nothing devil-like about it. A little paganistic maybe, with the reference to animal gods, but they were Christian Native Americans. *I got nothing better to do*. Frank decided to give it a try. He straightened his back and placed his palms toward the sky like he had seen before. He shut his eyes and did the breathing. Seven deep breaths and no coughing jag—a miracle had already happened. He said what he wanted, "Give me a purpose, or take me to my grave." Then he opened his eyes and read the words out loud over and over again, counting off each saying using a bead. It seemed to take forever, not one recitation said with ease. When it was done he put everything back in the bag and threw it into the table drawer with the playing cards. Then he went into the bathroom to urinate and toss his teeth into yesterday's cup of no-longer-fizzy Polident. He stripped down to his underwear and went to bed feeling the satisfaction of having at least accomplished something.

*

Although it was dark when Frank awoke, he knew it was late morning by the way his back ached from too many hours in bed. There was somebody knocking on his door. He thought about ignoring it and took a deep breath to see if he smelled another evacuation in the forecast. Nothing.

"I'm coming," he said to the door, on his way to the bathroom. He snapped his dentures in and threw on yesterday's clothes, going straight for the door without his morning pee. *It better be quick.*

"Is this a bad time?" Rosa asked, standing in the rain with Juan looming behind her.

"It's all a bad time, or a good time, depending on how you see things," he answered. *Again with the philosophy? What's up with that?* "Want some coffee?"

"Yes," Juan answered.

"Good. Make a pot while I finish some business in the bathroom."

*

"So let me get this straight. You want to lease some of my land, so you can plant alfalfa—and Teff?"

"It's a newer kind of hay grain out of Ethiopia," Juan said. "It's like Timothy—high in fiber, but not high in protein so it won't give the horses colic. It looks like it'll grow here, easier than Timothy. This was our plan for the acreage that was scorched. Even if we could get it ready by fall, it wouldn't be passable for growing Teff commercially. We couldn't do the first bud cut because we'd need it to re-pasteurize. Ideally, we need land that's had nothing planted on it for at least two seasons—"

"Like my land, rich and useless," Frank interjected. Rosa picked up the conversation.

"Frank, whatever works for you works for us. And if we're here to ask a favor, I say we get it all out on the table." Frank watched her glance at her husband, who gave a slight go-ahead nod. "We don't just want to use your land. We want you to oversee it. Juan and I can't be in three places at once. We'll pay you for your time."

Frank rolled over what they had said. Every bit of it sounded good, but what you agree to first is what you're stuck with last. "I'm not some young farm hand—my days of sweating it out in a field are done," he started his negotiating with the obvious.

"We can plow and harrow the land—do all the planting, see to the irrigation," Juan replied. "We need your brains not your brawn. It doesn't make sense for us not to take advantage of what you know,

Frank. Sure you might have to run a piece of equipment now and again, but nothing strenuous and not more than you're comfortable doing."

"If you're willing, we'll pay you a price per acre and a percentage of the net yield. We're still working out the numbers of what we can afford," Rosa tag teamed. "Juan's gonna stay on part-time at the rehab center till we get this thing going."

Frank was struck by the unity of their request—all thought out, presented in equal measures. Even their virus face bandanas matched. They reminded him of himself and Ervina Fay, always on the same path with the same goal in mind. Missing her was not going to stop. Maybe having a partnership and a new goal could help. "I'm in. We can hash out the details as need be."

Rosa jumped up to hug him. "Thank you, Frank. You won't regret it!"

"I'm sure I will," he replied, trying to maintain his cranky old man reputation—*with these two around it might be tough.*

June 11, 2020

CHAPTER 23 ~ JESS

Vacaville, California

Jess didn't always trust Sharon to do things the way she would do them, like giving the baby sugar-free strawberry yogurt. There are only so many fights you can pick with a woman who's taking care of your child for free, especially if that woman is your son's ex-girlfriend, and your best friend, and doing your daycare while taking care of her own baby—*and she's the person you're in love with.* Jess and Sharon's relationship was complicated, to say the least. Nothing about it was normal, like that November day when Sharon told her she was pregnant …

*

"If you're lookin' for Christopher, he's not here." Jess had bolted to the door the minute she saw Sharon's car pull into the drive. Sharon looked caught off guard, holding a letter she obviously meant to drop and run.

"I'm not looking for Chris. I wanted to give you this," Sharon responded.

"Unless it's bail money, I'm not interested." Jess began to close the door, then swung it wide in fury. "My son's not a violent man!" she spat out angrily. "You didn't need to bring the police into your little *lovers' quarrel!* Now he's got to take time off work, go to court—"

"Did he tell you I'm pregnant? That he was gonna knock the baby right out of me?" Sharon blurted. Jess took a step back, her righteous aggression gone. She opened the screen door.

"How far along are you?"

"Ten weeks. I'm due—"

"Around June first," Jess interjected.

"How'd you figure the date so fast?" Sharon asked, looking confused.

"*I'm* due on Memorial Day," Jess responded, letting the surprise of that information sink in. She held the door for Sharon. "You may as well come in."

*

"So Christopher's getting a brother and a son?" Sharon reiterated, sipping the tea Jess had brewed. "Or a sister and a daughter, or a son and—"

"Yes. A sibling and a child."

"Does he know you're pregnant?" Sharon asked.

"I told him last week. Me using a sperm donor upset him. I'm thirty-five and I wanted a baby. I just didn't want a father around for this one. Telling him that made him feel bad about *his* father. Everything makes him feel bad about his father."

"I'm sorry," Sharon said.

"For what?" Jess retorted. "Dating my son? Being an older woman? Getting knocked up?" The list was endless.

"He's nineteen, Jess! Not exactly a baby! And I'm only twenty-five! Not exactly a cougar!"

"Twenty-six next week," Jess replied, completely drained of her anger. "Do you even love him?"

"Yes! No—not the way I'm supposed to," Sharon's answer made pathetic sense to Jess. "I'm back to loving him like a little brother," she sobbed.

Jess watched Sharon break down, unable to comfort her the way she would have a few months ago. There was a punishment in letting Sharon stew in her misery. *Who am I punishing?*

"I'll get them to drop the charges!" Sharon continued to cry.

"Threatening bodily harm is assault," Jess said. "California doesn't let victims drop the charges. He's gonna have to go to court." She thought about Chris' father. *Maybe it's for the best.* "I'm not gonna make excuses for my son." Jess let more silence pass. It felt strange. She and Sharon had been friends forever, eight years working together at Timberline without much empty silence between them. "What are you going to do?" she finally asked Sharon.

"I don't know. Get a roommate? Work as much as I can until I have the baby? Apply for aid? I'm not asking for anything from you and Chris, and I'm not getting rid of this baby."

Jess' mind flashed back to a similar conversation she had with Christopher's father and *his* mother. She felt like putting her head down on the kitchen table. She was exhausted.

"You're gonna move in here," she said, without thinking. "There's no sense in us trying to run two households. We need to make the best of our resources." Jess had been watching out for Sharon since the day they met. This was no different.

"What about Chris? He hates me!" Sharon cried.

"He doesn't hate you. He was just blind-sided by two women he thinks had no business getting pregnant, and they did anyway. Things will smooth out by the time you give notice to your landlady."

*

And they did. Sharon moved in. She and Christopher's relationship became sibling-like again despite the baby she was carrying. All their money was pooled together for expenses and the future. Jess and Sharon went back to being best friends, comparing every aspect of their pregnancies. People around town either didn't know or didn't care. When it came time for labor and delivery, Sharon assisted Jess, and two weeks later, Jess assisted Sharon. The two baby boys were chubby, easy-going infants. Christopher called one Sonny and the other Bro. Jess went back to her manager's job at Timberline, and Sharon worked there four nights a week in sales. It was perfect—or would have been if Jess wasn't in love with Sharon.

*

The babies were one and nearly one, an event celebrated with a small family party and ending in a birthday cake mess. Jess had just returned to full-time work after the pandemic lockdown. They decided Sharon would be the last salesperson called back to work since her unemployment check was more than her paycheck. Chris' job in the stock room at the Grocery Outlet never closed down. They had kept their lives tiny, managing to bank their stimulus checks from the government. Their needs were simple—a walk to the playground, occasionally ordering takeout. The pandemic had its restrictions, but its upside was the family unity they forged. Christopher had begun dating a girl from high school, named Riley. She was crazy about Sonny and good for Chris. Riley convinced him to go to an online community college for a degree in landscape management. He was almost twenty-one, ready to get on with his life. Jess suspected they would soon announce plans to marry or move in together. Then it would be just her and Sharon—and their sons.

*

"Don't we look like a couple?" Sharon asked her, as they were walking their babies to their favorite activity, being pushed on the swings. Jess laughed it off, but the comment made her stomach flutter. Other than sex, they *were* a couple. They shared parenting, chores, finances—hopes and dreams. There were many times when their babies took turns being up all night and they ended up in the same bed, each with a child asleep on their chest. When news was bad, like learning their favorite co-worker had died of COVID-19, they fell into each other's arms and wept. The closest they ever got to talking about dating was when Sharon told Jess how happy she was for Chris, but that dating during a pandemic seemed like more trouble than it was worth. Jess never discussed her feelings on the topic. If Sharon suspected she was gay, she never let on. It wasn't until Jess met Sharon that she was certain of it herself. She thought her lack of wanting a man in her life was because of the hell Chris' father had put her through. Now that she was in love, she knew better. It was a situation that couldn't continue forever.

Finally, in an act of self-preservation, Jess began to pull away from Sharon. She started in the most obvious of ways—picking fights over nothing. Then she picked one fight too many.

*

"I don't know why you insist on putting the boys to bed in the shirts they wore all day." Jess snapped, after a long day at work.

"One less thing to wash," Sharon replied, seemingly unfazed by the attack.

"Well, how about this?" Jess shot back. "You go ahead and put *your* kid to bed in his dirty shirt and put *my* kid to bed in a pair of clean pajamas."

"I don't get what the big deal is?" Sharon responded.

"The *big deal* is that I work hard all day. When I buy pajamas for *my* son—with *my* money—I expect you to put them on him!" Jess' sarcastic words finally hit the mark she was thoughtlessly aiming for. Sharon stood up, looking ready to explode. Jess watched her take a slow deep breath, then bring her response in check. It was a trait Jess always admired after coming through an abusive relationship. *And now I'm the abuser.*

"Your money, your son, your house," Sharon said calmly. "I wondered when it would get down to this. I don't contribute as much as you do—just everything I have. I love your boy like he was mine. I thought you felt the same way about us." Sharon took another deep breath. "My sister just got a place on Alderwood, there's plenty of room for me and Sonny. We can be out by the end of the month."

"Wait? You're moving out? Without even discussing it with me? That's my grandchild you're talking about taking!" Jess wished desperately for a magic rewind button, a wish that didn't change the tone of her voice. To her own ears, she sounded like an angry lunatic. Sharon continued to be rational.

"Jess, you've been wonderful to me. I'm not gonna be the reason you're miserable. I'll go put those jammies on Bro. It won't wake him. He sleeps like the dead." Jess watched Sharon take the pajamas from the top of the pile of laundry she was folding and walk down the hall to the bedroom their sons had shared since they were born. She wanted to run after her, tell her she was sorry, that she loved her. What was the point? They would just end up right back at this place anyway. *The point is I love her.*

*

It was two long weeks before Sharon's move-out date. The tension between them was palpable. Jess found herself working as many hours as she could to keep some distance between them, certain if she let her guard down she would beg Sharon to stay. The babies caught the mood, teething and fighting for attention. The idea of separating them was too horrible to think about, like giving one of your children up for adoption. Jess suggested creating a visitation schedule. "Of course, you can see your grandson any time you want to! What kind of monster do you think I am?" Sharon had responded, like the good person Jess knew her to be. One night Jess heard one of the babies crying and rushed to their room, colliding with Sharon. It would have been a regular moment before their fight, now the awkwardness of seeing Sharon in her camisole and thong, with her hair piled everywhere and Jess' son smashed against her breast, was too intimate. Jess grabbed the baby and fled back to her room, where she and her son cried themselves to sleep. She blamed the excess emotion on perimenopause, but her heart was broken. Work was the only place Jess held it together.

*

The shoe department at Timberline was packed. It was June and people were buying footwear for hiking, yard work, and outdoor adventure—especially now, with indoor activities limited by the pandemic. Jess was filling in for a girl whose mother was waiting for a negative Covid test result, and it was standing room only at the cash register. At least she didn't have to smile beneath her mask. Like a robot, she rang up one order after another, from a line that appeared endless because of the mandatory six feet of distance between customers.

"I recognize those beautiful eyes," Jess heard the next customer say. She looked up from the register.

"Uncle Frank!" She hadn't seen her uncle since his wife died a few years ago. As bad as he looked at the funeral, she hadn't expected to see him again in this lifetime.

"Still just as pretty as your mother, God rest her soul."

Jess burst into tears, unable to add her mother's death to her list of sorrows. "I have a baby," she blurted. "A boy named Brian."

"There a husband that comes with that baby?" her uncle asked.

"Nope. Just me and him. Christopher's moving in with his girlfriend."

"Good for you!" Uncle Frank replied, to Jess' complete and utter astonishment. "Life's too short to not have what you want."

"Well I don't know if it's everything I want, but he's a real good baby. How're you doing?" she asked.

Frank began to cough. "Not Covid!" he choked out to everyone taking a few steps back. "Just a smoker's cough." To Jess he said, "I swear to Jesus it's less embarrassing to shit your pants than to have a cough these days."

Jess laughed for the first time in a week. "You're probably right, Uncle Frank! Let me ring up those work boots and then I got a break coming. We can go outside and chat. Good?"

"Whatever you say, girl."

*

"So, a job? Wow. You excited?" Jess wondered if her uncle's new job was due to a lack of money. It was pointless to ask since she couldn't help—especially now with Sharon moving out, there would be daycare expenses and no money going into the savings account.

"It's the same thing I always did—looking over the crops, telling people what to do. But I never start a new job without a new pair of boots, and I'm not gonna change that now. How old's your boy?"

"He's one, just started to walk. I have a grandson too, which I guess means you have a great-great nephew." Jess was figuring out the generations as she spoke. "Chris' boy."

"Ah. He just moved in with the mother." Frank surmised.

"No. That's a different girl. It's complicated," Jess responded, wishing for a simple end to the conversation.

"Sounds like it," Frank replied. "Being happy is no easy thing. Sometimes it takes a bit of magic to move it along."

"Yup," she said, having no clue what he meant. "This has been great, but I've gotta get back to work." Jess got up from the picnic table where they had been sitting. Her uncle reached over and grabbed her arm.

"Wait. I got something for you. It might be nothing, or it might be something—either way I'm giving it to you."

Jess felt a moment of panic like her uncle was about to give her something creepy or do something weird. *Don't be ridiculous* she told herself and waited politely for him to shimmy out whatever was in his pocket, his gnarled arthritic knuckles making the job harder. Finally, it came free—a stained, worn little drawstring bag. He handed it over.

"Believe what you believe, but this little potion bag saved my friends from a fire—it might have saved me too. You just tell it what you want and do what it says."

"Okay, Uncle Frank. Thanks." Jess skirted around the table and gave him a quick hug. "It was good to see you. I'll have to bring the boys to visit the ranch when this pandemic is over."

"That would be nice," his reply looked like it came with a bit of a tear. Jess hurried back to work.

*

It was after nine-thirty when Jess left work. Too late for dinner, not too late for a hot fudge sundae. She had gained a few pounds in the last year, stuffing her feelings. Overall, she was still passably pretty, with short dark hair and long legs that hid the extra weight. "One more sundae isn't gonna kill you," was what Sharon would have said. There was a kindness to Sharon, always looking for the best in people. It felt selfish sitting in the car eating Dairy Freeze without calling her to see if she wanted one. Everything suddenly felt selfish—separating the boys, creating financial hardship for their family, putting Christopher in the middle of an awkward situation. Jess began to cry into her hot fudge. *Dairy Freeze isn't going to help this mess.* She got out of her car and threw the half-eaten ice cream into the trash. When she returned to the driver's seat she realized she had discarded the napkin too, and searched her purse for a Kleenex to wipe the evidence of her selfishness from her face. Uncle Frank's little magic potion bag was right on top. She pulled the drawstring open and was surprised to see its very un-Uncle-Frank-like contents. *"This little potion bag saved my friends from a fire ..."*

*

"We have to do inventory. I'm going to be home late." Jess voice-texted Sharon, and then she drove back to Timberline and parked in a secluded spot behind the building. She took out the beads, reread the directions, and began. *Give me a way to tell Sharon how I feel ...*

*

Sharon never went to bed unless everyone was home and the doors were locked, so it was no surprise for Jess to see her sitting in the living room. What Jess didn't expect was to see her crying. In her hand was a letter.

"Are you okay?"

"No. I'm not okay. I've been lying to you this whole time! This is the letter I tried to give you the day I told you I was pregnant." Sharon stood up and held the letter out to her.

"I don't want to read it!" Jess pushed the letter away. *What if it says Chris isn't Sonny's father?* She thought about how alike the boys looked, but did they really? *What if it was a lie?* "Listen, you're moving out soon, let's not get into anything we don't have to." Jess' words accelerated Sharon's distress.

"Please, Jess! Just read it before I stop myself from telling you everything!" Sharon left the envelope on the coffee table and ran off to her bedroom. Jess put her purse down and picked up the letter. She sat in the chair Sharon had just vacated and contemplated the possibilities of the letter's contents. Other than the obvious—Sonny's parentage—she had nothing. Then crazy things went through her mind, like Sharon having a secret identity or being a missing kid on a milk carton. She opened the letter.

> *Dear Jess,*
>
> *I'm sure by now Christopher told you I'm pregnant. You tried to talk me out of dating him and I wouldn't listen. He's a good kid. I probably didn't have to call the police. Being pregnant made me more scared about bodily harm—like if he pushed me or something. You were right about us. It was a lot of heartache for nothing. Two weeks into it I saw that the reasons I wanted him were his ways that reminded me of you.*
>
> *I'm in love with you. I wanted to say it a while ago. I'm saying it now before you start to hate me for ruining your son's life. You've always been so good to me, making sure I was okay and caring about what I think. I can only guess how you feel about me now. Having your son's baby sure puts a complication on things, but I'm not having an abortion or giving the baby up for adoption, and I'm not planning on needing anything from you or Chris. I'm sure my sister will help me out. I'm going to quit Timberline and get another job before it's obvious I'm pregnant so you won't have to look at me every day—although I'll miss looking at you. I am so, so sorry,*
>
> *Sharon*

*

I'm in love with you. Jess read the words over and over again. They were jumping off the page at her. *I'm in love with you.* She thought about all the ways Sharon had shown it—waiting to eat dinner with her when she got home late from work, making sure her favorite pants (the only ones that still fit) were always clean, putting up with her bad moods—the list was long. It wasn't about being a good roommate. Sharon had included her in every one of their babies' accomplishments, even lying about Brian walking to make it look like Jess was witnessing his momentous first steps. *She loves me.* Now what? *Do I go to her room, crawl into her bed, and take her in my arms?* Jess felt like she was going to throw up. She went to the kitchen to get a glass of water and saw the homemade honey cornbread on the counter—her favorite. Did she even know Sharon's favorite bread? Banana? She thought of all the hints she could have dropped about her love for Sharon, full-out fear had stopped her. *Keep it simple, dummy*, her mind rang out, *just start with I love you, too*. Jess washed her hands in the kitchen sink, happiness overriding her nerves. Then she tiptoed to Sharon's bedroom and opened the door.

"You awake?" she asked, soft enough for a sleeping person to ignore.

"Yup."

"I'm in love with you, too. I guess we'll figure out what that means in the morning."

"Okay," Sharon replied.

"Thanks for making cornbread," she said, odd but not totally.

"You're welcome."

Jess quietly shut the door. *Thank you, Uncle Frank.*

June 20, 2020

CHAPTER 24 ~ SETH

Vancouver, British Columbia, Canada

The irony of him crushing three medium-sized Brazil nuts and adding them to his morning oat bran to create the perfect daily dose of selenium had not escaped Seth. He wanted the powerful antioxidant benefits of selenium for his heart, thyroid, lungs, and mental health. The sad thing was that too much of that same mineral creates a toxicity that could lead to anything from hair loss to death—which was why his team was working so hard to get the Canadian government to recognize the dangerous amounts of selenium leaching from the open coal mines into the Elk River Watershed. So far, not so good.

As an environmental scientist, Seth spent his adult life seeing the writing on the wall. He couldn't remember one project where the issue they hired him to investigate turned out to be no big deal. It was *always* a big deal by the time a municipality hired a consultant. Water was his specialty—degree and source of contamination, cure and remediation. He was beginning to see that as the easy part—putting together the report and the resolution plan. The impossible part was getting anything to change once the evidence was staring everyone in the face. People want to talk about water quality restoration, they just don't want to follow through with it. The Elk River Watershed area was on the precipice of unsalvageable. Realistically, it would take a thousand years to completely reverse the effects of the runoff from discarded mountain surfaces, mined for steel-making metallurgical coal for more than forty years. In the case of the selenium contamination in Elk River, Cutthroat Trout were the canaries in the coal mine— first with gill deformities, and later, with total reproduction failure. The Cuttys, though obvious, are smack in the middle of the ecosystem disaster.

Saturated insects and plant life—along with anything that eats invertebrates, like birds—became a poisoned casualty well before the Cuttys' absence from the river was fully noticed.

For whatever reason, this particular project was depressing the hell out of Seth. It wasn't as though pollution was ever a joyous topic, but he used to have a level of hope in the process that had diminished over the years. It felt oddly parallel to the level of hope he used to feel about his marriage.

*

Seth and Eileen met at the University of British Columbia. She was a political science major, he was studying environmental science and engineering. She seemed to like his quiet, studious nature, and he was enthralled by her ability to speak to anyone. They spent hours in bed talking about how they would save the planet together, environmentally and socially. Eileen called Seth her "California Boy," which was funny to him since he had not one characteristic Californians were noted for. He was pale, unathletic, and clean-cut. He couldn't even keep a tan, always going from burn to fade and missing the tanning step altogether. She, on the other hand, would have fit right in with the celebrities in Hollywood Hills. Eileen was tall, blonde, and striking. She grew up in Vancouver, British Columbia, the daughter of a famous author and her physician husband, and lived a life of relative entitlement—the details of which unfolded well after Seth was already in love. Even with its enormous acreage, his family's dilapidated ranch and farmhouse didn't stand a chance against the ten-million-dollar home on Marine Drive where Eileen and her sisters were raised. Her parents were gracious, they didn't ask too many questions. It didn't matter anyway. He was getting his Doctorate, so supporting their daughter wasn't going to be an issue. They accepted him because he was who Eileen wanted.

It didn't take long for the differences to show. Seth didn't know what a social calendar was, while Eileen seemed to hate alone time with just the two of them. The crazy thing was, when they were out with other couples, Eileen couldn't say enough about him—the projects he was working on, his indispensability at the organization. She talked more about him than she did her own job as a college professor. Seth let her do his bragging since he didn't know how to be impressive, or how to stop her. He was a no-nonsense farm boy at heart. On a ranch, there isn't a lot of room for complaints that don't matter—like whether you were snubbed at the social club. And most of the status ranking had to do with your horses or how your crops did that year. He didn't know how to play the game his wife thought was so important. They talked about having kids, but it never became more than talk. Every year, Seth could see the writing on the wall become more pronounced. Then something would happen to unite them. Five years ago, her father died. Two years later, it was his mother. If somebody else didn't die soon, Seth wasn't certain he could live much longer with his wife's total dissatisfaction of him.

*

Seth watched Eileen throw the empty plastic yogurt container into the main trash bin. She never recycled. "Why should I go to the trouble when no one else is doing it?" she said, a repetition of her case against recycling.

"That's the point," Seth answered, without looking up from his oat bran. Their old argument was now just habit with no fury attached on either side. *No fury.* It was a trait Seth was missing, the ability to become righteously furious. Eileen had been granted double the amount of righteous anger, a byproduct of her entitlement. *His* instinct was to go within and obsess about what he could do to change the situation. *Nothing.*

"What are you up to today?" he asked, to set the conversation back to polite.

"What do you think I'm up to? We're in a pandemic. It's not like there's a ton of options." Sarcasm. Another thing Seth hadn't mastered in eighteen years of their marriage.

"I'm writing another letter to the International Joint Commission about Canada's breach in the Boundary Water Treaty. Maybe—"

"Well, that sounds like fun," Eileen replied before he was finished. "I'm going to drive to my sister's, maybe sit on the beach." She left without saying goodbye, let alone kissing him. Her kisses had gone from his mouth, to the top of his head, to vanishing into the ionosphere.

… a bigger push outlining the impending damage of the Wigwam River in Montana will stop any new open coal permits … Seth finished his sentence in his mind. He got up and put his bowl in the sink, then went for a run. Another day in paradise.

*

The run was rejuvenating. Seth loved everything about British Columbia. It really *was* a paradise. Their home in Vancouver was just a short distance from over two dozen hiking trails, some on the Pacific coast and others inland in the surrounding forests. Seth tried not to get stuck on one route—a habit he had been working to break for years. Once you see perfection it's hard to look beyond it for the next miracle. Yes. He was a scientist who believed in miracles. He couldn't understand why all scientists didn't. Knowing the chemical reason for the dynamic attraction of water, or the biology behind the spawning ritual of a salmon might lead a scientist to think he had all the answers, but how could that knowledge not lead to the bigger question? *What force created this delicate system of biological balance?* It wasn't a question he pondered aloud. Sometimes in the lab he temporarily forgot his true beliefs. Then an unexpected rain, filtering the spectrum of light into an arc of separated wavelengths of red, orange, yellow, green, blue, indigo, and violet, would validate Seth's certainty of a higher power at work. This belief in a higher power was intertwined with a belief in his own higher purpose. He was on this earth to help save the planet. The only question that had ever been in his mind was whether he should go toward the salvation of water or trees. An internship with the Canada-B.C. Water Quality Monitoring Program tipped the scales to water. After that, he *dove right in*, as he used to say at parties before his wife pointed out how many times he had recycled that tired line. *At least I recycle,* he silently retorted, as his feet pounded their way to his long driveway. Seth ran in place while he pulled the mail from their mailbox, then one last power sprint up the drive. *A good run.*

*

Showered and ready to write the perfect letter to the International Joint Commission, Seth grabbed the mail from the counter to read in his office. A small yellow bubble-padded mailer caught his attention. It was from his cousin, Jess. Although she was much younger than him, they had always been close. She still lived in their hometown and had been very attached to his mother. He went to his office and opened the envelope. The package was strange, both the gift and the letter that accompanied it.

*

Hey Seth,

I hope this finds you doing good. I can't believe we haven't spoken since your mother's funeral. I still miss her. Every time I pull out my sewing machine I think of Aunt

Ervina spending hours teaching me how to sew. She was so good to me, I couldn't have done it being a single mom without her. Okay, enough with the hearts and flowers. You know how I felt.

Your dad came by Timberline to get new work boots and he gave me this little spirit potion bag. He said it worked for him and saved the people who gave it to him. I used it and guess what? It worked! I'm supposed to pass it along so that the next person can get their miracle. I decided there was nobody I'd rather pass it to than you—keep the miracles in the family, ha-ha. Please take this seriously without thinking that your father and I have lost our minds. We have, lol, but not about this. I can't explain it—you just have to do it.

Pretty interesting news about your Dad getting a job, right? He looked kind of excited, I mean as excited as Uncle Frank gets.

Also, I don't know if anyone told you that you have more relatives. Both Christopher and I have new babies that just turned one. Crazy right? I can't figure out what my son and grandson are to you. It's too confusing—maybe second cousin? and second cousin once removed? You tell me. They are so adorable I can't wait for you to meet them!

Take care of yourself, I love you, Jess

My father has a job? He didn't mention it when Seth called him after the latest wildfire came a little too close to the ranch. *Ugh.* Environmental disasters had become a commonplace arrow through his heart. He suddenly felt overwhelmed by it all—like he might go back upstairs and climb into his bed. *Don't be ridiculous. It's ten o'clock in the morning!* Seth shook off his despair and opened the little bag that came with the letter. "Okay, wow. This is so not like Dad," Seth muttered. He read through the directions, then held the beads up to the light looking for something that would make them dynamic. They were common, weathered, hardwood beads—maybe sandalwood. The threads that held them together appeared to be a natural fiber, perhaps a strong silk. He let his hands drop to his lap and leaned back in his office chair—a monstrously expensive piece of furniture Eileen had insisted on, then grew to hate when she saw how many hours Seth could sit in it without a hint of discomfort.

He thought about what he knew about his father. Quiet, pragmatic, a hard worker. Stable. Seth hadn't lived there in thirty years, but their attachment to each other was unspoken—*or was it?* His mother was the one he had called every Sunday. Then she'd hand off the phone, "Your dad wants to say hi." They would stumble through the first few sentences, eventually hitting on a topic of mutual interest—the weather, his current project. Seth suddenly wanted to dissect every conversation they had ever had. He realized he couldn't remember the details of his childhood. Just working the farm, together. Had they done father-son things throughout the years? Not Boy Scouts or camping. Science club was through the school, and other than coming to end-of-program fairs his dad didn't participate or brainstorm with him. Seth remembered his mother delicately gluing tissue paper onto the wing-shaped metal hanger of his Northern White Skipper Butterfly project. *Or is that a moth?* He was no longer certain of anything. He wanted to blame this absence of paternal closeness on Eileen for keeping them apart. She had nothing in common with his parents and had seen no value in going there more often than was necessary. Seth never spent another Christmas on the ranch once he got married. Christmas with Eileen's family was an over-the-top Disney Spectacular-like event. "Why would we go south for Christmas?" she would say every year, as if a snowy Christmas were the gold standard. The last time it snowed in Vancouver on December twenty-fifth was 2008. He could have pushed her or visited more on his own. His mother looked forward to those Sunday phone calls like he was the second coming of Christ. He continued to call weekly for a couple of months after she passed, but soon it became twice a month, then whenever.

Seth could no longer continue this train of thought. It was making his left arm ache. He would have to include hypochondriac to the list of negative personality traits he had developed over the years. He looked at the beads again and wondered if they had anything to do with his mother. Probably not. She attended the Methodist church, while his father attended the earth. "God isn't in a building," his father would say as he surveyed the lands of his ranch. "He's right here." Seth got up and pulled his stretching mat (he refused to call it a yoga mat after Eileen ridiculed his attempt at his and her yoga class) from under the futon in his office and spread it across the shiny bamboo floor—the *one* room of the house where he won the fight for sustainable flooring. He sat cross-legged with the beads and instructions in his lap. "Om satyam narayanam," Seth said, aloud. "Easy enough." Putting a desired miracle into words was the harder thing. You create a hypothesis, gather facts, evidence, and data, then prove or disprove your hypothesis. Scientists don't spend a lot of time wishing for miracles. *Or do we?* He closed his eyes, trying to empty his mind, and took seven deep breaths. "Let me feel the satisfaction of purpose again," he said without planning, then began to count out the mantra, one-hundred-and-eight times. "Om satyam narayanam …."

*

When Seth was finished, he took a few minutes to stretch and mentally rehearse his letter to the International Joint Commission. He couldn't focus. He had the urge to call his father. It was Saturday and Seth had just called him last Sunday, *or was that two weeks ago?* His desire to talk to him *right now* was too strong to ignore. He snatched his cell phone from the desk, then sat back on his yoga mat and dialed. His father picked up on the second ring.

"Everything okay?"

"Yeah. Good Dad. How about you?" Seth asked.

"It's Saturday."

"It is. I had a minute and thought I'd give you a call. Anything new with you guys?" Seth immediately regretted saying "you guys" as if his mother were still alive. His father appeared not to notice.

"As a matter of fact, yes," he answered. "Looks like I'm going back to farming."

"Wow. That is news."

"I'm renting my land to Juan and Rosa, down the way—their acreage burnt out and they're lookin' to plant alfalfa and a wheat called Teff. I'm gonna oversee everything. I've been reading up on this Teff—doesn't look too complicated."

For a man of low affect, his father sounded downright giddy. "This's great, Dad! If there's anything I can do to help—"

"There is. Irrigation's gonna be a problem. The groundwater's been low for a couple years, and the government's restricting surface water use—about goddam time they do something as far as I'm concerned. That San Joaquin Valley is a mess. Everyone talks about building tanks to hold high water reserves, and nobody's done a goddam thing! There's so many water committees, no one knows if they're blowing their nose with the toilet paper they just used to wipe their ass! Been going like this since Hector was a pup."

"So you want me to research the latest irrigation strategies, maybe combine—"

"I want you to come home and help me get this thing started."

"I'll leave this afternoon. Spend the night in Portland, and be there by dinnertime tomorrow," Seth's plan formulated as he spoke. *Why not?* He had already done all the groundwork on the Elk River problem, anything else could be handled remotely.

"Hey, I was just kidding. Isn't Canada closed from the virus?"

"I'll have no problem getting through the border with my US passport and science credentials. My environmental visa will get me back into Canada." *Or maybe I'll be stranded in California*, Seth thought with an adventurous flutter in his stomach.

"Shouldn't you check with your wife?"

"She hates me." The truth was out of his mouth before he could stop it.

"That's a shame, son," his father replied with his classic acceptance of what is. His lack of questions was something to suddenly appreciate—among other things.

"I know a guy who's working on the San Joaquin. I'll have him get me up to speed and have a day's worth of answers before I see you."

"Just to let you know, I haven't cleaned a thing since your mother died."

"Well you better get started," Seth answered, only half-joking. "I won't be sleeping beside any homegrown science experiments. And Dad, can you pick up some oat bran and Brazil nuts at the store?"

"Yup. See you tomorrow, son."

June 20, 2020

CHAPTER 25 ~ BELLA

East Vancouver, British Columbia, Canada

One more house and she would be finished for the day. Avoidance had caused Bella to save this house for last. She pulled into the driveway, happy not to see the wife's car. It was short-lived relief when she remembered the non-negotiable list the woman had left the last time she hadn't been there to personally supervise the cleaning of her McMansion. Bella opened the back of her Mitsubishi Outlander and began to pull out the vacuum cleaner. "Oh god. I almost forgot," she muttered, aggravated. She went around to the passenger side, opened the door, and searched through the cardboard box of extra supplies until she came up with a new Hepa vacuum bag. "God forbid the air from someone else's dust shoot out the ass of my Hoover and into your *precious* home."

She took a few deep breaths to calm herself while she removed the one-quarter-filled bag and replaced it with a new one. "Is that a new bag?" the wife had asked the last time she cleaned. "No," Bella had answered. "It's your bag from the last cleaning. I saved it with your name on it." "That won't do. I want a new bag."

"I'll give you a new bag!" Bella said, aloud, the memory of that day still fresh. "Right up the old kazoo!" She didn't hear Seth Campbell walk up behind her.

"You okay, Bella?" Mr. Campbell asked. He was dragging his suitcase. She almost died thinking he might have heard her.

"Oh! Mr. Campbell! I'm fine. I'm just complaining about the weight of these new vacuum cleaners. They're supposed to be getting lighter. Maybe I'm just getting older." *I sure as hell am—fifty at the end of the summer, too old to be doing this shit-ass job.*

Mr. Campbell rested his suitcase beside his car. "Let me help you with that," he said, then began to wrestle the vacuum from her. It felt wrong.

"No, Mr. Campbell, I can get that! You're gonna get dirt all over your clothes."

"I probably will. I'm sure it won't kill me. Bella, call me Seth. It's ridiculous for two people the same age to be so formal. Actually, what *is* your last name?"

"It's Graham, Mr.—Seth."

"Graham. That's Scottish. I expected something more Aboriginal, Squamish," he answered, while she watched him pick up the vacuum accessories that had fallen from their inconvenient compartment.

Indigenous, she mentally corrected, although many of her people still used Aboriginal. "It was," she answered. "But the Canadian Indian Act gave the agents the right to rename our people with Christian names—to assimilate us into the white population." She tried to say it without letting too much disgust show on the words. "Most of us don't know our original names."

Seth Campbell stopped so abruptly that Bella bumped right into him. He pivoted and looked at her, making eye contact less than a foot from her face. Bella ran through what she had just said, checking it for overt disrespect. Seconds passed. He finally spoke.

"Bella, I'm going out of town for a while—back to the States to help my dad. In the meantime, our house is perfectly clean. You don't need to clean it today.

Oh shit. I just got myself fired. She tried to think of an appropriate apology for saying true things. She said nothing, unable to suck down one more humiliation for herself or her people. Tears sprang to her eyes as she followed him to her SUV and opened it so he could put back her cleaning equipment. There was never a good time to make less money, but especially now. Half of her clients were canceling because they were afraid she would spread the coronavirus to them. Mr. Campbell firmly closed the liftgate.

"Bella, how much do you make cleaning our house?" Mr. Campbell asked.

"One hundred dollars, but it takes me—"

"Oh, I know how long it takes you, and I know what a bitch my wife is." She watched him remove his wallet from his back pocket and pull out three one-hundred-dollar bills. He pressed them into her hand. "If you had gotten here five minutes later, I would have been gone and the house would have been locked up. Let's pretend that's what happened. Take this week off, and maybe you should take next week, too. She's going to be in a foul mood when she sees that I've left."

Bella wanted to hug him. He looked so … satisfied. "Thank you Mr.—"

"Seth." Then he pulled something else from the front pocket of his pants, a small bag. "This is special magic. It's used to manifest your heart's desire, then you pass it on. It worked for me and I'm passing it on to you. I'm a scientist who believes in miracles." Her mouth hung open. This day was not what she had expected. "Now let's get the hell out of here," he said, "before my wife pulls into this driveway."

"Good luck, Seth," she said.

"You too, Bella. Namaste," he replied, as he whipped the suitcase into his car and sped off. She was right behind him.

*

Pulling into her *own* driveway at the end of work was a daily dose of stomach acid. She might be walking into a calm moment—or a shitstorm. Today was Saturday. It was normally her day off, but Bella's work schedule was now dependent on who she could get to stay with her mother. The options for care were shrinking with each

Alzheimer's stage. "Your mother is transitioning," the neurologist would say whenever her behavior took another turn toward intolerable. Transitioning was such a benign, almost colorless word to describe the hell her mother was putting everyone through. Bella had begun labeling the chaos. Sad Sally, Rocking Rhonda, Noisy Norah, Ravenous Rachel—the names explained her mother's behavior better than a ten-minute description could.

When she walked through the door, Bella immediately knew the flavor of the day— Susie Searcher. Stuff was everywhere. This stage had lasted longer than most. Her mother, whose real name was Agnes, now spent every moment from sunup to sundown frantically searching the house. She pulled apart closets, cabinets, and cubbies, looking for an unnamable item she couldn't seem to find. The aide for the day, Samantha, had her bags in hand and was ready to dash when Bella arrived.

"She ransacked most of the day," Samantha said, a combined greeting and update. "I tried to keep ahead of it."

"I know," Bella replied, wondering if cleaning the Campbells' house wouldn't have been preferable to coming home early to this. Three o'clock. It was nowhere near sundown. "Where is she?"

"In the bathroom. I put the dangerous stuff in a box above the washer where she can't reach it."

"Have a good weekend, Sam. I'll see you on Tuesday." The house was quiet. Bella washed her hands in the kitchen sink before checking on her mother. A necessary five minutes on the toilet was what she really needed, but things became unpredictable once her mother laid eyes on her. Fear of germs now stopped her from taking an uninterrupted bathroom break at the Chevron station on the way home. She had tried to talk herself out of it, knowing she could bring in disinfectant, "I'm a cleaning person for chrissake." Then she would drive right by, convincing herself it would be simpler to just go at home. It never was.

*

Her mother wasn't in the bathroom. Bella tiptoed through the small house and found her in the bedroom emptying out the closet. She crept back to the bathroom, careful not to hit the exhaust fan switch. Her five minutes turned into two when she heard something crash. Bella rushed from the bathroom and into her mother's bedroom. A chair was toppled over in the doorway of the closet, two huge boxes of pictures busted open on the floor around it. Her mother appeared uninjured but furious.

"I need to find it!" she yelled, pulling the boxes apart. The pained look on her face perpetually destroyed Bella more than the original diagnosis had.

"Mom, just let me help. I can find what you want," Bella pleaded.

Her mother fell apart. "No one can help!" she screamed, instantly becoming Rocking Rhonda, sobbing and careening back and forth while clutching an old photo album to her chest. Two years of this, and Bella was still unable to philosophically harden her heart to the sight of it. She wrapped her arms around her mother and rocked and cried with her until they both fell asleep on the closet floor.

*

Bella awoke to darkness. Her mother was gone. *Did I lock the doors?* Her resting heartbeat, no longer resting. She jumped up, ready to dash to the next disaster, then saw her mother sound asleep in her bed, still clutching the album. Sleeping through the night, especially without dinner, was hit or miss. Bella snuck out of the room, knowing she had better make the best of her time. That didn't mean cleaning up the mess—it meant a long bath, a decent meal, and paying some bills online.

*

This is good, thought Bella, as she stretched her body from side to side in her chair. *Not even two a.m. and I'm finished with everything*. The spinach and cheese omelet she had made was digesting nicely, no need to take a Prilosec before bed. Her silk robe, a present from her husband on their twenty-eighth wedding anniversary, hugged her more tightly these days from stress eating and no time to cook healthy meals. She silently made another resolve to eat better. At least she didn't drink alcohol, a decision made in her youth after witnessing the disaster of her Aunt Opal's life. It wasn't a myth that the People of the First Nation were better off without *spirit water*. "We can't hold our liquor, and we can't keep our men," she mused, wondering if the second part of that statement was true. Her husband left the same week her mother moved in. If that didn't cause Bella to seek refuge in the bottle, nothing would. She took a deep breath, clearing her husband from her thoughts. One more chore, a load of laundry, and she would hit the hay. Hopefully, her mother was out for the night.

Bella grabbed her ugly uniform from the bathroom floor—rich people don't like to see their cleaning lady dressed like a friend—and shoved it into the washer. It startled her to see Mr. Campbell's little bag fall out of the pocket. *Mr. Campbell left his wife.* That part of her day felt like a week ago. She started the washer and took the bag to the kitchen.

"Special magic," he had said, and that's what it looked like. She knew nothing about Mr. Campbell —Seth. He was some kind of scientist. "*Doctor* Campbell," Mrs. Campbell had corrected her more than once. *He hates his wife and believes in magic.* It was a lot to learn in one day. Bella read the directions. "What is my heart's desire?" she asked aloud. "To see my mother at peace," she answered herself. Her mother's peace would be her peace. It scared her to think Alzheimer's was hereditary, but lately, she had developed a theory that taking care of one generation was what caused the next generation to lose their minds. She didn't want to lose hers prematurely from the stress of taking care of her mother. "Give my mother some peace." Bella performed the magic.

*

It was done. She carefully coiled the beads and returned them to the gauze sack along with the worn faded directions. Then she had an idea to make a copy of the mantra for herself. It took some time to meticulously type up the directions, letter for letter. Her understanding of magic was based on movies and fairytales. She wasn't even sure it would work without the beads, but Bella didn't want to accidentally turn somebody into a frog. When she was through she printed it out, cut the paper to size, then rolled it up and put it in the cabinet with her good glassware. Three o'clock—*really time for bed*. As she went to shut down her computer, she noticed an Amazon advertisement had popped up across the top of the screen. Like everyone else, Bella hated unwanted pop-ups. Then she saw the content of the ad—a life-like baby doll. Her mind flashed to the album her mother had brought to bed with her. It wasn't photographs, it was Bella's baby book. She remembered the anguished cries, suddenly realizing her mother wasn't saying *it*. She was saying *her*. "I can't find *her*!" Was it possible her mother was looking for her baby?

"Oh my God, my poor sweet mother! She thinks her baby is missing!" Bella clicked open the ad. The doll was *very* realistic, with gender-accurate genitalia and soft latex skin. It came with a baby blanket, two diapers, and a one-piece terry-cloth romper. She ordered the female doll, selecting overnight shipping. Then she climbed into bed with her mother and thought about her own little girl, working and unable to visit for fear of getting them sick. Bella cried herself to sleep for the second time that day.

*

True to Amazon's word, the doll arrived Monday morning after an exhausting weekend. Bella unwrapped and discarded the packaging, marveling at the doll's beauty. She diapered and dressed the manufactured human infant, then swaddled her in the blanket.

Her mother was especially vacant and sullen that morning—refusing to get dressed or eat a bite of toast. She sat perched on a kitchen chair, staring out the back slider—no rocking or searching today. Bella walked into the room with the doll cradled in her arms. She had the baby book with her, which she placed on the kitchen table beside her mother.

"Agnes, look who I found," she said softly, then positioned herself between her mother and the door. The recognition was immediate.

"Annabella," her mother exhaled the name and reached out her arms. Carefully, Bella transferred the doll to her mother's arms. Their eyes met in a rare connection of understanding—woman to woman, mother to mother, soul to soul. Tears of joy ran down Agnes' cheeks as she uttered instinctive words of love and devotion, and rocked her "Little Annabella" to sleep. The real Annabella felt her body relax. Her mother was at peace for the first time in months. It was a miracle.

"Thank you, Dr. Seth Campbell," she whispered. "Namaste."

June 23, 2020

CHAPTER 26 ~ AMELIA

Kitsilano
Vancouver, British Columbia, Canada

In the movies, they would have called it a "cute meet," except the story sounded seedy when Amelia said it aloud—she, being a professor at the University of British Columbia, and Luka, her student. He had signed up for one of her night classes, *Advanced English as a Second Language*. It was immediately clear to Amelia that Luka didn't need the course. He was brilliant. And handsome. And funny. She fell for him the minute he walked into the classroom. Amelia would have called herself obsessed had she been able to recognize the signs, but at twenty-nine years old, she had yet to meet anyone who occupied her mind beyond a mild interest. Two weeks after classes began, she looked up his records (another gray area in professional ethics) and found out he was thirty-three years old and a student at Regent College's Master of Divinity program, studying to be an Orthodox priest. The Monday night class became the highlight of her week. Then Luka didn't show up one day, and Amelia hated the way his absence made her feel. She immediately emailed him with the assignment he had missed, and an enquiry about his health.

I am fine. I had no one to watch my children, he replied to her concern. She was crushed. There was nothing in his records about a family. Amelia pressed her luck with another email. *Oh, you have children! How nice! Does their mother work?* It sounded nosey. She read it twice and hit send anyway. *She is dead,* he replied. *Thank you for the assignment.*

She is dead? He was a widowed Russian immigrant with two children, juggling college, work, and daycare—and making it look effortless. Luka was amazing, and now their conversations included his children. Without the slightest hint her attraction was reciprocated, Amelia's mind ran wild with visions of their life together. She began attending a Russian Orthodox Church to get a feel for it. The priest, Father Stephan Kozlov, was married. His wife and six children sat in the front row each Sunday, looking proud and happy—a good sign. Everything became a good sign. Then the pandemic happened and the rest of the semester became online classes.

*

As difficult as it was not seeing his face—Luka never used the Zoom camera—their online relationship became wider than school, blossoming into a friendship. He told her funny stories about the kids. She told him about crazy things that happened at the university. Amelia was ecstatic when he asked her to be the subject of an interview for his master's thesis, *Cultural Inclusion and Orthodoxy,* to get her perspective as a language professor who deals with students of all nationalities. When Luka learned of her Squamish First Nation heritage, it generated more material for his thesis—and more Facetime together. It wasn't her imagination that they were getting closer. At the end of the Spring semester, he told her he had to leave for a month-long seminary trip but didn't have anyone to watch four-year-old Anya and two-year-old Alexander. Amelia jumped to offer her assistance. "I don't have classes for eight weeks. It'll be great to be around small children again," she said, having never been around them before. As an only grandchild, Amelia's exposure to young families was limited.

*

Her initial meeting with the children was promising, with Alexander only crying a bit when his father left for a trial hour. But Anya was open, helpful, and funny. She showed Amelia around the tiny apartment as though she were a real estate agent. "Vannaya," she waved her hand into the bathroom. When they got to the bedroom, Anya patted her bed. "Mine." Then the crib, "Alex." On the wall was a picture of a young woman holding a baby girl. "Mama," she said, without a trace of sentimentality. The woman was beautiful, her long, blonde hair cascading over one shoulder to give a full view of both her face and the baby she was holding.

Amelia's stomach turned icy from the beauty of it all. *How does anyone top that?* "Is that you?" she asked the obvious.

"Da," the sweet girl answered and continued her tour.

*

Amelia and the children were playing a guessing game when Luka returned. "I spy, with my little eye, something that is the color red!" Amelia said, deliberately looking toward the kitchen counter where a cluster of clean radishes was draining on a dish towel.

"Redis!" Anya screamed back triumphantly.

"Yes," Amelia said. "The thing we are looking for is red." She heard Luka laugh behind her.

"You are right, Anya!" he said, adding to Amelia, "Redis is Russian for radish."

"I'm going to have to study hard to beat this one!" Amelia replied, laughing. Anya rushed to her father and hid behind him.

"Papochka! Ne pozvolyay yey bit' menya!" she cried.

"No one is going to beat you. She said you are going to be pobeditel'—the winner." Luka assured his daughter. "Amelia is very nice. Ona - moy drug. She is my friend."

"Well this was eye-opening," Amelia said. "My ESL training is useless."

Luka picked up Anya and swung her around the room. "Everything is useless with this one! She is too smart for us all!"

“YA tozhe! YA tozhe!” Alexander yelled, putting his arms up for Amelia to twirl him in the air. Soon they were taking turns swooping the kids back and forth as they screeched with delight. *This is just like a movie!* she thought, her heart bursting with happiness.

*

Not knowing if she would be able to go back and forth to her condo, Amelia moved into Luka’s apartment, lock, stock, and barrel. It was good she did, parenting two small children left no time for anything else. A tough day—no naps, extra whining—made her think she wouldn’t get through the month. Then the very next day would be fun and easy, with both kids in great moods and sleeping through the night. Their routine took over in a way that erased the life Amelia had been living. *What did I use to do with all my free time?* she wondered. Now breakfast and getting dressed took up an hour. Walking to the Connaught Park playground, thirty minutes. Two hours of swing pushing, running through the water spray, and some occasionally frightful toddler-gymnastic moments, made Amelia feel more exhausted than any CrossFit class ever had.

*

“Alexander! You can do this!” Amelia hollered. His thick, blond hair was blown back by the wind, revealing an angel’s terrified face. His hands clutched the side rails of the slide.

“Nyet! YA ne mogu.”

“Yes, you can! I’ll catch you.” She crouched down and held her arms out. She could hear Anya, encouraging him—or perhaps bullying him—from behind. Amelia’s limited grasp of Russian made it difficult to know which. “Anya! Give him a minute.” Within seconds the sister pushed her brother hard, sending him flying down the slide. Amelia caught him, losing her footing. They tumbled to the ground, then scrambled out of the way before Anya had a chance to land on top of them. "Anya! That was not nice!"

"Ty skazal, podtolkni yego!" she replied, indignant.

"No, I did not say give him a push. I said give him some time." It appeared they all needed work on their language skills—except Luka. He was fluent in five languages—Russian, English, German, Greek, and Latin. *Luka was fluent in everything.* Amelia forced herself to concentrate on the children in front of her, and not their father. "I'm starving! Who's ready for lunch?" To a chorus of "Mne!" she swung Alexander into his stroller and they headed home for lunch, naps, and maybe a load of laundry. She would have to place another online grocery order, the month was going by quickly. In a week Luka would be home. *Then what?* she wondered.

*

Every evening the children Face-timed with their father, both clamoring to talk about what they had done or seen that day. After Anya and Alex went to bed, Amelia would call Luka back so they could catch up on an adult level. They spoke of the kids, the virus, the city—the Black Lives Matter protest at the Georgia Viaduct, which again had forced her to cancel their Science Museum outing. Eventually, their conversation would turn to personal questions.

"I'm interested in what this means to you—how becoming an Orthodox Priest is accomplished," she said, after hearing about his day.

"There is a stack of theology books and pamphlets on the shelf in my bedroom closet. Read whatever you would like," Luka replied. "You may not find it as interesting as you think."

"*You* might be surprised," she answered, grateful for a legitimate excuse to breathe in the smell of his clothing.

Their call lingered as if neither wanted to hang up. Luka ended with, "I do not know how I will repay you for this, Amelia."

"Please, no! I have loved every minute." *And I will die when it's over.*

*

Anya and Alexander were asleep. It had been a busy day filled with cookie-making and planting tomato seeds in an egg carton. Amelia had never planted a thing in her life—another first. The kids called her Mimi, unable to say Amelia. It was a good fit and made her happy whenever they called for her, even in the middle of the night. With the kitchen clean and another load of laundry humming in the washer, Amelia settled into Luka's bed with a stack of his books and papers. It didn't take long for her to find a discovery that would unravel her dreams. It was a pamphlet from the Orthodox Church of America covering the basics of Orthodox religion, including their stance on married priests:

> *"Concerning ordination, married men may be ordained to the diaconate and priesthood. However, they must be married only one time to a woman who also has been married only one time. If a man is a widower, he too may be ordained, provided that he has not remarried, and he may not marry after his ordination. The Tradition of the Orthodox Church is that both the priest as well as his wife must have been married only one time—to each other. And this would apply regardless of whether the person is no longer married due to divorce or to widowhood."*

Amelia read the passage twice, each time feeling a stab of pain at the last words—*And this would apply regardless of whether the person is no longer married due to divorce or to widowhood.* She jumped from the bed, grabbed her laptop, and desperately searched for anything to counter this new piece of information. There was nothing. Every article ran to the same disastrous end—a widowed man could not remarry and also be an orthodox priest. "How could I have missed this!" She cried into Luka's naked pillow, the pillowcase removed to enhance the smell of him. Just as she was really falling apart, her cell phone rang. She tried to pull it together as she searched the bed sheets for her phone.

"Hello?" She couldn't see who it was for the crying.

"Amelia?"

Hearing her mother's voice caused Amelia to lose the little control she had mustered.

"Mama!" she cried.

"Amelia! What's wrong!" her mother demanded, fear in her voice.

"Everything!" She poured her heart out about the man she had known for six months and loved for five of them. Her ranting woke up Alex, who cried out for his Mimi to get him from the crib. Within minutes, everyone was in Luka's bed, crying and bi-lingually babbling. Her mother had heard enough.

"Give me the address, I'm on my way," she said.

"You can't come over, it's ten o'clock! Who's gonna watch grandma?"

"Your grandmother is sound asleep with her new baby—I'll explain when I see you. What's the address?"

*

The drive from East Vancouver to Kitsilano would take her mother at least twenty minutes, maybe longer the way she drove. Amelia spent that time settling the kids back to bed. There was no use introducing them to a grandmother they could never have. She cried some more at that thought. To add extra torture to the moment, Amelia read an essay Luka had written about why he wanted to be a priest. *Making Sense of the Loss of a Life* was the theme of the piece—obviously about his wife, despite the generalizations. She was back to hysterical when she opened the door for her mother. No masks. No distancing. They hugged each other for five full minutes. It was ten weeks since they had been in the same room together.

"What do you want?" her mother asked, gently.

"I don't know what you mean," Amelia answered.

"What do you want from this situation? What's your heart's desire?"

"I want Luka—and the kids. I want us to be a family."

Her mother removed a small sack from her purse. "This is powerful magic," she said. "Doctor Campbell gave it to me. It worked for him, then for me. It will work for you, too."

She sounds insane was Amelia's first reaction. *Hereditary Alzheimer's.* She couldn't think of a response that wouldn't reflect those thoughts, so she played along.

"I don't want to trick him. Being a priest is what he's always wanted. He will hate me if I take that away from him," she verbalized this truth. "I don't even know if he loves me!"

"Amelia, you deserve children and the man of your dreams." Her mother was making her cry again. "Take the beads and follow the directions. The right thing will happen." Amelia felt the little bag being pressed into her hand. "Promise you'll do it for me," her mother implored. "I've gotta go. I've pushed my luck long enough with your grandmother." Another hug and her mother was gone.

*

Amelia wrestled with what to ask for—*after* wrestling with whether to do it in the first place. She knew a Sanskrit mantra was not dark magic, but it felt like she was pitting voodoo against Christianity. Did Jesus even speak Sanskrit? He probably spoke Aramaic and Hebrew, though Sanskrit had been around for five thousand years before His birth. It was a question Luka would have been able to answer. The thought caused her a bout of hysterical laughter, so close to tears. Of course, she would do the beads! How could she not? But what would she ask for? The fantasy part of Amelia fought with her realistic, though recently dormant, side. "Make Luka love me beyond all else." *Really? Beyond the love of his children? Beyond the love of their mother?* her mind sarcastically asked. Or "If we are not meant to be together, free my heart." A good person would choose number two. She didn't feel like a good person. She felt like a desperate woman. She sat on the floor on Luca's pillow, back straight with legs folded yogi-style, and began the seven breaths. Her unsettled mind pelted through her situation, finally saying, "Free me from the pain of loving someone I cannot have." Amelia began to chant.

*

The new day brought with it two children and one adult grumpy from lack of sleep. Breakfast was less synchronized swimming and more of a belly-flop event. Nobody wanted to go to the park. Amelia's mind ran to overanalyzing. Were the beads working by trying to make her stop loving the children? She dismissed the thought. Nothing could change the way she felt about Anya and Alexander, certainly not one bad morning. Half a Disney movie later, the kids were passed out on the couch. Amelia couldn't resist staring at the perfection of their sleeping faces, one so dark, the other so fair. Neither particularly resembled their father, yet both reminded her of him. As if on cue her phone rang, flashing his name across the screen.

"Hi," she whispered. "Everything okay? You never call this early."

"I did not want to worry you, but one of the Bishops here tested positive for coronavirus. He is in the hospital, doing poorly—we have already been quarantined for nine days. I am free to leave as of this afternoon."

Amelia stammered her first thought. "I'm not ready for you to come home."

Luka laughed. "Don't worry about how the place looks. I know how difficult it is taking care of two children—"

"It's not that," she replied, suddenly panicking over the impending end of her motherhood. "I'm not ready to leave Anya and Alexander. I have five more days!"

There was silence on the other end of the line. Amelia didn't have a next sentence. Finally, Luka spoke.

"We should talk. I will be home by six tonight. Do you need me to get anything at the store on my way?"

"No. We're good." *We are good.* "I'll see you tonight."

*

Remarkably, the next four hours flew by. Amelia cleaned the bathroom, changed the sheets on Luka's bed, and made a meatloaf dinner with the kid's less-than-helpful help. A backdrop dialogue ran through her head like a chain letter. *What if I say this? What if he says that?* Suddenly Luka was at the door, suitcase and flowers in hand. Anya and Alexander ran to him, making the initial hello chaotic, but not awkward. Soon they were seated at the table eating dinner, the bouquet of flowers in a centerpiece pickle jar.

"So I'm sure your trip wasn't what you planned, but was it still worth going?" Amelia asked once the children's stories had subsided.

"It may seem crazy, but being forced to quarantine made it a true retreat. Studying is one thing. Knowing your heart is another. I got to better know my heart." His answer was sending butterflies through her stomach.

"And what has your heart told you?" She tried to keep the question light as if its answer was unimportant.

"That I was meant to be a priest. And that—"

Crash! Both Alexander and his chair fell sideways to the ground, a timely interruption of Luka's answer, but not before Amelia's heart was broken. "Ow!" Alexander screamed, as his father rushed to him. "I want Mimi!" he yelled even louder at Luka's attempts to check his wounds.

"Grab some ice," Amelia commanded, then cradled the crying two-year-old in her lap on the floor. "I told you not to push at the leg of the table," she said to him with soft reproach.

"Or I will knock off my block," he answered, a month of English under his belt.

"That's right," she soothed, Anya now peering over them like a second mother. *A third mother.*

"I'm glad this happened on your shift," Amelia said to Luka as he handed her ice wrapped in a facecloth.

"And I would have been happy to hear about this over the phone," he joked back. *Another Hallmark moment,* quickly followed by the echo *I was meant to be a priest.* She couldn't take it much longer.

"Why don't you clean the kitchen while I give the kids a bath? My guess is they'll be in bed early based on how little sleep we got last night." She tried to throw in a smile, but suspected the word "defeated" was stamped on her face.

"No sleep, and you wanted them for five more days." His grin was heart-melting.

"They're hard to resist," she answered, attempting to hold Alexander and pull herself up. Luka hurried to assist her.

"So are you." He didn't let go of her arm. His eyes pierced through her, as if … *He loves me!* The realization flooded her body with embarrassing warmth. The mala beads had been useless. She couldn't have him, and now her heart was more trapped than ever. Amelia pulled her arm away.

"I have to go." She kissed Alexander's head and thrust him into the arms of his confused father, then bent down and desperately hugged Anya. "I love you, little angel." Both children were crying and calling her name as she pulled her already-packed suitcase to the door.

"Amelia, please! Tell me what is wrong!" Luka followed her to the hallway, two wailing babies at his side. She couldn't answer him. "I know you have feelings for me!" Amelia paused at the closed elevator, then raced to the stairs, unable to listen. *I am meant to be a priest.* Luka continued to follow her, begging her to stop. "Please, just talk to me!"

"I can't." She kept going without looking back. Four steps into the stairwell, she lost control of her suitcase. It tumbled the two flights with an alarmingly loud reverberation. Amelia ran after it. Behind her ran Luka, still juggling two crying children.

At the bottom of the stairs, Amelia found her suitcase burst open, her belongings scattered over the first-floor landing. She sunk to her knees and tried to smash everything back into the luggage. Her shampoo bottle was broken. The thick pink goo splattered across Anya's crayon drawing—a sunny day picture of the four of them looking like a family. Amelia wiped across the absorbent construction paper with a shirt, causing more damage to the picture. She could feel Luka and the kids behind her. It was too much.

"I love you," she cried, without turning around to look at him.

"I love you, too," Luka replied.

"A widowed priest can't remarry," she said.

"Amelia—"

"I won't be the reason you don't become a priest!"

"Come back upstairs so we can talk."

Resigned, she stood up and put out her arms to Alexander, who was sucking his thumb and looked scared. He went to her immediately, wrapping his arms around her neck. Luka reloaded the suitcase while Anya fussed over the ruined picture. They took the elevator back up to his apartment.

*

Anya and Alexander were asleep and the kitchen was spotless. Luka brewed two mugs of tea while Amelia set out the cookies she made the day before. They took seats across from each other and sat silently cradling their cups. The only thing left to do was talk.

"Luka—"

"Please. Let me speak first," he interrupted. "Canada was our new start, a place where no one knows our real story." Amelia felt a pang of fear at his words. *Their real story?*

"You and I have never spoken about Anya and Alexander's mother—there are things I should have told you. The few times I tried, you made certain that I stopped."

"I couldn't bear to hear about a woman you loved so much. That picture …"

"Yes, I loved her. She was beautiful and smart—a woman of incredible potential." Luka paused. "Her name was Polina, and she was my sister."

"Your sister!" Amelia could not believe what she was hearing.

"Yes. She and her husband were drug addicts." He looked pained, as though reaching for words that would soften the damage to his sister's memory. "At times they had great success battling their addiction. Then one would fall and the other would follow. They overdosed together on a bad batch of Afghan heroin. Alexander was three weeks old."

Amelia's mind raced with questions. Who found them? How long were they alone? Did Anya see her parents dead? Luka continued.

"I lived with them, on the lower level of their house. One morning I was getting ready for work and I could hear the babies crying in their cribs above me. By then Polina and Eduard had been dead for hours. The ambulance came. They took away the bodies—no questions, no investigation. Just another side effect of a damaged society. There was a very public custody battle, I could not leave Polina's babies with Eduard's dysfunctional family. In the end, everyone signed off on the adoption." An ironic smile crossed his face. "Who could find fault with a man studying to be a priest?" Luka sipped his tea and gestured to his surroundings. "Now we are here, where the stigma of their parent's death cannot follow them. Anya and Alexander know me only as their Papochka—the beautiful woman on the wall as Mama. Someday I will tell them more. But for now, they need only safety and love."

"I don't know what to say," Amelia began.

"You have already said the only words that matter," a smile lit his face. "You love me."

"When do we have to get married?" The question sounded normal in her head, but ridiculous out loud. Luka's laugh was spontaneous, deep, and genuine.

"Amelia! Let me do *some* of the wooing!" He became serious. "I will be ordained next summer, so it must be before that." Luka got up from the table and pulled her into his arms. "Perhaps I should at least kiss you before we plan a wedding."

*

His kiss was better than Amelia had dared to imagine. Her body filled with warmth. She searched Luka's face for a mirror of her feelings. The love in his eyes was all the confirmation she needed.

"Ya lyublyu vas, moya dusha," he whispered, finding her lips again.

Moya dusha. My soul! Amelia's heart sang! She would figure out the rest of the sentence later. Knowing all the words suddenly didn't seem necessary. She was content with kissing her future husband—the father of her two beautiful children.

Thank you for the magic beads, Mama. Namaste.

June 26, 2020

CHAPTER 27 ~ DIANE

Vancouver, British Columbia, Canada

He hadn't said it, but Diane knew her husband doubted her story. He had reason to be skeptical. Greg had seen her text in every conceivable situation—on her way home from work, driving their girls to sports, even during a two-minute trip to the store. And when she wasn't texting, Diane was talking on the phone—without the Bluetooth. Greg had offered repeatedly to set up the connection in her new car, but she refused. She hated the way the call wouldn't transfer from her speaker to her iPhone when she was done driving. "No hands-free devices for this girl!" she would brag, making fun of those mothers with the wireless speaker clipped to their ear. *But I swear to God I was not texting that day.*

*

Diane had a lot going against her on this one. She had a huge presence on Facebook—over nine hundred friends and fifteen hundred followers. Everyone knew her habits, her irreverence for convention, and her smart-ass comebacks. Both of Diane's teenage daughters had developed an aversion to social media after experiencing one too many *eew!* moments, courtesy of their mother. They would no longer allow her to post pictures of them, so Diane's Facebook page was bereft of the normalcy of family life. She prided herself on being a left-wing American, which loosely translated to just-left-of-liberal Canadian. She had an infatuation with Justin Trudeau and joked that he should be married to a woman his own age—namely her. Up until late one Thursday afternoon in May, when she killed a fourteen-year-old boy,

Diane thought she was the funniest thing to ever hit Vancouver. Now she knew better.

The accident was front-page news. *Wife of UBC Dean Hits and Fatally Injures Fourteen-year-old Boy in Shaughnessy neighborhood.* Social media blew up with the story. Very few posts suggested she be given the benefit of the doubt, "Of course, she was texting when she ran him down with her brand new Audi SQ7!" Diane knew if she were to be tried by the media she would certainly serve prison time. The accident was so devastating it took her two weeks to open her computer (her phone had been seized by the police) to see what people were saying. The same friends who, not long ago, filled her page with laugh emojis and thumbs-up-likes were either jumping on the social hate bandwagon or as absent as the sound of crickets in the night. She screamed and sobbed about the lack of support, and against the advice of her barrister pushed to post her side of the story. After forty-eight hours of vociferating, her husband ended her rant with a booming, "Wake up, Diane! Social media is not your friend! How in God's name are you gonna convince strangers that you're innocent when your own daughters won't even talk to you?" Diane shut down her computer and increased her Xanax to catatonic levels. Her new concern became whether or not her doctor would refill her prescription. It would be months before this nightmare was over—maybe double the time of a normal vehicular homicide due to the pandemic delays. She occasionally tried to look on the bright side—*Maybe I'll get coronavirus and die before I have to go to prison.*

*

One day her husband came into her bedroom—something he hadn't done since moving to the den when she accused him of being no comfort whatsoever. He placed a package on the bed beside her.

"This parcel is addressed to you. It's from Amelia Graham. She's a professor I work with at the University,"

"I assume it's not naked pictures of the two of you?" Diane asked, too depressed to care.

"I have no idea what it is," Greg answered, his detached, uncurious nature still intact.

She opened it the minute he shut the door. Inside was a small gauze bag of beads and a letter.

Dear Mrs. Jansson,

I can only imagine what a difficult time this is for you. My name is Amelia Graham. I'm an English professor at UBC. It may seem odd that I'm writing to you since we've never met, but your husband was extremely kind to me when I first began at the University. I struggled to fit in and felt very much the newcomer. His door was always open for a question or necessary introduction. I am hoping to return his kindness with this gift.

These are miraculous mala beads. They were given to my mother by an environmental scientist named Dr. Seth Campbell. She used them to create a space of peace for my grandmother who has Alzheimer's disease, and then passed them along to me. When I say they manifested a wish beyond my wildest dreams, I am not exaggerating. I am passing them to you in the hope that using them can ease some of the pain you must be feeling. Please know this "gift" is being sent to you with sincere intentions and should be taken seriously. I wish you all the best.

Namaste, Amanda Graham

Diane threw aside the letter and opened the sack. She held the beads while she read the mysterious instructions.

"Jesus! No wonder the girl had a hard time fitting in! What a freak!" She tossed the beads back into the bag, leaving them, and their cryptic directions, to fall upon the floor from her exaggerated fluffing of the bed quilt. "Lunatic," she muttered, hoping her medication would take effect soon.

A few minutes later, Diane heard the door creak open. "Dad sent me to check on you," her seventeen-year-old daughter, Janelle, said quietly.

"You can tell him nothing's changed. I'm still indicted for murder." Diane didn't bother to roll over to face her daughter.

"What's this?" Janelle asked, picking up the beads.

"Some *mystical* thing one of your father's weird friends sent me."

"Can I have it?"

Yesh," she slurred. *Oh good. The Xanax is kicking in.* "Close the door on your way out."

June 26, 2020

CHAPTER 28 ~ JANELLE

Vancouver, British Columbia, Canada

There was a tiny part of Janelle that wanted to see her mother go down for this accident. She had been such a handful over the years. Janelle remembered the exact moment she went from thinking she had the coolest mother in town, to realizing her mother was an obnoxious asshole. It was her thirteenth birthday party.

"Call me Diane," her mother had said to Tim, the boy Janelle was infatuated with. "It's not like I'm that much older than you guys." *Yeah, you are. You were thirty-three when you had me.* Her mother stayed in that basement almost the entire party, missing easy shots at the pool table and cracking jokes. Janelle's friends thought she was great. Tim thought she was great. She finally left with a flashy, "I'm going upstairs! Now you kids can play spin-the-bottle or whatever it is you play these days!" From that point on everything about her mother became too much—too much opinion, too much drinking, too much trying to be cool, too much bragging about how people thought she was cool—and too little actual parenting. Thank God for her father. How he put up with it was anyone's guess and a testament to his ability to accept people for who they were. "How very Canadian of you," her mother would say whenever her father refused to badmouth someone. Janelle hoped she possessed more Canadian than American. She worried about her thirteen-year-old sister, Suzette. Who knew how their mother's current situation would affect her?

*

The mala beads were intriguing—the scrolled directions reminded Janelle of the map from *The Goonies*, her mother's favorite movie. *Who would send this to her?* She couldn't name the reason she didn't ask her father, other than the obvious. Everyone in the house was in a stupor, voluntarily sequestered in their own rooms and pretending nothing had happened. She hadn't been surprised when her father asked her where they kept the blow-up bed. Now with him in the den, their four separate bedrooms occupied all four corners of the house. It was like living alone.

Her mother wasn't going to do the mantra, she didn't have a spiritual bone in her body. "If seeing isn't believing anymore, why would I believe something I can't even see?" Her *Diane-isms* were repeated with such frequency that quoting her became a family joke. When Janelle had asked her for details about the accident, her mother told her that on the advice of her attorney, she couldn't talk about it. *The amazing Diane is suddenly speechless.* Janelle knew she needed to get a better attitude. Of course, she didn't want her mother to go to prison. But what *did* she want? She thought about the mantra, knowing she was going to do it. She could ask for the truth, but how would that help? It wouldn't keep her mother out of jail, and if it were an ugly truth it could cause Janelle to despise her even more.

Let the truth of what happened change my mother for the better. There was something hopeful about that request. "Please let the truth of what happened change my mother for the better," she said aloud, then began the magical mala bead meditation.

DIANE (Continued)

Mornings no longer felt like a fresh start. Now drug-induced fogginess and cotton mouth eventually gave way to the new normal of her current reality. Wakeful consciousness had become a never-ending pity party, followed by the relief of vacant blackness.

*

Something was different today. Because Diane awoke with a clear thought, she assumed she was still asleep. *I'm sorry for your loss.* The words floated across her visual mind like a ticker tape. *I'm sorry for your loss.* She squeezed her eyes shut, testing the theory she was still asleep. *I'm sorry for your loss.* Maybe she needed stronger tranquilizers. She opened her eyes. Her bedroom looked normal. Greg's archaic alarm clock said ten past nine, the earliest she had wakened in seven weeks. Her head felt clear. She tried to shut her eyes again. *I'm sorry for your loss.* The words were in cursive, her own handwriting. Diane put the pillow over her head. It didn't help, she could hear the sentence recited by the egoic voice in her mind. *I'm sorry for your loss.* She sat up and dug her hands through her hair, settling them over her ears. She couldn't block out the sound. Suzette opened the door and looked startled to see her mother upright, holding her head in her hands. They made eye contact.

"I'm sorry. Mom," Suzette said, then scurried out the door. Diane put her hands down. *I'm sorry for your loss.* Suzette and the dead boy were almost the same age.

*

In the corner of Diane and Greg's bedroom was a shiny mirrored desk, a plush ergonomic office chair, and the most fashionable shelving and storage cubbies. Diane had searched Pinterest for months to find exactly the right look for her office nook. She had insisted on a new printer—she didn't like the color of Greg's—and spent an extra four-hundred-twenty dollars to purchase the pink version of the Canon PIXMA. Mounted on the wall was a twenty-three-inch industrial panel monitor with a touch screen, wrapped in a bezel-cut stainless steel finish. Though no expense had been spared, Diane rarely used it—preferring to sit on her bed with her iPhone and laptop and just stare at the beautiful look she had created. This morning, with the force of a never-ending sentiment ringing through her head, Diane rushed to her desk. She was so desperate to write something down that she couldn't take the time to wait for her expensive computer to boot up. Instead, she pulled a sheet of paper from the fancy printer and began to write by hand …

I am contacting you against the advice of my barrister and my husband, but you are his mother. First, I must tell you that I am sorry for your loss.

It was a Thursday afternoon. I was driving through your neighborhood on my way back from looking at a small antique table that a woman had listed for sale on the Facebook Marketplace App. I am somewhat familiar with that area of town because I once had a tennis instructor who lived around the corner from you. Nonetheless, I used the GPS map on my phone to find the house. On my way back from looking at the table (which was not to my taste and totally overpriced) my phone was resting on my lap. I hadn't shut off the directions and the annoying voice kept telling me to "resume the route." I looked down at my lap and shut off the program, then turned to take a left on Leonard Street. I could see a boy walking toward me quite a distance away on my side of the road. He was well onto the shoulder and I didn't give him one bit of thought, except to note that all the boys have long hair again from no haircuts during this pandemic. As I got a little closer, the wind picked up and blew his hair back from his face. His eyes were so beautiful, very brown. He looked right at me, making direct eye contact. Then I saw his mouth move. Only this morning did I realize what he was saying—"I'm sorry, Mom."

While still looking at me, your son stepped off the curb and directly in front of my car. It happened so fast that I didn't slam the brakes until after I hit him. I sat in shock while one of your neighbors did CPR and called 911. The police eventually removed me from my car and brought me to the hospital in a separate ambulance.

As his mother, I felt you should know these details. If it were one of my daughters, I would need to know. Again, I can only say how sorry I am for your loss. Diane Jansson.

*

Diane opened her desk drawer and pulled out a monogrammed envelope left over from a Christmas party she had hosted before the world went into lockdown. She folded the sheet of paper in quarters and slipped it inside, then wrote out the name and address that had been permanently etched in her mind since the first day she saw it in print. Using the same courier service she had used for the Christmas party, Diane made arrangements for her letter to be hand-delivered to Noah Sunderlin's mother. Then she took a shower, got dressed, and put on some makeup. She had no idea what the future would bring, but she wasn't going to waste one more precious minute with her family.

JANELLE (Continued)

The noise was random and needed to be checked out. Janelle walked into the den to find her mother deflating the blow-up bed and folding the linens. She looked calm. It was ten o'clock in the morning.

"Hey, Mom," Janelle hung back, unsure if a morning hug was appropriate these days. Her mom solved her dilemma with a quick kiss on the top of her head.

"Janelle, yay. You're up. Can you give me a hand dragging this to the hall closet?"

"Sure?" Janelle wasn't going to ask if folding up the improv Motel 6 was a Dad-approved move.

"Thanks for holding down the fort while I was … out of it."

You're welcome seemed risky to say aloud. "I was gonna go grocery shopping today if you want to come," Janelle said tentatively. Her mother looked confused and indecisive. "That's okay, I can go by myself," Janelle amended.

"Yeah. I don't think I'm ready to get into a car. How 'bout if we do a big online order and have it delivered?"

"Works for me."

Janelle had seen her mother in re-group mode many times. In the past, it was an arrogant regrouping, usually instigated by an imagined slight from someone or something. Her mother would square her shoulders and push forward with a project or party that would re-solidify her position as supermom and socialite. This morning's return of the matriarch bore no resemblance to the past. It was twenty hours since she had recited the miracle mantra. Janelle dared to hope.

*

Dinner was almost normal—a few conversational lags here and there. Janelle watched her sister supply a story or joke when necessary.

Suzette was an empath, reading the room and filling in the spaces so nobody would feel uncomfortable. *I'll have to keep an eye on that*, Janelle decided. Being an accommodating pleaser wasn't in any woman's best interest. Her father's phone rang. Ever polite, he got up from the table to answer it with his classic, "Gregory Jansson, here." Suzette comically mimicked him, making her voice sound masculine and important. Her mother's laugh was genuine, a sound Janelle hadn't realized she missed. Her father returned to the room, his face oddly emotional.

"That was your lawyer, " he began. "The young man you hit was going through a hard time, suffering from depression. A neighbor came forward with an account of the boy's deliberate intent to step into your path—they've deemed it a suicide. The charges have been dropped." A fuzzy tingling ran the length of Janelle's spine. Her father plucked a napkin from the table and stoically wiped his tears and cleared his throat. "Diane," he said, "it's over. This nightmare is finally over."

All eyes were on her mother, waiting for the *I told you so* to begin. Instead, she reached across the table, a hand toward each daughter which Jenelle and Suzette quickly filled with their own. "It may be over for us," her mother said, "but the nightmare is just beginning for his family. I feel so sorry for them—I can't imagine losing either one of you."

Janelle watched the tears run down her mother's cheeks, tears shed for someone else. *A miracle.* She would have to ask her father who sent the mala beads, but she knew who they should go to next—Zachary….

June 27, 2020

CHAPTER 29 ~ SELMA

Vancouver, British Columbia, Canada

Selma wasn't her name. It belonged to an aunt she had never met. In typical Jewish tradition, her parents named her after a dead person. The original Selma's demise had occurred shortly after birth, so she was referred to as 'dead baby Aunt Selma' to differentiate between the two.

By the time 'alive Selma' reached the age of eleven, even her body knew she had been dealt a hand from the wrong deck of cards. Without any artificial hormones or surgery, her physique had begun taking on masculine characteristics to match her emotional psyche. She towered over her older brother and was stronger than him in every way. Her arm bulk was significant, her thighs were chunky and powerful. Over the years her mother had attempted to grow out Selma's dark, tightly curled hair, each time giving up once the length became hideously unmanageable. It was cut short—*a pixie* her mother had called it. It wasn't as though Selma wanted to work on her appearance. Styling her hair, picking out clothes, or primping in front of a mirror were the last things on her list. At seventeen, Selma had never worn a bit of makeup or purchased an item of clothing. She could count on one hand the number of times she had been forced into a dress. She spent every day in black chinos and a black button-down shirt, clothing purchased for her first job as a ticket attendant at a local movie theater. Selma had convinced her mother that she needed three sets of uniforms for what amounted to two weekly shifts. When the theater job ended because of the pandemic, at least she had some clothes she felt comfortable wearing. But without that job, working out in the basement was the only thing keeping her alive—*that, and Janelle*.

*

Selma met Janelle in science lab. They were the two brainiacs of the four students assigned to that lab table. Each had been given a substandard lab partner who spent the period talking and pretending to contribute. Janelle was intellectually funny. Selma fell in love with her the first time they shared a joke.

"What did the scientist say when he mixed boric acid and 99% alcohol and blew up the lab?" Janelle had asked her lab partner, Keira, who stared blankly at her as though it were a question on a quiz.

"Oxidants happen," Selma replied, without looking up from her task, causing Janelle to burst out laughing with a sound so pure and delightful that Selma couldn't get enough. After that, she did everything she could to make Janelle laugh—jokes, eye-rolling, muttered comments about the teacher or the assignment. It was as though they were the only two people in the room. Eventually, Selma got Janelle a job at the movie theater. The first time Janelle snapped a selfie of the two of them—dressed in jet black and hovering over the candy counter—Selma panicked, certain she was headed for social humiliation.

"Hey. You're not gonna put that on Instagram or anything, are you?"

Janelle laughed her beautiful laugh. "Are you kidding? I hate that shit. You have to be pretty insecure to count the likes you get for posting a picture of a bowl of Dim Sum!"

"Did you just call me a Chinese dumpling?"

"You're more of an Italian meatball," Janelle answered, a smart-ass grin on her face.

"Yeah, right! More like a Jewish Matza ball," Selma replied.

"Same thing!" Janelle volleyed back.

If only that were true, thought Selma, while rejoicing in how fun work had become. They had a plan and a game for everything. Selma bagged the popcorn. Janelle squirted the fake butter. Janelle sold the tickets. Selma ripped them in half and pointed the patron toward the correct theater. When the movies ended, they raced through the rows of barely lit rooms, each seeing who could clean their section the fastest. Their shifts included plenty of time to study chemistry, criticize other students, and vent about the shortcomings of their families. Janelle had a car so she picked Selma up for the shifts they worked together. Selma told her manager she needed to work the same days for transportation reasons—a little manipulative, but worth it. The rides back and forth added a different intimacy to their conversations.

Revealing sentences turned into further riddles. Selma couldn't get to the bottom of her own sexuality, let alone Janelle's, who had never mentioned a boyfriend, or guys in general. *Is she gay? Am I gay? Is it still considered gay if you want to be a man?* Being with Jenelle swirled through her head even though she had no idea what "being with" meant. Selma was a virgin. Finding out the details online wasn't for her. It wasn't guilt that made her stay away from the internet, it was sullying the romance of her feelings with the seediness of some stranger's graphic sexual display. *How am I going to have first love if I don't know what it is?*

Hanukkah came and they exchanged eight gifts. Selma bought Janelle things for her car—a fur steering wheel cover and a heated windshield scraper. Janelle's gifts were more personal—a black t-shirt that said *I hate social media,* a pair of fingerless gloves, and a soup bowl inscribed *"Please sir, I want some more"* based on their shared love of Oliver Twist. Selma was excited about the gift she chose for Janelle on Zot Hanukkah, the last night of the Jewish holiday. The words on the silver heart-shaped pendant were a customized version of the traditional friendship necklace. One side said *two in black*. On the other side, *i've got your back*. She couldn't wait for Janelle to open it.

*

"I love it!" Janelle quickly pulled the necklace from the jewelry box and held it up to her neck, turning her back to Selma. "Help me do this." Selma nervously pulled the lobster claw back and slipped it around the tiny ring, trying not to touch any part of Janelle.

"Done."

Janelle whirled around, her hand on the little heart, still trying to look at it despite the short length of the chain. "I love this," she said again. "I hope you like your present." She pulled an envelope from her back pocket and thrust it at Selma. Selma opened it. It was a gift certificate for *One-Exit Escape Room,* already scheduled for the Tuesday night of Christmas vacation week.

"Oh my God, this is great!" Selma felt like jumping up and down. "Who's going with us?"

"Nobody," Janelle replied. "I signed us up for the hardest room and we're gonna break the record time to escape!"

Selma couldn't wait.

*

The escape room was called The Labyrinth. The answer to each intricate clue led to an east, west, north, or south direction—or to answers that were virtually the same thing, up, down, left, right. Thrown in for added confusion were questions that resulted in dead ends and turnarounds. The record was nineteen minutes, set by four college students. Selma and Janelle didn't break the record. Janelle did, however, break a toe tripping over a chair while they attempted to solve the first clue, whose answer would gift them with the key to the light switch. Once they knew it was hopeless, they sat on the floor to take a good look at Janelle's toe.

"Maybe we should go to the emergency room," Selma said, envisioning herself carrying Janelle through the building.

"No way. I paid for a minimum of sixty minutes and we're staying for sixty minutes!" Janelle said. "But you'll have to carry me outta here when our time's up."

"I plan to," Selma answered, feeling her throat get thick from the way Janelle was staring at her. There was a long pause.

"You know I'm not gay, right?" Janelle said quietly.

"I'm not either," replied Selma.

"Wait? What?" Janelle looked confused.

"I'm not gay," Selma repeated. "I'm a man trapped in a woman's body. My true self is just a guy who likes girls." Selma let that sink in for a bit, weirdly unconcerned about how her friend would take it. Finally, Janelle's golden laugh rang out.

"Well, okay then! Sounds pretty simple!"

Selma laughed, too. "Simplest life ever!"

"What do your parents think?" Janelle asked, suddenly serious.

"They don't know," Selma answered.

"But they know you're gay?"

"If they do, they're not saying," Selma tried to make it sound like it didn't matter.

"Well, that's not good. Isn't there a window to get hormones … and surgery and—"

A loud buzzer went off and a voice came over the intercom. "Time's up ladies! How did you do?"

"We broke a toe!" Janelle yelled into the air.

"Stay right where you are," the faceless voice commanded, and without shutting off the speaker said, "Jason, get the wheelchair for number four. It's another broken toe." Janelle and Selma fell over laughing.

*

From that day forward, every discussion between them centered around the mystery of the transgender world. Selma was surprised to find Janelle knew more about the topic than she did. The hopelessness of her possibilities had caused Selma to put a brick wall between herself and the information she needed to achieve happiness. Now she wanted to know everything.

"Being a man is out of the question," she said to Janelle, during their final clean-the-entire-theater shift before the pandemic shutdown. "It would kill my parents," she continued. "I mean, it's not like they get me—or even like me—but I still don't wanna kill them."

"This is your life!" Janelle retorted.

Is it? Selma wondered. It didn't feel like it.

*

The month of April was immersed in transgender education, sending each other links on surgery, hormones, clinics, and psychologists who specialized in making transgender decisions. After debating what it should be, Janelle began to call her by her chosen male name. In between remote school classes they texted and Face-timed, their conversations always ending in the same conclusion—nothing would change until Selma told her parents.

*

May brought new challenges. Janelle's mother had killed someone in a driving accident and was being charged with homicide. Things were so awful for her friend that Selma's gender identity problem was no longer discussed. She watched Janelle's joyous, wise-cracking personality quickly morph into depression and rage against her mother, a woman Janelle had assured Selma was so selfish she barely factored into their family's dynamics. Selma hadn't seen Janelle in person for two months when she asked her mother to help her make a meal for their family, giving her an excuse to visit.

"Selma!" her mother exclaimed. "I'm so happy you want to cook with me!"

No, Ima. I would rather you make the food yourself, then I drop it off.

"We'll make Cholent!"

"Can we just call it a beef stew?" Selma asked, hoping for a less Jewish choice. At least her mother hadn't suggested Matza ball soup.

"Or maybe we should make Matza ball soup, in case they don't eat beef. Do your friends eat beef?"

"They eat beef," Selma replied, though her mother wasn't listening and had begun to hunt the freezer for stew meat, muttering something about Kishka. *Regret. Regret. Regret.*

*

The Cholent came out magnificent. Selma's mother transferred it into one of her thrift store finds—a covered serving bowl that "wouldn't kill her dead if it didn't get returned." The honey cake, normally a dessert reserved for Rosh Hashanah but chosen because the ingredients were already on hand, smelled delicious and sat perfectly centered on another bargain bonanza plate. Ima had a basement full of things that wouldn't "kill her to go missing."

"Bring it over while it's hot," her mother ordered, a needless command since Selma couldn't wait to see Janelle. "And when you get home try on the dress I bought you for the family portrait!" Selma had already lost the argument about wearing the inherited pearls with one of her black button-down shirts. "You're not going to wear your Aunt Selma's pearls with an old black work shirt!" *Maybe dead baby*

Aunt Selma should have taken the pearls to the grave with her. More words Selma couldn't say out loud.

*

Selma texted before getting out of the car. *I'm in your driveway. I made you some food.* She waited a few minutes before tentatively exiting her mother's Toyota Corolla and slowly walking toward the Janssons' front door. Janelle whipped open the door before Selma had a chance to ring.

"We just found out my mother is innocent! They dropped the charges because the boy had mental problems! He walked in front of her car on purpose!" Janelle looked euphoric—and wonderful.

"Oh my God Janelle! That's great!" Selma said, balancing the platter and the casserole dish.

"Do you want to come in?" Janelle took the cake from her. Selma had never been inside Janelle's house. Janelle's family was blond and beautiful. Selma was embarrassingly neither of those things.

"No. I gotta go. We're having a family portrait done—I gotta try on this lame-ass dress my mother bought …" Selma felt the desperation rise into her throat and project out with her voice.

"A dress, huh?" Janelle grinned. "Like a shave-your-legs kind of dress?"

"Don't go there," Selma groaned back at her, though secretly happy to have her friend point out the humor of her personal tragedy. Janelle suddenly looked inspired.

"Wait right here!" Selma, still holding the Cholent, did as she was told while Janelle raced back into the house. She returned a minute later minus the cake, but dangling a small gauze drawstring bag.

"This is your answer! I swear it's magic! Just hear me out before you tell me I'm crazy." Selma listened as Janelle told her how this bag of beads had saved her mother. For a couple of science geeks, buying into the concept of magic was easier than Selma would have thought. She couldn't wait to go home and try it.

*

"Have you tried on that dress yet?" Selma's mother's voice boomed through the closed bedroom door.

"I will!" Selma bellowed back. *I could squish her like a bug.* Her mother was so tiny. They were all tiny, even her brother. Selma dreaded the unveiling of a new family portrait. They hadn't taken one since she was ten—before she became a monster. She could lie across the family sofa carrying them all on her back. Selma forced the image from her mind, concentrating instead on the mantra in front of her. *Om satyam narayanam.* She cleared her mind, hoping that screaming at her mother and imagining squashing her hadn't ruined the magic. "Send me the courage to be who I'm meant to be." Selma began to chant ….

*

The dress wasn't horrible. It was black knit with long sleeves and a modest neckline. Not a dress for June, but more suited for winter. Maybe her mother didn't hate her. *Or maybe she knows the less hairy skin I show the better.* Selma stood in front of her dresser, another family heirloom filled with the musty smell of the dead, and stared into its fun-house-quality carved mirror. She looked passable. The few feminine qualities she had were accentuated by the delicate neckline of the dress. Her eyes were dark and large—if a little too close together. She opened the velvet box and lifted the pearl necklace, draping it against her throat, knowing it would fit her like a choker. Tucked into the large flat box was a picture of baby Aunt Selma wearing the pearls at her naming ceremony. The pearls went halfway down her tiny body. A delicate kippah on baby Selma's head made her look like a little old man. Selma pulled out the picture to peer closely at the baby's face. It was covered with fine, dark hair below the hairline and in front of her ears, like a baby monkey—like her own infant picture.

What did baby Aunt Selma die from? It was one of many undiscussed family topics. Selma secured the pearls around her neck and left to get her mother's approval on the dress.

*

"Oh! Selma! You look so beautiful! You did a great job on your hair!" Her mother rushed toward her, reaching up to touch the hair Selma hadn't bothered to brush that day. "Did you try on the shoes?"

"It doesn't matter if they fit. We'll be sitting on Bubbe's couch. I'll just fake it."

"No. I want them to fit. What if we go out for a nice meal?' Her mother persisted.

"We're in a pandemic! We're not going out to eat! I can't believe you're letting a photographer into our house." Selma was done with the fashion conversation. "How did Aunt Selma die?"

Her mother looked shocked by the question. "She was born with a disease."

Well, that tells me nothing. "What kind of disease?" Selma pushed.

"What difference does it make?" her mother answered and turned to busy herself with nothing.

"It makes a difference to me. I'm named after her. I'm wearing her necklace."

Her mother turned, looking weirdly defeated. "It's called Congenital Adrenal Hyperplasia. My mother called it salt wasting. It was something they didn't know about until it was too late."

Selma had the sudden urge to hug her mother. They weren't huggers. "Thanks, Ima." Then her mother went back to business with the commands.

"Take off that dress and come eat before the photographer comes."

*

There were pages and pages of information online about Congenital Adrenal Hyperplasia, CAH. When Selma hit *IMAGES* she was assaulted with everything from malformed infant genitalia to masculinized, hairy women who looked just like her. Multiple times she had to turn away and take a deep breath. She didn't realize she was crying until a string of snot landed on her new black dress. She made herself continue.

There were multiple forms of this genetic disease—from serious and deadly, to hardly any symptoms. Apparently, Selma's adrenal glands were the problem. They were producing excessive amounts of androgens, making too much testosterone. Based on what she read, Selma decided she had Non-Classical Congenital Adrenal Hyperplasia.

"Non-classical congenital adrenal hyperplasia (NCCAH or NCAH) is a hormonal disorder characterized by early signs of puberty namely excessive hair growth, increase in height, and acne. It can also involve decreased fertility as well as menstrual problems in females. This non-classical form is much milder than the classical form of CAH, and can be treated effectively using steroid hormones."

Her search quickly moved to gender dysphoria and CAH, then CAH and transgender surgery. An hour later Selma was emotionally spent, less confused, and more confused. Why hadn't her parents recognized the signs? *Did they know but do nothing?* There were treatments, but Selma knew it was too late. Her mind had already decided. *I am a man.*

She checked the time. Ten minutes until the photography session. Using a dirty sock and an old bottle of water, Selma wiped the mucus from her dress and smoothed out the wrinkles. She pulled on the low black shoes. They were not comfortable, but fit perfectly. As she walked past the mirror, her battered psyche recoiled at the image. She stopped and looked down at the mala beads on the dresser, then picked up the picture of baby Aunt Selma, communicating with her for the first time.

"I'm sorry that you're dead, little aunty, but I've had enough." Selma pulled off the pearls, breaking the clasp. "This is bullshit. I'm not a girl." In a matter of minutes, she had re-dressed in her nicest black pants and shirt. Using what was left of the bottled water, she doused her hair and combed it straight back then rolled the shirt sleeves up to expose her hairy forearms. As a concession to her mother, Selma wrapped the pearls around her wrist like a bracelet, securing the ends in a knot. She slipped on the black patent leather flats. They looked great with the pants. After one more glimpse in the mirror to admire her unwaxed upper lip, she strode through her bedroom door and into the parlor just in time to hear her mother holler, "Where is she? Somebody go get Selma!"

"My name is Zachary and my preferred pronoun is *he*—where is *he*?" Zachary smiled at his shocked father and brother, then kissed his mother on the top of her head. "I'm right here, Ima. Let's get this photo thing over with."

June 28, 2020

CHAPTER 30 ~ CHILI

Vancouver, British Columbia, Canada

Chili had learned to tread carefully when it came to asking things of his mother. She had a delineated cut-off point. As a single parent with two jobs and a full college class load, sometimes Chili didn't dare ask what was for dinner let alone push her on the topic of who his real father was.

"If it mattered even one bit, I would tell you," was her latest response.

"It matters to me," he had argued, his teenaged voice whinier than he intended.

"It shouldn't." And just like that, the conversation was ended. "Go see if Nana is eating with us."

Dissed and dismissed, Chili grabbed his cell phone to call his grandmother, who lived in the cottage next door. Of course, she was eating with them. She ate every meal with them.

"I said 'Go see' not call. She might need help getting over here."

*

Nana was somewhere between the most capable and the least capable person Chili had ever met. She was a powerhouse of information, and in her prime had been able to fix anything from a wall to the heating system. But now she had a disease that was getting the best of her. Breathing was hard. Walking was hard. Not being strong anymore was hard. She was frustrated by the pain and it made her bitchy.

"Look at this shit," she said as they walked the short distance between houses. "Everything needs painting," followed by, "The front steps are rotting out." It was the same thing she said every night. Chili didn't think it looked all that bad. He could probably do more, maybe learn to paint, but no one asked him to.

"Nana, Mom's almost done with school, she's gonna make fifty bucks an hour. We can pay someone to fix up the house. You need to stop worrying," the same thing he said every night.

"You think I'm gonna worry less if your Momma's a nurse working on a Covid floor? That's where they put the new nurses." The same reply, to the same response, to the same problem. Chili loved his Nana, but she was making him want to push her off the steps.

"Let me get the door for you, Nana." He jumped ahead to open the door, the smell of chicken pie met him in the doorway. Store-bought pie crust, rotisserie chicken, and a packet of gravy powder—Chili's mouth watered in anticipation. He hoped there was cranberry sauce.

*

Chili remembered the exact moment that learning the identity of his father became a thing. He was six at the time, eleven years ago, and figuring out family dynamics was not yet in his skill set. He had a mom and a nana. His friend, Joey, had a mom and an aunt. His cousin, Ronnie, had two moms. Everything made sense. Then he learned that Joey and Ronnie visited their Dads every other weekend and did fun things like go bowling or buy a John Cena action figure. For two weekends a month, Chili had no one to play with. "When am I going to my Dad's?" he asked his Nana. "You'll have to ask your mother," Nana had replied, always careful not to commit to something his mother would be furious about. "You don't have a dad," his mother later told him. "Why?" he asked. "Some kids just don't," she answered, an ending to the conversation and a beginning of Chili's feeling of lack. Everyone had something he didn't have—a father.

*

With the odds estimated at fifty-million-to-one, Nana, Mom, and Chili had been born on the same day. To further increase the improbability, that day was the first of July—Canada Day. In his baby book was the newspaper article with a picture of the three of them, his infant face barely visible in the blanket. His mother looked beautiful, young, and terrified. Only his Nana looked happy, beaming like it was the best day of her life. Every year, someone from the newspaper or social media wanted to make a big deal of this one thing that gave him celebrity status despite his lack of a father. His mother always refused. "I don't need everyone in Vancouver knowing our business." This July they would each be celebrating a milestone birthday. Nana was turning fifty, Mom thirty-five, and Chili was going to be eighteen. His mother had already turned away a bunch of phone interviews and laid down the law with his grandmother to do the same. A month before the big birthday, his own phone rang.

"Is this Chili Colmer?"

"Yeah?"

"Nice name, kid. This is Tim with *Fan Daily Magazine*. We'd like to do a telephone interview about your upcoming family birthday."

"I don't think so," Chili replied, only hearing the words *Fan Daily.* Excitement pitted his stomach. Fear, too. His mother was studying in the next room.

"Great!" the guy replied. "You must be pretty pumped. Any big plans? How does your dad handle all this attention?"

"I don't have a father." It was out of his mouth before he had a chance to skim it past his brain.

"Everyone's got a father," the guy replied, as Chili dealt with his panic.

"I meant I don't know who he is …" he was making it worse.

"You need to do a DNA test!" the reporter enthusiastically persisted, as though this were his new story.

"I gotta go." Chili hung up. *Fuck. Fuck. Fuck!* His mother was going to kill him. He tried to slow his breath as he calculated the probability of this not turning into a disaster. *Zero. Less than zero.* What if they called his mother? What if they went ahead and printed something saying the one-in-fifty-million baby doesn't even know who his daddy is? His life would be over. Chili sat on his bed and leaned into the wall that abutted his mother's desk. He could hear her music playing—Drake, *In My Feelings*. They had watched the video together, with his mother finally concluding, "a story about playas being playas, and pretending they ain't playas." Chili had patiently explained the lyrics, the nods to Drake's mentors, heroes, and co-producers—the dance video challenge. His mother acted unconvinced but then began listening to Drake non-stop. She was so stubborn, so private, so unforgiving if you did her wrong. None of this was helping. He redirected himself to eavesdropping, wishing he had a glass to put up against the wall. So far her phone hadn't rung—unless she had it on silent. He decided to do nothing. He might as well enjoy whatever time he had left before the bomb went off.

*

Nothing happened. On day three he began to relax. Then, like the instigator his mind was, his obsession turned to what the reporter said about DNA testing. Chili searched 'DNA tests' on Google. Ancestry came up first, available only online—$151 through Amazon, $193.46 with taxes and shipping. He had the money, he didn't have a charge card. In the past, he made purchases by giving his grandmother the cash and using her debit card, but then she'd have a record of the purchase. But would she? On her charge card would it just say *Amazon*, or would it say what the purchase was? He couldn't take the risk. Chili rifled through his bureau for the Visa gift card he got for Christmas last year, knowing he had already used most of it. It wasn't there. He searched 'buying a Visa gift card' on Google. It looked pretty simple, but you had to be eighteen. He was a big bi-racial kid with an afro, he probably wouldn't get asked for an ID.

*

"Nana, can I borrow your car?" A simple yes or no question that was sure to turn into a fifteen-minute interrogation.

"Yup. If you pick me up some milk."

"Thanks, Nana." Chili grabbed her keys from the hook, stashing his 'drop something off for a friend' excuse for another day.

*

London Drugs had Visa gift cards and milk. He was in and out in twenty minutes with two one-hundred dollar cards and a liter of one percent Dairyland. No one asked him for an ID, probably because kids don't normally pick one percent milk. *Thanks, Nana.*

Purchasing the DNA kit turned out to be trickier than he thought because of using two charge cards. He ended up calling Amazon to put in the order with customer service. His skill set was growing. The package would arrive on Thursday, which was good because his mother would be at work and he would be home alone. Chili's job at the movie theater was still on hold because of the virus, and he wasn't babysitting much because nobody was going anywhere. This was supposed to be his summer to make big money for college. That wasn't happening.

*

Create an online Ancestry account, spit in the tube, fill in the return address, and ride his bike to the nearest postal street box, which were always easy to spot—bright red and covered with postal codes. It went ridiculously smoothly. Now he would wait for Ancestry to send him an email with the DNA results. Even if his real father never did a DNA test, Chili hoped to find one of his relatives who could lead him to the guy.

*

"Let's go for a ride after dinner."

Fawk! His mother hadn't asked him to go for a ride since the talk on how babies were born. He was twelve and so embarrassed he wanted to jump from the moving car.

"Why, what's up?" *DNA! DNA! DNA!*

"Nothing. Can't a mother take her kid for a ride without a reason?"

"No—I mean some moms could, but not you. Just tell me what's up." Chili answered back, wondering if this time she would *throw* him from the moving car. His mother was fierce.

"After dinner," was all she said, then went into her bedroom and shut the door.

*

Dinner was a disaster. She made his favorite meal. *The Last Supper.* No matter how much gravy he slopped on it, he could barely choke down the chicken pie. Nana obviously knew what was about to happen because as soon as they finished, she stood and began to do the dishes, "I got this if you guys want to go." *No, Nana. We do not want to go.*

*

"Do you drink?" They were barely out of the driveway.

"No!" he shot back. "When would I even drink? I don't even go anywhere?"

"Have you ever been drunk?" his mother volleyed.

"No," he lied. Once he and his co-workers, Janelle and Selma, sat in the parking lot behind the movie theater and drank a couple of bottles of wine Janelle stole from her mother's "Whine Cellar." His mother had been studying for finals and was satisfied with his text, *I'm home from work. It was busy. Nite Mom.* It was a clean getaway.

"I've been drunk," she continued. "Very drunk—fully loaded—shit-faced."

Well, this is getting interesting. Maybe the conversation was about the perils of drinking. Relief flooded Chili's body. It was only temporary.

"The night I met your father I was blackout drunk."

Chili stopped breathing while his mother took a sip of her iced tea and stared directly ahead. The wait for the next sentence was excruciating.

"My mother had finally said yes to me going to a concert with my friends—*Jane's Addiction* at the Pacific Coliseum, November third, two-thousand-and one." Another pause. "We got to the coliseum early and drank some very cheap wine in the parking lot. I don't even know what kind it was—dark and red, the first glass tasted like poison. My friends were carrying me by the time the concert began. I was an easy target for a guy looking for an easy night."

"Mom—"

"Chili. The story is the story. I'm not gonna dress it down for you, but there's no way you were ready to know before now." They stopped driving. She had pulled into the London Drugs parking lot—*the scene of the Visa card crime.* He wanted to jump into the back seat and pretend he was five again.

"We didn't have backstage passes, but my friends thought it would be fun to try and get in anyway. Somehow we all got separated. The next thing I knew, a guy was sitting in a stairwell with me, listening to me cry and tell him about how I couldn't find my friends. He was tall—like you—and decked out. I threw up on his shoes. He said he would drive me home. He was very sweet. He carried me to a limousine. The inside had a bar and fancy lighting—like Christmas lights. One thing led to another and we had sex. He was gentle and kind. I wasn't forced—I was stupid maybe, but no one forced me into anything."

She still hadn't looked at him. Chili was trying to figure out how he factored into this. It was like she was telling a story about somebody else.

"I was drinking a bottle of water from the little auto bar when another guy opened the door and started yelling at us. 'She better be outta this limo in five minutes!' Then the door was slammed shut. Your father handed me a one-hundred-dollar bill from his pocket and told me he was sorry that he couldn't drive me home and that I should call a cab. I had never been in a taxi before. I wandered around the parkade until I found a security guard who told me where the payphone was. Then I called my mother and she came and got me."

Chili had to say something. "Nana must have been really steamed—"

"She was." His mother turned, looking at him for the first time. "Her anger died down around the time I realized I was pregnant. It was two more months before I told her. She caught me heaving one day from morning sickness and I insisted it was the chili she made for dinner the night before. That's when I began to think of you as Chili."

"What about the guy—my father?"

"For a long time, I had no idea who he was. I stalked the band online and eventually found out he was a security guard. Later, I figured out his name—Archie Belle. He was married with six kids and already had two ex-wives. Our lives were complicated enough. I didn't need the kerfuffle. We had no money and no power. What if he tried to get custody of you? How could I fight that? I'm sure he's a nice enough guy, but he's a player. Who knows how many kids he has by now?"

Chili should have been concentrating on his mother's story—his story—but all he could think about was how much DNA was out there. This was going down the shitter fast. Relatives would be *coming out of the woodwork*, as his Nana was fond of saying. Speaking of Nana …

"Does Nana know who he is?"

"No. After I told her he was the kind of guy who might force me to give you up, she dropped it and never asked again. No one knows." She smiled a little. "But me and Nana did a great job raising you. You're smart, respectful, trustworthy—the kind of son anyone would be proud of."

Not trustworthy. "So what do I do now?" his question to her, and himself.

"That's up to you. I can't stop you from trying to contact your father, but I don't know how he'll react. It could be the greatest thing ever or a catastrophe. Do you want to open up that can of worms before senior year? Maybe we just get through one more year and then I'll contact him myself if you want—find out if he's open to getting to know you."

"This's why you hate the birthday publicity."

"Yup. You look just like him and I don't look all that different, although he probably forgot me the day after we met. Chili, whatever you want to do, I'm in. You're a great kid and I wouldn't change anything. It's how I got you."

*

Chili checked his email for the fourth time that hour. Nothing. It said the saliva took six to eight weeks to process. He was at week three. His birthday was in a couple of days. They would have one more shared birthday before his mother found out he had betrayed her. He should have told her that night in the car. His phone buzzed with a text. *Janelle.*

Hey, Frosty! What's up? She had nicknamed him Frosty because she refused to believe he had been named after a food and, instead, insisted his mother had misspelled the synonym for cold. Chili closed his email and walked through his house to make certain no one was home. Then he called her. In ten minutes he had blurted out the entire story to Janelle—as if she could do anything about it. As if he hadn't made things worse by telling another human being.

"What do you want to happen?" she asked.

"I want the whole thing to go away," he answered.

"Well you can't un-know about your father, but maybe we can do something about the DNA thing. Did you call them?"

"Uh-huh," he answered. "They said my record isn't in the database yet, but that after it's processed I can go into my account and delete everything. They can't guarantee it will happen fast enough that somebody won't be notified about me as a new relative. I've been checking my email every couple of minutes so I don't miss when it's ready."

"Stay put. Me and Zachary are coming over."

"Who's Zachary?"

"You'll see." Janelle hung up.

Great, another person is in on my mother's secret. I am so screwed.

*

Chili was still looking for this Zachary character when Janelle and Selma arrived. A few sentences later, he realized they all had complicated lives. By then he was hyperventilating.

"Dude, seriously. Calm down. You're gonna give yourself a seizure," Janelle was rubbing his back.

Selma—*Zachary*—stood to the side holding a small bag. "We have something for you."

*

There was nothing in the mala bead directions about doing the mantra alone, so his two friends stayed and walked him through the process. Chili didn't believe for one minute it had the power to change anything but felt oddly resigned once they finished. *So be it* was the unfamiliar phrase stuck in his head. He didn't hear the back door open.

"What are these girls doing in here? Your mother will flip if she finds out you had someone in the house with this virus!"

"I know, Nana! They're just dropping off a birthday present." For a woman who could barely walk, his grandmother seemed to do a good job sneaking up on him.

"Call me when the miracle happens," Janelle said, rushing toward the door. "Happy birthday, Frosty!"

"Those are some odd friends you have."

"I know, Nana."

*

Tuesday, June thirtieth. As the big day loomed, the requests for interviews increased. When Tim from *Fan Daily Magazine* called to see if he had changed his mind, Chili finally lost it.

"Don't call me again!" he screamed. "If it wasn't for you my life would be perfect right now!" He didn't care that his mother was in the next room. Chili hung up before the guy could answer. His mother was standing in his doorway ten seconds later.

"What the hell was that about?" she demanded. It occurred to Chili he lived a life with no privacy, and an overload of privacy. He was about to scream, "None of your business!" when the doorbell rang. His mother fumbled in her pocket to grab her mask and went to answer the door. Two minutes later she was back in his room dangling a white postal bag marked DAMAGED/UNDELIVERABLE MAIL.

"What the hell is this?" she demanded on repeat.

He didn't answer. He grabbed the bag from her and ripped it open, spilling its contents onto his bed. The box was mutilated. It looked like it had been run over by a semi. When he pulled it apart there was no vial, no DNA. "It worked," he whispered with awe.

"What worked?" his mother asked. The lie took a split-second to develop, as though it had been waiting there all along.

"Janelle wanted to see if you could send a damaged package from one address to another without postage if you put the person you're sending it to as the return address." He was stuffing the pieces into the postal bag while he lied. "I can't believe it worked," he said again.

"Your friend Janelle has too much time on her hands—and what was all that yelling I heard earlier?"

And now for the triumphant truth. "A guy named Tim from *Fan Daily Magazine* keeps calling me for an interview. I told him not to call here anymore." His mother's look softened to mush. She hugged him with her head buried in his chest.

"You know you're the best mistake I ever made, right?

"I know Mom."

Thank you Janelle and Zachary for saving my life.

July 6, 2020

CHAPTER 31 ~ PETER

Vancouver, British Columbia, Canada

Peter couldn't stand to see anyone happy. It caused him indescribable physical pain, as though someone was scratching at his insides in a place he couldn't reach. Happy people were empty-headed idiots—useless in a miserable world. Over the years he had developed coping mechanisms. They weren't savory, but they did the trick to quell some of the angst he felt. The shrink his parents had sent him to, more than three decades ago, had inadvertently given him the key to staying sane—though he was certain the therapist had something else in mind when he advised, "Find little things to give you pleasure. It's the little things, not the big things, which will get you through this life." It was great advice unless your pleasure was achieved by causing somebody else's pain. Peter took his counsel to heart.

As a shift manager at a Fast Lube on Kingsway, Peter was friendly, helpful, and had endless opportunities to create suffering for others. A few drops of motor oil squirted in with the windshield washer fluid was sure to make a chirpy, blond, soccer mom a little less cheery next time it rained. It became even more fun once Peter saw the book of car wash coupons clipped to her visor. He pictured her marching back to Rub-a-dub Car Wash to ruin their day with accusations that their wax filmed up her windshield. *A two-for-one special.*

He could write a book on the fine art of screwing people. It was all about going undetected. Every move was designed to ruin the other guy's day without him knowing it was you who ruined it. His desire to see people suffer had increased during the pandemic. It wasn't from being isolated, he had already embraced that lifestyle. It was from being saturated in the daily newsfeed of misery. The world's pain and suffering fueled his desire for more pain and suffering. His schemes were becoming intense.

Peter had recently pulled off his biggest feat to date—arranging a lift accident at work by poking tiny holes in the hydraulic line, then hiding one of the safety lock pins. He knew the happy-go-lucky, lazy idiot he was trying to rid himself of wouldn't work too hard to find another locking pin. No one died, the car was totaled, and the jackass was fired. The missing pin miraculously turned up right on the service cart. He couldn't pull off another stunt like that without getting caught, so his job was off-limits for the time being.

*

It was the Monday after the Fourth of July. The jerks he worked with were bragging about the cookouts, beer, and fireworks they perpetrated over the weekend. *Ass-wipes and imbeciles*. Why would Canadians care about the Fourth of July—just another excuse to drink with your buddies and blow your fingers off with pyrotechnics? Peter could feel himself sinking into the persona of his youth—an undersized, bullied, abandoned baby boy. He would need to do something soon to get his power back. His mind flew to his latest obsession—the perfect little family that had moved in next door to his run-down, old house. He hated everything about them. One morning Peter glimpsed the wife rushing out to the driveway to kiss her husband goodbye before he left for work. It got worse, she waved when she saw him staring.

"Good Morning!" she hollered from her patch of perfect grass across from his dirty mulch. He cultivated fantasies after that morning. Nothing sexual, he didn't covet her. His were violent fantasies. He wanted to destroy her happiness—run her kids over in the driveway, orchestrate a fatal car accident for her doting husband, and watch her crumble.

His childhood therapist would have reminded Peter that a healthy mental attitude was the basis for happiness, and vice versa. That rejoicing in the happiness of others was the cure for his own misery. *What a load of shit*. The guy was an idiot—a court-appointed idiot—if he couldn't understand how joyous the misery of others made Peter feel. Maybe there was a point in his life when things could have been turned around, but Peter doubted it. Therapy was a joke. Not once did Peter reveal the real story. His mask was impenetrable. Like uncle, like nephew—though Peter was not into diddling little boys.

*

One more customer and the shop would be closed. He was unusually exhausted. *The longest fucking Monday in the history of Mondays*. Strangely enough, Peter hated this last customer for the opposite reason he hated most people—she was a miserable bitch. Ginny Colmer was cranky and demanding. When he saw her name on the schedule for the end of the day, two thoughts occurred to him—*Why would she be coming in at night?* and *I hope I die before this day is over*. He was relieved when her grandson, Chili, drove into the lot.

"My grandmother said to *actually* vacuum the inside of the car this time," the kid said as he handed Peter a discount coupon that expired in a few hours.

"Will do!" Peter sang out like he was living his best life. *Fucking bitch.*

*

The car was spotless before he began. With robotic monotony, Peter reclined the front seats to vacuum the crevices. That's where he found the little gauze bag. Without a hint of hesitation, he stuffed it in his pocket. He didn't know or care what was inside. Hopefully, it was something the old bat treasured. Peter didn't vacuum the car.

*

A bad day made for a worse night. Peter unlocked the front door of his house and walked straight through to the back deck without turning on a light. He sat down at the cheap, plastic bistro set and unwrapped his Subway Veggie Delite, eating the whole of it in a few large bites. He washed it down with the bottled water that was included in the meal combo—the chips he had eaten in the car. A gust of wind blew the bag and wax paper away. He didn't lift his hand to stop it. Peter didn't smoke, drink, or do drugs. Those were habits for the weak. He settled into the pitch blackness of the night and indulged in what was currently his only vice—fantasizing about killing the family next door.

Over the next several hours, Peter's body didn't so much as twitch. He had spent years self-soothing, learning to slow his breathing and live within his mind. It used to be enough for him. Now he yearned to act out the scenarios his mind concocted. He heard sounds coming from next door—laughter, a child crying, the slam of the back door to let the dog out, and later, the husband calling the dog in for the night. The sounds magically fit into his plot points. Their back slider sounded like the scrape of a shovel blade. It was time to go to bed—there was nothing left to work out. The decision had been made to go forward with his plan to murder the family next door.

*

Peter was shocked to realize how ill he felt when he stood up to go inside—dizzy, sweaty, somewhat nauseous. Food poisoning from the sub, he decided. The light-headedness turned into breathlessness.

He barely made it to the living room couch. He pulled off his pants while trying to decide if he could navigate to the bathroom to take a piss. He couldn't. The stolen bag fell from his pocket. He leaned over to pick it up from under the coffee table and fell forward, hitting his head on the hard metal edge just as his hand grasped the bag. It wasn't the blow that killed him. It was the pulmonary embolism from the COVID-19-related blood clot that had begun in his leg and traveled to his lung.

This is not in the plan, was Peter's last thought.

July 20, 2020

CHAPTER 32 ~ DAPHNE

Holly Hills, Colorado

The call from Peter's boss was out of the blue. Daphne hadn't realized her brother knew what state she lived in, let alone the actual address. Moving out of Vancouver and denouncing her entire family had created space to heal—*to forget*. "You don't forget, you forgive and make peace with the abuse," her counselor had said many times. That turned out to be a colossal load of bullshit. You run. You erase. You re-create. *Does anyone make peace with their abuse?* Daphne doubted it. Maybe if someone had believed her the first time. "Don't be ridiculous! Uncle Peter loves you!" Then Uncle Peter died, and her brother took over where the sick bastard had left off. Three times, Daphne ran away from home. Each time she was hauled back—twice by the police, and once voluntarily when her father had a heart attack and died. *Another thing to feel guilty about*. Daphne was back to drowning in her past.

*

"I didn't know you had a brother?" Donny's voice was calm and controlled, as though it were normal to find out your wife of twelve years had a brother. Daphne's mind ran through a list of possible replies and settled on nothing.

"Another thing you don't want to talk about?"

At the beginning of their relationship, she had told him that her childhood wasn't good, never adding one substantiating detail. After seeing the pity (or worse, revulsion) on the faces of previous boyfriends, Daphne didn't trust anyone to view her the same way once they knew her history. The crazy thing was that Donny wouldn't have been put off by it. He accepted things and people for what they were. Now, too much time had gone by. How do you say, "This is who I've been all these years …"

"Canada," she finally answered, like a code word for top secret.

"Canada," he parroted, again okay with her explanation. "Is there any part of this brother-thing you *do* want to tell me?"

"No. He's dead now. It's pointless."

"Anything we should do? Call somebody?" he asked, ever practical.

"It was just me and him." *Me and him.*

"We'll have to go clean out his place."

"Canada's still closed to Americans," she felt like a robot. *Canada is closed forever.*

"Tomorrow morning I'll make a couple of calls—see if you need a probate attorney—maybe call his boss. Good?" her perfect choice of a husband asked.

"Yes," she answered, then crawled onto his oversized leather chair and into the safety of his enormous embrace. "Thank you, Donny."

"You bet." She felt him kiss the top of her head. *I am worthy of happiness. I am worthy of love.* Let the litany of self-soothing affirmations begin.

*

One of the perfect things about Daphne's husband was he had been married and divorced before she met him. Donny had two half-grown children and a vasectomy. His concern that he was robbing her of the miracle of birth was trivial compared to her concern that he would one day find out she had a baby (a twenty-two-year-old baby) out there somewhere, along with a tubal ligation arranged and paid for by her mother. Keeping all these secrets wasn't difficult. *Having* them was. There wasn't room in her head for a normal life, so she tried to keep it simple. Work Monday through Thursday, wash the dishes, make the bed, buy a ham, turn down the neighbor's offer of coffee. Tuesday was bowling, and Friday the trash was brought to the curb. Life in Suburbia, USA—better known as Holly Hills, Colorado.

When she ran to the United States one last time from Vancouver, Daphne thought she would live in Seattle forever. Forever lasted approximately two boyfriends and a dental hygienist degree. Then Colorado sounded good, fresh air, plenty of teeth. She applied for a job at a dental clinic in Denver and snuck out of the basement apartment she and the current deadbeat were living in. She left a month's rent on the TV stand but took the car which was registered in her name. After three more bad choices, she met Donny. He was working at H&R Block doing seasonal taxes for extra income. His day job was claims associate at the Social Security Administration in downtown Denver. Donny was easy to love. He wanted to do everything for her, starting with her taxes. She made his life better with good sex and the second income he needed to offset his child-support payments. They were married six months after they met, on December 31, 2008, just in time to get the married-filing-jointly tax status. For twelve years they lived their shallow, but perfect, little life. Then Peter died, and Pandora's box was officially opened.

*

"So it's all working out. The probate lawyer—barrister if you will," Donny made a royal flourish with his hand, "hired a company to clean out your brother's house. The landlord wants it done ASAP so he can get it fumigated for the next renter. Apparently, you have to hire a special cleaning company if someone has the coronavirus. Weird, since we didn't have to hire a special moving company."

Daphne had no answer for him, so she nodded her head, which was beginning to unravel.

*

Days passed, with continual updates from her husband. "Apparently, there's a will … Apparently, his car was paid off … Apparently, his job had a life insurance benefit …" *Apparently, I don't give a shit!* She wanted to scream. *Apparently, you're having the time of your life organizing my disgusting brother's happy ending, while I'm feeling suicidal!* Daphne's positive-speak mantras were no longer working.

*

One day a package came, the sender's name unfamiliar with a return address similar to her brother's.

"Here," Daphne said to Donny, handing the package to him. "You open it. You're the one handling all his stuff." Donny ripped it open, spilling a small bag onto the table.

"There's a letter. Want me to read it?" he said, with gleeful anticipation.

"Sure."

"Dear Mrs. Farnham,

My name is Janice Abbott. My husband, two children, and I live next to your brother. First, let me say how sorry we are about his passing. This pandemic has been a tragic nightmare for so many people.

I'm writing to tell you the circumstances of his death. Although we didn't know him very well (he seemed to work a lot and kept to himself), I would want to know the details if it were my brother.

On the night of July 6th, our dog got loose and took quite some time to return home. The next morning, when we let him out, he made a beeline for the hole in our fence and ran into your brother's backyard. My husband looked over the fence and couldn't see him. Then he realized your brother's back slider was partway open. Not having access to the backyard—there's no gate—my husband went around to the front, where your brother's car was parked. After repeatedly rapping on the door, Jules (my husband) walked around the property and tried to look in the windows, but to no avail. Everything was closed and shuttered. Having no other choice, we called the police. The rest, as you can imagine, was sad and rather ghastly. They called the BCAS to come, though by then it was hours too late.

The small bag I enclosed with this letter was clutched in your brother's hand and fell into the driveway where one of the attendants kicked it under your brother's car. For three days we left it there, for fear of the virus germs, and then Jules scooped it up using a broom and dustpan. After tremendous persistence, we found your name and address as next of kin. My husband is an insurance actuary by trade.

I don't know what is in the bag (of course we didn't open it) but it must have been important to him if it was in his hand on his dying moment. I thought you would want to have it. I know I would, if it were my brother.

Very sincerely and with deep condolences,

Janice and Jules Abbott"

Donny put down the letter and picked up the bag. "I wonder what it is?"

Daphne was frozen. The years spent turning Peter into a meaningless, non-person had vanished. The woman's detailed description had made him disarmingly real again. Her brother was finally dead but felt more alive than ever. Her husband held the bag out to her.

"Open it," he suggested, a look of intrigue splashed across his simple face. She stood up from the table.

"No," she answered. "I'm gonna go lay down."

*

He can't hurt you anymore. He can't hurt you anymore. He can't hurt you anymore ...

The bedroom door creaked open—a sound from her nightmares. Her husband poked his head in.

"I'm not gonna ask you to explain. I know better." The concern in his voice was genuine. He put the bag on the bed beside her. "Why don't you just hang on to this? You might change your mind about opening it—or I can throw it away if that's what you want." Daphne didn't answer. Donny quietly closed the door on his way out. Then, like a mind reader, he said, "I'll put some WD-40 on these hinges later."

Daphne let herself imagine the worst possible contents in the little bag. *Body parts. Folded dental tools. Something sexual—clamps.* She compressed her eyelids with the palms of her hands. *Just open it.* It wasn't a command, but a gentle suggestion. *Just open it.* She did as she was told.

*

Why would he have these? What was he trying to make happen? Opening the bag had created more questions than answers. She read the instructions again, becoming even more confused.

Reverse the curse, the words floated through the confusion. *Reverse the curse*. Was this her brother's do-over? The lady next door didn't sound afraid of him. Peter clearly hadn't tried to get at her kids. Maybe he was different. It was twenty-one years since she last saw him—their father's funeral. If he had managed to find peace, Daphne deserved to find it too. She was exhausted by the perpetual, terror-filled inner dialogue that ruled her life. With tremendous effort, she cleared her mind and read the directions one more time. *Let me make peace with my past ...*

*

"… Om satyam narayanam." One-hundred-and-eight times. Daphne put the necklace over her head and absentmindedly fondled the tassel. Like it was yesterday, a forgotten memory formed sharply in her mind. She and her brother were running through the woods. The necklace Uncle Peter had just given her was bouncing up and down against her chest. Uncle Peter was chasing them. Daphne liked the game of chase, but her brother was pulling her arm so hard as they ran. "You're hurting me," she said breathlessly.

"We can't let him catch us. Uncle Peter is a monster!" Her brother dragged her through bushes and briars. In her child's mind, the game of monsters was fun. In her adult mind, looking clearly through the window of time, she could see the terror on her brother's face as he pushed her down behind a fallen tree. "Shh," he whispered. "Don't let him hear us." Peter's hand was over her mouth, suffocating her. His knee was pressed into her back to hold her still. Eventually, the woods became quiet. Uncle Peter was gone. Daphne was mad at her brother, crying that he hurt her. He pulled her into a hug.

"Look at me!" he said, fiercely. "Don't *ever* let Uncle Peter catch you, Daphne! He *really* is a monster!"

The window to the past snapped shut, its echo creating an avalanche of emotion culminating in loud convulsive gasps for the innocent children she and her brother once were. It was several minutes before she realized Donny was on the bed, rocking her like a baby.

"We—me and Peter—we had a *horrible* childhood!" she sobbed, suddenly wanting him to know every detail.

"It's okay, Daphne. I got you. Nothing's gonna hurt now. I got you …"

*

Fifteen hundred miles away, in Vancouver British Columbia, two men were packing up a dead man's possessions to put into storage.

"This is a complete waste of time," the younger man said.

"Yup," replied the seasoned furniture mover. "Nothing but junk that's not worth saving."

Together, they turned over the old dining room table to remove the legs for transport. On the underside of the table, scratched deep into the wood in childlike scrawl, were the words ~~UNCLE PETER IS A MONSTER!!~~ I AM UNCLE PETER!!

The young guy laughed, but the older man felt a chill run up his spine. He couldn't wait to get home to his nice wife and a hot shower. He was always grateful that the furniture couldn't talk. *Or maybe it could.*

July 27, 2020

CHAPTER 33 ~ BETTY

Englewood, Colorado

The dental office returned Betty's call within an hour.

"Sounds like an infected tooth," the dental assistant, Daphne, said. "I'm sure Dr. Kissell will call in an antibiotic. What pharmacy do you use?"

"Walgreens on East Hampton, and can you ask them to deliver it?" Betty answered, relieved to not have to beg for medication.

"Of course," replied Daphne. "And I'm putting you in the book for next Monday at nine a.m. That should give it time to settle down so the doctor can evaluate it. Maybe she can do a root canal and save the tooth."

"Sounds good." Betty hung up without thanking the girl. She grabbed the bag of corn from her freezer. She had used it so many times it was now a solid block of ice instead of individual face-conforming kernels. Tooth pain was a unique kind of hell. Betty was no wimp—three natural births, a broken foot—but she had never been in this kind of discomfort before, wracking nerve pain from eyeball to collarbone. She threw the bag onto the tile floor and stomped it apart with her slippered foot. Then she wrapped it in a dish towel and sat on the living room couch where she could watch the new neighbor kids play street hockey while she kept an eye out for the pharmacy delivery.

*

On day three the Amoxicillin kicked in and Betty was beginning to feel human. Without the pressure of constant pain, her thoughts turned to Monday. *How the hell am I going to go to the dentist when I haven't managed to leave the house in seven months?* Her agoraphobia had reared its ugly head again—just in time for a global pandemic.

The last time this happened, in 2002, Betty had a husband. Granted, he wasn't much of a husband, which explained why she didn't have him now, but when forced he was able to do the errands, take the kids to their activities, and keep food in the house. That housebound bout lasted almost two years. At least Gerald had waited until she was mobile again before meeting the woman he wanted to spend the rest of his life with. With her 'disability' gone and nothing standing in the way of her working, the alimony wasn't great. Over the years, Betty had taken a dozen menial jobs to supplement her income. None of them were worth the effort. The pandemic came just in the nick of time. Two months into her current situation, she filed for pandemic relief unemployment. Her doctor (actually his secretary) wrote a note saying Betty's health was at risk. Between the CARES Act and Gerald's monthly check, Betty was making more money than she had made in years. She had also tipped more DoorDash/Uber/Instacart drivers than she could count. Maybe she could consider it a medical tax deduction …

*

The middle of the night was when Betty made decisions. She bought things she didn't need on the home shopping network, got up and ate the food she had managed to resist all day, and gave herself haircuts she was surprised to wake up with in the morning. It was three a.m. Monday when she decided she could pull out her own tooth. *How hard could it be?*

*

YouTube wasn't as helpful as she thought it would be. The first video was an animated infomercial sponsored by the dental association, clearly designed to let you know what *the dentist* might do for the extraction. There were a few valuable pointers, mostly on what type of tooth deserved to be yanked. She was sure her rotten tooth qualified. It had been infected twice, filled to the brim with mercury, and had a distal crack of indeterminate depth that made her dentist wonder if a crown would even work. She tried the cold spoon trick to see if the nerve was already dead and felt the icy cold penetrate all her teeth except the bad one. It was as dead as a doorknob.

Betty watched videos of tattooed truckers using huge plumbing pliers, and parents trying to wriggle out baby teeth. Finally, there was one that looked promising. It was posted in 2018 by a man who lacked money and dental insurance so he devised a simple extraction tool to remove his infected tooth. He drilled a horizontal hole through one end of a small dowel, to which he tied a ten-inch piece of string. The other end of the string was secured in an infallible noose—she would have to look up noose-making. The goal was to tighten the noose over the bad tooth right at the gum line, then turn the dowel so the string would wind around it, eventually causing the dowel to rest up against the other teeth for leverage and force the string taunt. Then give it one more firm turn—popping the tooth from its socket. It looked painful, but feasible. Without further ado, Betty hopped out of bed and headed for the cellar to collect the necessary items.

*

Her cellar proved useless, so she improvised with a large wooden salad fork and a triple-strand length of dental floss. She decided a slipknot was as good as a noose, and tied it to a fork tine, rolling it candy cane-like till she reached the end of the fork handle. Her plan would work just as well as his manly contraption. She laid everything out on a towel on the bathroom vanity. Then she went to the liquor cabinet and poured herself a tall Jack Daniels Honey, which she took back to her room—she might as well look at shoes on QVC while she waited for the 'anesthesia' to take effect.

*

When the telephone woke Betty, five hours later, she was three pairs of shoes richer, still sporting a rotted tooth, and now a nasty hangover.

"Hello," she mumbled into the phone.

"Betty? This is Daphne from Dr. Kissell's office. You were supposed to be here twenty minutes ago."

Shit. "Oh, I should have called you. My tooth fell out last night." *Did it?* Betty stuck her tongue in what should have been a hole. *Goddammit.*

"Oh my goodness! You need to come in right away so we can make sure the whole tooth is out and not just fragments!" Daphne's concern was killing Betty's head. She began to feel sick, left the phone on the bed, and ran to the bathroom. Daphne was still talking when Betty got back to the call.

"Okay. Okay. I get it. I need to come in and see the doctor. But here's the thing …" Betty explained her dilemma to Daphne, the nice dental technician. As crazy as it was to blurt out the whole story, Betty felt like she had found the right audience. Daphne assured her that all would be fine and promised to call her back after she spoke to the doctor. Betty hung up relieved but not certain if she had included the part where her tooth hadn't fallen out. *Holy freaking mackerel.*

*

Betty's doorbell rang at six p.m. while she was heating a can of soup. *Probably Amazon.* She grabbed her mask and went to the door. If it hadn't been for the green scrubs she wouldn't have recognized the visitor as Daphne, having only met her one time at a cleaning two years ago.

"Miss Betty, this is as close to a house call as we can get, right now." Daphne had a white paper bag in her hand. Betty ushered her in.

"Dr. Kissel sent antiseptic mouth rinse, some dental wax, and gauze pads. She said if the infection flares up again—like chills and a temperature—call her and she'll renew the antibiotics. She also gave me this list of therapists. They'll do appointments on FaceTime or Zoom." Then Daphne looked embarrassed. "I circled a couple I know are pretty good."

"Oh, Daphne. I can't thank you enough." Betty wanted to hug her.

"We're not done. Dr. Kissell wants me to take a picture of the tooth cavity to make sure it's good." Daphne pulled out her phone.

Betty's face reddened. "It didn't fall out."

"I figured that," Daphne replied. "So let's get a picture of the tooth so Dr. Kissell can sleep tonight."

Betty slipped off her mask, opened her mouth, and pointed to the back molar.

"Number thirty-one—just like she thought. Open wide." Daphne's phone camera flashed. She opened the picture to make certain she got it. "Good. We're all set. In the bag is another appointment card for the end of August. Call us if you can come in sooner."

"I will. Thanks again—"

"I have something else for you—from me." Daphne again looked embarrassed. She pulled out a gauze bag from her scrub pants pocket. "This was given to me—by my brother. It healed something inside me that was broken. Maybe it can work for you too."

Betty didn't know what to say. "I don't want to take something … so precious … I mean, it's from your brother?"

"It's meant to be passed along," Daphne said. "I think you're the right person to have it." She pressed it into Betty's hand and was out the door a second later.

Betty didn't waste any time discovering what was in the mysterious little bag. Her disappointment was almost physical. She had hoped it was some kind of anti-depressant pill—or at the very least some CBD gummies. It was a necklace. She put it back in the bag and tossed it onto the coffee table next to the dental supplies, then went to eat her soup.

*

Afternoons were the hardest. Her morning chores—if you could call them that—were finished, and it was too early to lay in bed and watch television. There were no demands on Betty. Her kids lived out of town and no one knew or cared if she was agoraphobic or just being pandemic cautious. She ate her big meal midday and was satisfied with peanut butter crackers and a cup of tea for dinner, which she took to the living room so she could gaze out the window while she ate. It was strange not knowing what the front of her house looked like. She had a kid mow the lawn but had done no weeding or planting. Pretty soon the shrubs would cover her windows like one of those crazy old hermit women. Her car hadn't been driven since February. *I am a crazy old hermit woman, too anxious to do anything and then aggravated by the boredom of my life.* She went back to looking out the window.

Betty could tell summer was wearing on the kids who lived across the street. Two brothers, so close in age she couldn't decide who was the oldest, played street hockey or rode their bikes and scooters all day. Lately, they fought about everything until their mother would come to the door and scream at them to knock it off. It was entertaining, like a reality TV show. Today the kids were nowhere in sight and Betty's uselessness slammed at her once again. She set her tea down on a coaster bearing her ex-husband's laminated picture—a long-ago gift from her children—and picked up the worry beads the hygienist had given her. That's when she realized there was a note inside, rolled tightly in a tube shape. She spread it out on the coffee table and read the odd directions. Out of sheer boredom, Betty followed the instructions. *Give me something to get me outta this house.*

*

The doorbell rang as Betty was wrapping up the mantra. She tossed the beads aside and opened the door to discover a large box from QVC. "What the hell?" She hadn't ordered anything, though the three pairs of walking shoes in the box were her exact size and style. *Why would I need walking shoes?* As she tried on the first pair, she had a vague sense of lying in bed and watching a young sexy woman in hiking clothes prattle on about all the trails in the Denver area …

The shoes fit perfectly. Betty began walking back and forth through her house, something she probably should have been doing forty pounds ago. As she walked past her living room picture window, she heard the backup signal from the UPS truck pulling out of the driveway across the street. Her casual glance took in the entire situation with computer-like accuracy. The boys were fighting again, one brother knocking the other to the ground, where he lay motionless. After a quick attempt to rouse him, the conscious boy saw the truck coming their way and threw himself onto his brother to protect him from impact. Betty raced out the door in her new walking shoes. She yelled and slammed her fist into the rear of the truck to alert the driver. He stopped, the back of his big box truck covering the fallen boys.

"Call nine-one-one!" she screamed to the driver and ran to check the kids. The oversized shirt of the boy on top was wedged beneath the truck tire. He was clutching his brother and waiting to die, seemingly unable to comprehend the event was over.

"It's okay… you're okay," she soothed, as she laid down and scooted under the truck to get a look at the unconscious boy. "What's your brother's name?" she asked.

"Anthony. His name's Anthony. My mother's at the store. We were supposed to stay inside!" he wailed.

Betty reached for the pulse in Anthony's neck. It felt fine to her untrained hand. "Let's see if we can get you off of him—give your brother a little air." She helped the boy slip out of his shirt and move to the side. "What's *your* name?"

"Vinny."

"You're a good brother, Vinny. Everything's gonna be just fine." Betty could hear a siren getting louder. The UPS driver was on his knees throwing up beside the truck.

*

The paramedics had things under control within minutes, strapping the boy to a board and easing him out from under the truck. Betty insisted they take the older boy to be checked out, too, since he refused to leave his brother's side and looked as though he might go into shock at any moment. Thinking she was the grandmother, they hustled her into the ambulance and buckled her and Vinny into the same jump seat. Despite his full-blown anxiety, Vinny was able to recite his mother's telephone number. The paramedic handed Betty his phone. "Try to call your daughter and explain the situation without causing undo panic" —which Betty promptly did, then called again when Anthony regained consciousness during the short ride to the hospital.

*

A concussion without fracture or hemorrhage was the diagnosis. They would keep the boy overnight for observation. His mother, whose name turned out to be Bettina, couldn't stop thanking Betty and insisted on paying for her Uber ride home. Betty had the driver stop at Popeyes so she could grab a fried chicken meal, and then to the Dairy Queen on West 66th for a mocha fudge Blizzard. She might as well eat all the fattening foods she wanted before beginning her exploration of the hiking trails in Denver. *Thank god I bought three pairs of walking shoes*, she thought, grinning at the mysterious irony of her life.

August 9, 2020

CHAPTER 34 ~ CHERYL

Londonderry, New Hampshire

Like most mothers, Cheryl had grand goals when it came to getting through the pandemic. She and her husband, Steve, were both college-educated, so remote-schooling their two children should be a breeze. Cheryl welcomed the idea of setting up a home office since her new supervisor, Cody, was a nightmare and some physical distance from him would be a relief. The only thing Steve hated about his job was the ninety-minute commute from New Hampshire to Boston, now shorted from their first floor down to his office in the basement. They were going to rock this pandemic, keeping their family safe while creating the bonds their busy daily life didn't normally allow.

The initial clue they were in over their heads came quickly. Five hours into his first remote school day, their twelve-year-old son, Larry, smashed his laptop through the window of his bedroom, then panicked and ran away from home. "Our internet sucks," was what he told the officer who found him just before sunrise. The police were sympathetic. Cheryl and Steve were relieved but perplexed by their son's lack of coping skills. After a lecture on "rolling with the punches," then boarding up the window and finding the Chromebook—which had miraculously survived—Steve began his week-long quest for better internet service. He ended up hiring someone to install a whole-house booster and hard-wire his and Cheryl's desktop computers. Problem solved. Except it wasn't. Sometimes it was the school's internet that was on the fritz or the teacher's home wireless. Each time their son's connection was dropped or he couldn't log on his frustration grew, culminating in the absolute destruction of his school-issued Chromebook. More lectures ensued, with Cheryl taking the lead and insisting on a Zoom appointment with the guidance counselor, who turned out to be totally useless. How do you ground a kid stuck at home during a pandemic? What's left to take away after they've lost their friends and the coming baseball season?

Soon they found out what was left when their family dog, Thor, died of kidney failure. Despite everyone being home, they had missed the signs of his bladder cancer—lethargy and the constant need to urinate. Those were 'old dog' signs and Thor was a young dog. Cheryl assumed he was being a nuisance, only whining to go out every two minutes because everyone was around to cater to him. His death was swift and harsh—one visit to the veterinarian from which he didn't return. Around this time their seven-year-old daughter, Moira, started having problems.

*

"I can't—I can't … breathe!" Moira was white by the time she got upstairs to Cheryl's third-floor office. Cheryl held her, trying not to panic.

"Steve! Something's wrong with Moira!" she screamed at the top of her lungs. Of course, he didn't hear her, his office was in the basement. Larry appeared in the doorway.

"Want me to go get Dad?" he asked, unemotionally, like he was going to let him know dinner was ready.

"Yes! Run!" By then Moira's breathing was labored, her chest popping up and down with lips blue. Cheryl grabbed her phone to call nine-one-one but didn't have cellphone service. *Fucking New Hampshire mountains!* Steve appeared, immediately trying to 'handle' the situation.

"She's probably hyperventilating," he said calmly, as though he were an expert.

"Do you have service on your phone?" Cheryl screamed. "Call an ambulance!"

"I left my phone downstairs," Steve replied, grabbing a paper bag full of office supplies, dumping them out, and creating a funnel for Moira to breathe into. "She'll calm down once she takes a few breaths into this bag." Moira fought off the bag, gasping for help. Steve forced it over her face.

"Jesus, Steve! Call a fucking ambulance!" Cheryl was losing it.

"Just give this a minute," he persisted, as they both watched their daughter fall to the floor, unconscious.

Cheryl slammed Steve out of the way and lunged down, her ear against her daughter's chest. "She's not breathing!" She began mouth-to-mouth resuscitation. Steve stood paralyzed over her. *Any second he'll spring into action* her mind told her. He didn't move. In the magical timelessness that all emergencies possess, Cheryl could suddenly hear Larry's voice in the distance.

"She's up here." The room filled with people. A man put his hand on her shoulder and then reached down to check Moira's pulse.

"You did great, Ma'am. We're gonna take it from here." Cheryl moved aside and watched the paramedic put an Ambu bag over Moira's face, pumping short, even compressions to provide air. While the other two paramedics competently went about their duties—starting an IV and checking oxygen and Co2 levels—the bagger continued to talk.

"It looks like your daughter's got a little restricted airway. Has she or anyone in the house been exposed to Covid-19?"

"No," Steve said, sounding in charge, making Cheryl hate him.

"We're gonna try a breathing treatment, see if we can open up her airway a bit." He nodded to his co-worker who was putting together the nebulizer. "How long has your daughter had asthma?" he asked.

Cheryl and Steve exchanged looks. “She doesn’t have asthma,” Cheryl replied.

“Your son told us it was asthma.” They both looked at Larry.

“I know a kid—at school. He had an asthma attack in the cafeteria,” he looked embarrassed to be right.

Soon they were ready to transport Moira to the hospital. “We can only take one of you, they won’t allow both parents inside.”

Steve stretched to attention, somehow assuming he was the obvious choice. *Is he fucking kidding?* It would take an army to separate her from her daughter. “I’ll call you when I know something.” Cheryl began walking down the staircase behind the stretcher, then spun around to embrace Larry, who trailed behind her. “Good thing someone had phone service—”

“Yeah, I didn’t,” he interrupted. “My battery was dead. I told my math teacher to call nine-one-one. I don’t think he believed me at first. I’m getting a D in his class.”

“Okay. I don’t care about your grades,” she answered, amazed by how smart her son was when it counted.

“I do.” Steve piped in from the back of the line. Cheryl stopped herself from pushing him down the stairs.

*

The follow-up with Moira’s pediatrician led to a consultation with an allergist, which led to a battery of allergy tests and a pulmonary function test. Everything came out fairly normal, with only slight reactions to the most common allergens—pollen, mold, dust mites, and dog dander (though their poor dog, Thor, was already dead). Food testing was equally inconclusive. Moira was diagnosed with asthma and given an inhaler.

The next week was uneventful. Cheryl began to prematurely relax, believing everyone had found their groove in this new at-home world. Steve had picked up a few of the household duties. Suddenly he was an expert at removing laundry stains and efficiently loading the dishwasher. He seemed to have more free time than she did. Whenever she went downstairs he was making himself a sandwich or watching something funny on his laptop. *I'm here taking a break too* she would say to herself in his defense. Only her breaks didn't look like his. Hers involved running down two flights of stairs to check on Moira or grab a box of tampons. Working from home contained more protocols than at the office. Logins were timed and documented. Zoom meetings were endless. Every Monday there was an employee productivity evaluation. Cheryl was more stressed than ever before.

*

On week two, Moira's asthma attacks began again like clockwork—mid-morning, right before lunch break. Treating her quickly with the inhaler was key. Steve was no help. The first time he claimed to be oblivious to everything while he was working (including his daughter's cries). The second time he said he couldn't hear her over the noise of the washing machine's spin cycle, which was in the laundry room adjacent to Moira's room. After a tone-deaf comment about their daughter intentionally bringing on these attacks, Cheryl created a classroom space in her office for Moira. Her supervisor was less than gracious about the occasional interruptions, at one point sermonizing, "We all have kids. What if every employee wanted to work their schedule around their family? How would we get anything done? You should consider hiring a nanny." Cheryl didn't bother telling the twenty-seven-year-old pipsqueak about Moira's condition. Instead, she moved her daughter's desk into the storage area under the eaves so no one from work could hear her reciting her lessons with the rest of her class. It was humiliating, but they were getting through the ten-thirty hour without asthma eruptions. She wished she could say the same about the hour after lunch. They were back to exploring food allergies.

*

Two months in, focusing became impossible. Any household sound pulled Cheryl's mind from whatever task she was attempting to finish, causing her heart rate to accelerate with dread. A thud from Larry's bedroom below her, the sound of the unbalanced washing machine walking itself across the laundry room, a wheeze from Moira's learning closet—all things she would have jumped up to investigate if her supervisor wasn't such a bitch. She considered putting a complaint in with human resources but worried it might make things worse. Cheryl was exhausted. Not Larry. He had never looked better, living in his spandex. "I adjusted my work schedule to get in a longer morning run," he stated triumphantly. Then he re-functioned the back of the garage as a workout area. "It's amazing how many repetitions I can get in during my breaks." *Breaks? What are breaks?* It was the end of May and her husband already had his summer physique and knew all the neighborhood gossip, while she was drowning. Cheryl hated his guts.

*

School finally ended, providing a different challenge—working while your kids run amuck. Cheryl asked her mother, who lived in Denver, to fly East and help with the kids for the summer. The request was greeted with a flat no, her excuses drowned out by the pressure in Cheryl's head. *Thanks, Mom, for not being there when I need you.*

If difficult had a spectrum, her mother was on the high end. Cheryl rarely called her with anything important because her mother talked right over her and then would end the call abruptly once she finished complaining. "I gotta go," she'd say. "Somebody shut the bathroom door and the cat's trying to get in to use the litter box." *Somebody shut the bathroom door?* Her mother had lived alone for nearly a decade. Maybe her refusal to help was a gift. Cheryl researched babysitting certifications and found an online course through their local Red Cross. *Congratulations Larry. You just won your first paid summer job!*

*

"That kid can't watch his sister! He could barely get through seventh grade!" Steve's faith in his children was a thing of beauty. Cheryl had had enough.

"Your son is smart! A lot of kids had a tough time this year. Give him a fucking break, Steve." Swearing had become her thing—especially when dealing with her husband.

"So you're gonna have him do an online course—which he hates—then hope he gets enough out of it to keep our daughter from dying?" Steve was going for the jugular. Cheryl went right back at him.

"He did a better job of keeping her alive than *you* did!" Her sarcastic tone was reminiscent of her mother, but she had been itching to say those words.

"The paper bag would have worked!" he yelled.

"It only works for panic attacks! Not a bronchial restriction!" Cheryl screamed back at him, shocked that he still didn't get it.

"I'm still not buying the doctor's—"

"Moira is in her room crying." Neither of them had seen Larry approach. "She heard you say she's gonna die."

Cheryl's anger deflated like a football pierced by an arrow in mid-throw. "Oh, my God!" She rushed from the kitchen, but not before she heard Larry's words to his father:

"I'm taking that course and I'm gonna babysit Moira. She needs somebody with her all the time."

*

True to his word, Larry spent every minute of the summer with his sister. He taught her how to shoot baskets, kick a soccer ball, and swing a bat. They played every imaginary game he could invent. Cheryl watched them in the backyard from her high office window. To satisfy Steve, she had taken the class with her son, both becoming CPR certified. Larry kept a journal of each day's events, including what they ate and whether Moira had suffered an asthma attack. Cheryl watched him jot down notes between rounds of croquet, Moira's inhaler swinging from a little bag attached to his belt. When she did have an attack, he would first call his mother, then administer a puff of medication—all accomplished within seconds. Cheryl was proud of her son. Steve acted sullen to be proven wrong, now focusing entirely on the house and nagging everyone to pick up after themselves, as he neurotically scrubbed every surface. Cheryl didn't love these evolving family dynamics but was relieved to be able to stop worrying about Moira and concentrate on her job.

*

August brought rain, and more time stuck inside the house. Moira's asthma grew worse, sparking new allergen theories. To satisfy Cheryl, Steve had the basement tested for radon and got an air quality specialist to come in and look for black mold. After finding some minimal problematic mold areas—the inside of the bathroom exhaust vent and an area in the garage where water had seeped in—Steve amped up his cleaning. It didn't make a difference. Moira got worse, with two 911 calls in one week. Again Cheryl was at the end of her rope. To add kerosene to the fire, her mother had begun sending pictures of herself and her two neighbor boys hiking the trails of Denver while *their* mother worked. It was too much. Cheryl hated everyone except Larry and Moira—with Steve and her supervisor at the top of the list.

*

"I'm leaving my job," she announced to her husband one morning at breakfast.

"Why?" he demanded, as though everything were just hunky-dory.

"I can't be two floors away from whatever is going on with my kid!" She could feel her blood pressure rise.

"Cheryl that's bullshit! You hate your job and you're looking for an excuse to quit!"

"You think I'm using Moira as an excuse? Fuck you, Steve! You seem to have all the time in the world and you do *nothing* with our kids!"

Cheryl glanced out the front window to make sure the kids were out of earshot. They were playing hoop beside the family SUV, which was loaded with gear for their last-minute camping trip—a tough decision given Moira's precarious breathing issue.

"I lost my job," Steve said quietly.

"What?" Maybe she misunderstood him.

"I got laid off. I thought I'd find another job before I had to tell you."

"When?"

"In March," he answered. "At the beginning of the shutdown."

Five months! I've been pulling a rabbit out of my ass for five months and he hasn't even been working!

"Cheryl. Say something."

He started to lean into her like he might take her in his arms. She lost it.

"Get out! Get out! Get out! Get out!"

"Cheryl—"

"Get out! Get out!" She felt like a crazy person. "Get out! Get o—" The kids came into the room. Moira was crying. *Oh my God, what have we done?* Cheryl grabbed Moira into a tight hug and cried with her. Larry wrapped his arms around them both. Steve stood impotently for a minute then did as she commanded, and left.

"So Dad told you he lost his job," Larry said.

"You knew?" She looked up at him, suddenly realizing her son was taller than her—or less small and broken.

"I figured it out a while ago," he answered. "It was none of my business."

His words made her cry harder. *How did he know when I didn't?*

*

Steve moved in with his brother which made things easier—and harder. They still had three weeks of summer to get through, but the calm of not having her anger triggered at every turn made the extra juggling worth it. Moira's asthma attacks stopped completely. Cheryl didn't allow herself to consider Steve might have been right—it was a psychosomatic illness triggered by fear of the virus *or their strained family relationship*. She concentrated on getting through work and figuring out the finances, which weren't as horrible as she imagined. It appeared Steve, too, had been juggling, cutting back, and wisely using the unemployment checks she hadn't known existed.

*

"Your sister told me your husband moved out," was her mother's opening line when Cheryl picked up her call.

"Did she tell you the whole story?" Cheryl asked.

"Yup. You gonna forgive him?" Her mother cut to the heart of it. "Or are you gonna punish him?"

"It's not one or the other Mom," Cheryl replied, pissed that her mother was suddenly an expert on marriage.

"Sure it is. If you're gonna punish him you may as well divorce him right now. And if you're gonna forgive him you should do it sooner rather than later."

"Jesus, Mom!"

"I'm just trying to save you some time, Cheryl. I wasted a lot of time being mad at your father when it really just came down to 'either get on with the marriage or divorce him'."

I'm glad my life is so simple for you Cheryl wanted to say, but began crying instead.

"I sent you something in the mail. You'll get it today or tomorrow," her mother continued over her crying. "Don't take it lightly. It's a miracle maker."

Great. Probably a prayer request from some television minister. The urge to hang up was physical.

"Cheryl, I love you. Don't become a resentful old bitch like your mother. It's a lonely life." The call ended.

A resentful old bitch! How dare she! Cheryl embraced this new focus for her anger. It was a relief to not think about Steve. She could concentrate on all the ways her mother had let her down in life—not coming to her field hockey games or driving her off to college, acting like mother-of-the-groom instead of mother-of-the-bride. It was quite a list, which she added to every time her mother disappointed her. She had once written it all down in a journal when her mother refused to fly out after Larry was born, using the list as part of her post-partum depression. "Compiling evidence to support your feelings isn't productive" was what her long-ago therapist had said, so she had burned the pages. No matter, the list was forever seared into her mind. *Fuck you, Mom.*

*

The mala beads were a huge surprise, obviously not purchased new with a big church donation. Her mother's note said, *Hang in there. Things will get better. I love you.* Cheryl was still pissed about the *resentful old bitch* comment. Did that mean she was feeling resentful? It wasn't the first time she googled the word: re·sent·ful /rəˈzentfəl/adjective - *feeling or expressing bitterness or indignation at having been treated unfairly.* Cheryl wasn't stupid. She knew it was a short hop from her life to her mother's—and looking more like a self-fulfilling prophecy every day. What did she want? Larry had told her that Moira thought their father left because of her. A mother-daughter talk wasn't going to erase that guilty idea from her child's mind. Her mother was right. Whatever she was going to do, she had better do it sooner rather than later. Maybe it was time to include the kids in the discussion.

*

"When families are going through tough times, it's good to stick together." Cheryl felt like a hypocrite—*Get out! Get out! Get out!* "So I thought we should talk about what each of us wants."

"I want Daddy to come home," Moira said without hesitation.

"Me too," said Larry.

"Me too," finished Cheryl. She pulled out the bag her mother had sent. "Grandma sent me this magic necklace. She already used it and it worked for her. I say we try it." There was nothing in the directions requiring the mantra to be done alone. Cheryl explained how it worked.

"What did Grandma ask for?" Larry wanted to know, skepticism splayed across his face.

"I don't know. She didn't tell me." *I didn't ask.* "But I think we ought to ask for more than Dad coming home. What if we say, 'Make our family happy and healthy'? That should cover everything, you think?" Cheryl watched both children nod their heads. "Okay! Let's do this thing! Seven deep breaths, we say our wish, and then do the mantra a-hundred-and-eight times!" They sat on the living room rug, facing each other in a triangle, and performed the magic.

*

The email from Cheryl's corporate manager said "I set up a Zoom meeting to discuss a few matters. I hope 4 p.m. today works for you?" She spent the rest of the day reading into it. The only thing that could put her on corporate's radar would be a review from her supervisor. Was she getting fired? If so, why wait till the end of the day?

*

"Your supervisor, Cody Long, is no longer with the company. We know this is short notice and a substantial learning curve, but we'd like to offer you his position effectively immediately."

"I had no idea Cody was planning to leave," Cheryl stammered in answer.

"Neither did he," replied her manager. "I've sent a DocuSign proposal to your inbox. It should answer all your questions but don't hesitate to email me if you have more. We'll need an answer by 8 a.m. Monday morning. And Cheryl, I hope you take the job. I think you'll be the right fit. Have a good night,"

"Thank you, sir. You have a good night, as well." Cheryl kept a frozen, benign smile on her face until he hit the end meeting button, then rushed to open his email.

*

The job came with all the responsibilities she would have expected, plus four weeks of vacation and an extra forty-two thousand dollars in pay and bonuses. It was the position Cheryl had been searching for in her plan to quit her current job. She read the contract one more time, signed the document, and hit send. *Hallelujah!*

Her phone buzzed with a text. It was Steve.

We need to talk.

Come for dinner tonight—we're having pizza and a firepit, she replied, still high on the moment. **Text me when you get here and I'll meet you in the driveway**.

Sounds good! Do you need anything?

Nope. See you at 6:00.

Now to figure out exactly what she did need from him …

*

"I screwed up. I should have told you." Steve looked miserable. "I wanted it to seem like I was changing jobs, not losing my job."

"Well I was wound pretty tight—maybe I didn't make it easy to tell me anything." Cheryl realized the truth of it as she spoke. "Steve, I don't want to be a pandemic divorce statistic."

"Me neither."

"Then come home. I've been researching marriage counselors and I think I found one in Cincinnati that might work for us."

"Cincinnati?"

"Yeah. We do remote sessions and never have to worry about running into them. What do you think?"

"I like it." he looked hesitant. "I still don't have a job."

"Good. Cause we need a full-time nanny." Cheryl told him about her new position—the hours, the money. When the kids came out to see what the hold-up was, their parents were making out in the front seat of the car.

*

Pizza, s'mores, and a crackling fire—the perfect family night. While Steve gathered the pizza boxes to burn in the fire pit, Larry made an announcement.

"I've figured out what Moira's allergic to." He had everyone's attention, standing on the deck and holding his Moira Journal in his hand. "I graphed out her food and activities, along with the current environment—you know, was it raining, were we inside, or at a store, everything that was going on around us—and decided she's allergic to bleach.

"Bleach?" Cheryl exclaimed.

"Yup. When Dad was home he used a lot of bleach—the laundry, the bathroom cleaner, the mold stuff. She had six bad asthma attacks while the washing machine was going, and a couple at other times when Dad was cleaning. The only time she had an attack away from home was when we went swimming at that hotel pool for her birthday. There was a lot of chlorine, especially in the hot tub. It's definitely bleach. I looked it up and it can give people asthma attacks."

Steve rushed to Larry, slapping his back. "Our kid is a genius! Thank God you figured it out, Larry. I was convinced she was allergic to me!" Moira and Cheryl joined in the group hug.

"Now we can get back to being a happy and healthy family," Steve rejoiced. Cheryl felt an immediate vibration, like a Teutonic shift of the Earth. *He couldn't possibly know the weight of those words?* Both children lifted their eyes to search her face. She gave them a teary nod.

"It worked," Larry said in awe.

"Thanks, Grandma," Moira whispered.

I love you, Mom. Namaste.

August 24, 2020

CHAPTER 35 ~ WILLOW

Atkinson, New Hampshire

"You have the most beautiful voice. Have you ever thought of doing book narration?" The physician assistant at Children's Hospital had snuck up on her in the waiting room while she was reading to Morgan. She shook her head "no" as he unlocked the wheels of her daughter's wheelchair and began pushing her toward her appointment while relaying everything he knew about narrating an audiobook.

"I have a friend who makes steady money recording books in her spare time …"

That should have been Willow's first red flag, the use of the term *spare time.* Did he not see who they were wheeling down the hallway? Morgan was a full-time labor of love. A brain injury from a traumatic birth led to her diagnosis of severe mixed cerebral palsy. She was seven years old and had a smile that could light up a ballroom. Today, they were at Children's Hospital in Boston to talk about her painful spasticity and consider another botulism injection to stop her muscles from contracting. It was a never-ending process—hard-won milestones mixed with bits of physical relief. Willow lived a complicated life, and there wasn't room for much else. Though the idea appealed to her. She did like to read, perhaps she could make a career out of it?

*

Willow could not believe how involved it was to get started. So far all she had accomplished was setting up her profile page and creating a recording space, which consisted of an old wooden infrared sauna that hadn't worked for years. It was three feet by four feet with glass for the door and side panels, allowing her to keep an eye on things while she recorded. That was the plan, anyway. She had yet to be hired by anyone. Willow was one of 765,390 book narrators vying for a job on the popular site, Audible. She spoke three languages, Italian, Greek, and English—a niche that was either going to work for or against her. There was no point, with an accent as thick as hers, in checking off more boxes to put herself in a larger search category. Once they heard her demo recording it was yay or nay—actually, just nay.

The reading box, as she came to refer to the sauna, quickly became a central player in Willow and Morgan's life. The only area with enough room for it was the kitchen. It sat where the dinette used to be. As a single woman with a child who needed to be spoon-fed, she had no real use for a dining room table and four chairs. She sold the mismatched set on Facebook. The first time Willow wheeled Morgan into the little booth she squealed with delight, drool covering her bibbed sweater, her left arm rotating with excitement. She put the padded headphones over her ears and played classical music. Morgan was in heaven. Eventually, Willow decided to paint the exterior of the box, choosing a pallet of beige, whites, and grays which she mixed herself using a leftover can of ceiling paint. The effect of the lateral slats randomly tinted in subtle shades was very satisfying. She couldn't walk into the kitchen for a cup of tea without standing there for a few minutes to admire her work. She ordered a string of Christmas lights to drape along the top. Morgan was beyond thrilled.

*

Willow's nightly routine was dinner, dishes, then giving Morgan a bath and body massage—a ninety-minute process—after which they began the bedtime routine, an event that took another hour or more before Morgan settled into sleep. In the past, Willow would fall into bed shortly afterward, but now she was obsessed with getting a narrating gig. Because she no longer had a kitchen table, she did her author research inside the reading box, where she had attached a small shelf for her laptop, then snaked an extension cord through one of the air vents at the top of the sauna to mount a surge protector under the shelf. An LED book light and folding canvas chair completed her mini studio.

Willow jumped on every listing that might be a good fit, quickly sending out the link to her profile and demo. She had chosen a low hourly rate to make hiring her more attractive. The royalty option was also checked off, though the idea of doing so much work and then hoping for book sales seemed depressing. The truth was it had all become depressing—except sitting in the box. She loved being in there and would spend hours researching, reading, listening to books on tape, or just putting together the week's grocery list. It was her smaller world within an already small world. Sometimes the baby monitor went off, signaling the need for a quick check on Morgan. Then right back into the box she would go—protected, warm, comforted. The box had become her thunder jacket, her weighted blanket. She never felt anxious inside the box. As time went on, Willow wondered if she should find someone to fix the electrical board for the sauna. At least then she would have something to show for all this trouble.

*

Since she already did all her shopping online and didn't socialize, being in a pandemic hadn't really impacted her. Finances weren't an issue. The courts had *awarded*—a ridiculously gift-like term—enough malpractice money to take them both through this lifetime. To protect her daughter from the virus, Willow stopped the visiting aides and physical therapy sessions. It was easier to do the therapy on her own than to wonder whose germy home they had just come from. Same with doctor's appointments. By now, Morgan's team knew Willow well enough to call in a prescription for a bladder infection or severe constipation without having to physically see her child. The pandemic had made her life easier, a guilty thought at best. She stopped following her online CP community support group, most of whom viewed the pandemic differently as though progress was being lost. Willow wasn't seeing much difference either way. Morgan was her happy self.

*

One night Willow couldn't stop crying. It came out of nowhere. Well maybe not nowhere. She had received another rejection email from an author.

Dear Ms. Walker,

Although your voice is lovely in tone and richness, your Italian is perfect, I am going to keep searching for a narrator who has Italian language skills but sounds like an American for the portions of the novel that are in English. Thank you for auditioning. I would have loved to have you narrate my book, if only for your very cool name–Willow Walker is so catchy. Good luck with whatever your next project turns out to be.

Sincerely,
Jonathan Thomas Jefferson

"Che stronzo pretenzioso!" *What a pretentious asshole!* "I *am* American, you dick-wad Puritan!" Her ex-husband had used the term dick-wad on occasion. It felt good to say it out loud. It felt good to curse in Italian. Then everything felt bad. Willow climbed into her box with tissues, a blanket, and her cell phone. She curled onto the floor of the sauna and let the floodgates open, finally acknowledging the misery of her life.

Once she let it out, there was no stuffing it back in. She cried about her divorce, her family so far away in Italy, and the one memory she had of Morgan's birth—watching the staff perform CPR while they sutured her abdomen. She cried some more because she hadn't known to bank the umbilical cord blood. *Who knew stem cell infusions would become a treatment for cerebral palsy?* She cried because she used to have friends who didn't wear lab coats or call her Mrs. Walker. She cried because as much as she loved her daughter, taking care of her—being Morgan's mom—had become her entire identity. Her cell phone rang. She picked it up without composing herself.

"Hello?"

"Willow? It's Cheryl. You were on my mind today so I thought I'd give you a call. It's been ages since we caught up!"

Willow mumbled some sort of greeting. Cheryl rolled along.

"This pandemic has been crazy, huh? We've had such a year! Steve lost his job. I got a better one. Larry practically flunked out of seventh grade. And Moira's been in and out of the hospital with asthma! How are you guys doing?"

Hearing Moira's name increased Willow's inability to hold back the flood. Their daughters were six months apart—a pregnancy fantasy of them growing up as best friends. She was choking on her sobs.

"Hey. Are you okay?" Cheryl asked.

"No."

"Is it Morgan? Is there something I can do?"

"No." She couldn't find words. "I'm—I'm sinking."

"Okay?" Cheryl responded. "Are you safe?"

It was a good question whose answer should have been yes. "I don't know. I can't stop crying." Willow waited for her practical friend to come up with a plan. She did.

"We're gonna do four square breathing. I learned it for Moira. You're gonna take a slow deep breath to the count of four. Hold it in for a count of four. Let it out to a count of four. And then keep it out for another count of four. Ready?" Willow put the call on speakerphone and nodded her head as though they were Facetiming. Together, they began to breathe.

*

Ten rounds of breathing and Willow was back in her body.

"Thank you, Cheryl."

"You are welcome, my friend. Everything sucks for everyone right now. I can't imagine what you're going through trying to do this alone."

Somehow that made Willow laugh. *Alone would be easy!* It was the type of thought she normally refused to have—an honest one.

"I'm coming over. I have something for you. It's in a bag I haven't touched for like two weeks, so there's no need to decontaminate it. Just buzz me into the complex and I'll leave it at your door."

"It's kind of late. Are you sure you don't want to come by tomorrow?" Willow countered, it was after 9 p.m.

"I'm working all day tomorrow and this can't wait. It's a mala bead necklace. My mother sent it to me when our family was in crash-and-burn mode. Me and the kids did the mantra and it worked," Cheryl said. "I can't explain it—so I won't try. See you in ten minutes."

It was a half-hour drive to her house. Willow crawled out of the box, checked on Morgan, and took a quick shower. If Cheryl weren't coming over she would have stayed in the shower all night. Maybe she just liked phonebooth-shaped boxes—*coffins*. She tried to think of anything in her past that would link her to this feeling of comfort. Nothing came to mind. Her tea was steeping when she got the signal to buzz Cheryl through the gate. Willow was thankful it was late. Otherwise, she would have felt guilty not inviting her friend in. An ice pick of pain shot through her right temple and passed before she could fully acknowledge it. *Where does guilt factor into this?* Her subconscious knew, but the information trickled from her mind's grasp. She heard Cheryl's tap at the door.

"You look great," Willow said through the small pane of glass.

"You do too!" Cheryl replied, pulling a white-handled paper bag into view and then slipping it over the door knob. "What's with the giant crate?"

"It's a therapy box," Willow answered, knowing Cheryl would assume it was for Morgan.

"Cool. Call me tomorrow after six." A thumbs up from Willow and Cheryl was gone.

Willow opened the door and reached around for the bag. It felt empty. She grabbed her hand sanitizer from the counter and squirted some on the bag handles and her hands. She dumped out the little bag of mala beads and took them and her tea into the box.

*

Am I asking for a miracle? She wasn't going to wish Morgan away, or her husband back. It would take a lobotomy to erase the road she had traveled, but she had been pretending happiness—or okay-ness—for seven years. The strain of it was too much. What would my real happiness look like? She made a list:

Morgan being healthy, happy, and moving forward with her skills.
Hiring a helper to free up some of my time, then actually trusting them.
Re-connecting with my friends without feeling the pain of their perfect-looking lives.
Getting a narrator call-back and using my reading box for more than a hiding place.
Ridding myself of the feeling that I did something to deserve all this.

It was a good list. How would she make it into an intention statement? She added a title: *Willow's Happiness List,* then said it aloud, "Make Willow's happiness list come true." She began the ceremony.

*

Morgan's monitor went off at 4 a.m. Willow pulled the monitor closer to get a better look. Her daughter was fine, just shifting a bit in her Sleepform bed. There was a seizure alarm on the bed, but a good look at the video monitor always put her mind to rest. Willow rolled over, fluffed her pillow, and readied herself for her favorite part of sleep—the luxury of knowing you have at least an hour left. She fell into a deep dream, unlocking a forgotten scene …

*

Labor was slow but steady. It was thirteen hours since her water broke, three weeks before her due date. Willow was handling the pain without medication. She let Kevin think his support was making a difference, but the pain management was taking place exclusively in her mind. *Childbirth is natural. A miracle is happening. I am creating life.* She had imagined this moment since childhood, always knowing she would someday be a mother. Having it be a daughter was the sparkler on a confetti-covered cake.

From the moment she found out she was pregnant, Willow felt everything else drift into the background—her career, her friends, and her marriage were all dwarfed by this primal urge to protect. She stopped running and began taking leisurely walks along the Merrimac River. Her diet was meticulous, every morsel purposeful. She reveled in her growing belly and fuller breasts.

Sixteen hours into labor, the baby's heart rate decelerated. They shifted her onto her hands and knees. It rebounded. Over and over again, they repositioned her. Each time the baby's heart rate returned to normal. Eighteen hours in, the doctor decided a cesarean section was necessary.

"No! I don't want a C-section! I can do this naturally!" she cried, desperate to see her birth plan to fruition. She began to physically fight off their attempts to ready her for surgery. The institutional clock on the wall read 2:18 a.m. The dream faded. Willow woke up.

The nameless guilt from the lower depths of her soul had forced itself to the surface. She had delayed saving her baby's life in favor of fulfilling her birth plan—she alone was responsible for her daughter's oxygen deprivation. Willow began her day in a trance.

*

Somehow they reached the dinner hour. The house was a mess, she had skipped PT in favor of letting Morgan play in the reading box, soiled clothing and diapers remained where they had been tossed. She had lost her ability to push through. A dozen times she dissolved in tears. Halfway through the day, Willow realized Morgan was dehydrated—another failure. Dinner was the mashed leftovers from yesterday which Morgan hadn't loved on the first round. Willow finally gave up and let her play with the rubber spoon and suctioned bowl, no longer caring if she covered herself with gruel. She checked her emails on her phone. There was a message from one of the authors she had queried. Without a shred of hope, she opened it.

Dear Ms. Walker,

Thank you for auditioning for my book, Baklava, Biscotti, and an Irishman. I had feared, after six months of searching, that I would never find someone with your language skills who has a voice that doesn't sound like an old woman. When people fake a Greek accent it can be so painful and witch-like! I would very much like to talk to you about narrating this novel along with the other two in the series, An Irishman's Son and Costas' Story. I can be reached at the above email address and phone number. I'm also thrilled to see you are so close, two hours from where I live on Cape Cod. I look forward to hearing from you.

Sincerely,

Kathy Aspden

What just happened? Willow's brain snapped to attention. "I got a job!" she sang out to Morgan, who rewarded her with a wide smile and ear-piercing screech of joy. "Look at this place! Mama's got to clean up so we can get ready for your tubby!" Willow whipped through the house, throwing everything into a large basket which she shoved out of sight in the laundry room to deal with tomorrow. She cleaned the kitchen in record time and whisked Morgan out of her belted chair and into the tub in the hall bathroom. "I think Mama should install a garbage disposal in this tub!" she joked, as all the food targeted its way to the drain. Morgan laughed.

"M-m-m-a-a-a," she voiced. Willow stopped in her tracks. "M-m-m-a-a-a," Morgan said again, her right arm slapping wildly at her naked belly.

"Did you just say Mama?"

"M-m-m-a-a-a," her daughter yelled repeatedly, apparently loving the look on her mother's face.

Willow swung her out of the tub and twirled around the bathroom. "You are so smart! That's right! Mama!" She danced her to the bedroom, where they began the nightly routine of massage and bedtime.

As if by chance, Morgan's favorite book was the one Willow had made for her—The Morgan Manual. It was a laminated loose-leaf binder filled with pictures of Morgan and everything special to her, from the stuffed cow she had had since birth, to a homemade growth chart of her progress. Willow added to it regularly, but the older pages were Morgan's favorites. She was obsessed with herself as a baby. No matter what Willow chose to read, they ended the night with The Morgan Manual. Tonight was no exception. As Willow tiptoed out of her sleeping daughter's bedroom, she realized she still had the book in her hands. She also noticed that she had missed a call from Cheryl, which was just as well since the day had been such a mix of emotions. She plopped herself and the book on the couch and listened to Cheryl's voicemail.

"Hey there! I hope today was good! Me and a couple of friends started a book club. You should join us! Right now we're at the part where we figure out what to call ourselves and what our first book is gonna be. Ha! Okay, so we really haven't started it yet, which means it's a good time to jump in. One of the women is Adrienne, who you know from my cookie swap. If you know anyone else who we should ask to join, let me know. We're thinking six is a good number. You'd make four. Call me and let me know how you made out with the magic. Or just text me and let me know you're alive."

How did I make out with the magic? Willow leafed through The Morgan Manual while she thought about the answer. Her eyes lingered on the page containing Morgan's birth announcement.

Kevin and Willow Walker

are pleased to announce the birth of their daughter

Morgan Erin Walker

Born at 2:38 a.m. on December 15, 2012

Weighing 5 pounds 12 ounces

And perfect in every way!

Something felt weird, like a puzzle she had yet to solve. *Two-thirty-eight a.m. Two-thirty-eight a.m.* Why was that important? Willow leaned back and shut her eyes, trying to capture something just out of her grasp. Her dream! The Clock on the wall said two-eighteen! The obstetrician had recommended a C-section at two-eighteen a.m. Willow picked up her phone and Googled *How long does it take for an emergency C-section?*

"An emergency C-section is one that happens very quickly due to immediate concern for the health of the mother and/or baby. The goal is that no more than 30 minutes pass between the decision to perform an emergency C-section and delivery, but it can take up to 75 minutes."

They got Morgan out in twenty minutes! She hadn't delayed a thing with her plea to continue trying to deliver vaginally! It was her doctor's failure to act earlier that caused the trauma. *All is as it should be,* stated a voice in her head. Willow went to the kitchen and put the folding chair into her reading box. There was no need for Kleenex and blanket this time. She looked at Willow's Happiness List, tacked above the shelf. There was one more box to check off. She logged onto her CP Community site and queried: "Hello everyone! I'm looking to hire a reliable aide for my seven-year-old daughter in the Atkinson, New Hampshire area ..."

Namaste, my dear friend Cheryl. I can't wait to join your book club.

September 23, 2020

CHAPTER 36 ~ MATTHEW

Salem, New Hampshire

Change was difficult for Matthew, even if he were the one making the change. His mother was fond of repeating a story from his childhood to illustrate just how true that was. She told it something like this:

"We used to have this ratty, old blue chair. We got rid of it one day and replaced it with a nice, brown, leather recliner. Matthew came home from school and went ballistic! 'I hate this stupid chair!' he yelled. 'I want the blue chair!' I tried to console him by showing him how fun it was to push the up and down button for the footrest, but it was no use. He wanted the old chair and kept screaming, 'I want my blue chair!'

When he found out the blue chair was still in the basement waiting to go to the dump, he marched downstairs and refused to get out of it. Our basement was creepy, filled with cobwebs and water-stained boxes from the time the well pump let go. Joe had to drag him up the stairs, kicking and screaming, when it was time for bed. Every day after school he went right to the old, blue chair. He would take his snack and do his homework surrounded by that moldy cellar smell. I was so worried about damaging his little psyche that I wouldn't let Joe bring the damn thing to the dump! We finally got rid of it eight years later when he went off to college! I'm pretty sure that's what caused his allergies and all his sinus infections."

Matthew wished he could say some part of his mother's story was a gross exaggeration, but it was more like a metaphor for his life. He was still dealing with his crappy sinuses.

*

Today Matthew was going to meet a woman about a job. She was a friend of a friend, and the hours she was looking to fill would fit perfectly into his doctorate schedule. He hoped she wouldn't ask a ton of questions. It was complicated to explain getting a Ph.D. in sports medicine without becoming a medical doctor, but Matthew had no interest in treating patients. His goal was to research new technologies in the field of sports medicine. Keeping athletes alive, conditioned, and safe had turned into a passion for him after his best friend was paralyzed during a high school hockey game. Matthew was also on the ice that night. It had changed everything for both of them.

*

Mrs. Walker was younger than he thought she would be. Or maybe she just looked younger than her age. At any rate, she was a surprise. Her European accent, the curly hair bundled in a contraption on the top of her head, and the summer skirt and sandals made her look younger than him. Everyone was looking younger than him these days. He was thirty-three, mostly bald, and bespeckled with glasses he had worn since second grade. For graduation, his parents offered to get him Lasik surgery to correct his vision, but the glasses were part of his face. Taking them off felt like driving without a windshield. Plus he hated change.

"Matthew, this is my beautiful Morgan." Mrs. Walker swept her hand across the air in front of her as though she were introducing the next performer on a variety show. Morgan was a beauty. Had her features not been contorted by cerebral palsy, she would have been her mother's twin. Her slack jaw muscles and open mouth had created problems common to the disease—protruding and misaligned upper teeth and drooling. Matt stopped himself from analyzing the little girl and kneeled to say hello.

"Wow, Morgan! It's so nice to meet you! You look just like your mom." Her eyes shined, completing her award-winning smile. She made a noise of delight.

"I'm Matthew," he continued. "Your Mom tells me you're seven years old."

"Eight before Christmas," Mrs. Walker added. "We had a snowman party last year, but this year it's going to be all Angels." She smiled at her daughter as she spoke. "Do you want to go in the box while Mama and Matthew talk?"

In the box? He stood awkwardly as Mrs. Walker began wheeling Morgan out of the living room.

"You should come see the box. It's part of the reason I need you." Now he was nervous.

*

Within minutes it all made sense. Mrs. Walker needed someone to take care of Morgan while she worked. Her career as a book narrator had taken off, and evenings were no longer enough hours to get the job done. It was a little weird that most of the time she would be home while he took care of Morgan, like a mother's helper. *Well, that's what I am.* Whatever arrangements they made today would be contingent on things working out over the next few visits.

"Morgan has never had a man in her life," Mrs. Walker said, then reddened. "Except doctors, of course."

"She didn't seem scared," he replied. Mrs. Walker nodded.

"My schedule is flexible," she continued. "I do not care if we change things from week to week—you can just let me know what is your availability." Her accent thickened as she talked. "Are you ready to be a good pod mate?

"Excuse me?"

"A pod mate. For the pandemic? I canceled all of my daughter's therapies because I could not have someone who was going from house to house. Do you have a small life?" she asked.

"Yes," he answered truthfully. "Very small."

"Good," she said. It was the first time Matthew had impressed a woman with his virtually non-existent social life.

"This week I have Thursday and Friday available," he said. But most weeks it's Tuesday and Wednesday."

"Good. Let's do this Thursday at ten," she replied.

"Thank you Mrs. Walker. I will see you on Thursday."

"Call me Willow."

"I will-ow," he said, oddly, when he meant to say, "I will Willow." Matthew dashed for the door without a goodbye for Morgan or a thank you to his new boss. The job was off to an odd start. Now to go home and tell his girlfriend.

*

"I can't believe you didn't check with me before taking that job!" Faith was still in attack mode after forty-five minutes of beating a dead horse.

"I didn't think—"

"That's right Matthew! You didn't think! I'm a respiratory therapist! In a pandemic! As careful as I am, it would be nothing for me to bring this virus home to you! You'd be fine! That little girl you're taking care of wouldn't be! How could you be so stupid?" A question she had asked him every few sentences for almost an hour. A braver Matthew would have thrown out an Alzheimer's joke about now. It was easier to let her keep ranting, a skill he had learned from his father—although at this point his Dad would have been all "yes dears." Matthew was young and stupid. He kept going.

"She asked if my life was small and I said yes because, Faith, our life *is* small! We don't go anywhere!" He knew that sentence would take her right back to how stupid he was.

"We don't go anywhere because I work with Covid patients! How could you be so stupid?"

Hmm. Maybe I am learning to predict women, Matthew thought, fighting a nervous smile.

"Call her up and tell her you can't take the job," Faith demanded.

"No," Matthew's answer surprised them both. "I'm already committed, and I think she really needs me." He could have left out that last line and saved himself from a full-out breakup.

"She needs you? You moved in here—with your contained, little life—so we could weather the pandemic together! I rearranged *everything* for you! Kicked out a perfectly good roommate, changed my hours at the hospital—all so we could be together through this fucking thing without having to worry!" Faith paused and took it down a notch. This was normally the moment in a fight where she would tell him what he had to do to absolve himself. She didn't disappoint.

"You know you're gonna have to move out, right? I'm not gonna be responsible for giving a deadly virus to a handicapped kid."

"I know." He wondered what his face looked like. Sad? Relieved? Whatever it was, his soon-to-be ex-girlfriend saw it.

"You fucking bastard. You didn't get rid of your apartment, did you?"

"I—I sublet it. The guy—"

"I want you, and everything you own, gone by the end of my shift tomorrow." Faith turned her back on him. Matthew knew he had gotten off easy, he had behaved like a first-class ass. Then she whirled around, tore off the diamond necklace he had given her for her birthday, and screamed, "You can start by taking this! It should have been a fucking ring on my finger! I can't believe I wasted five fucking years on you!" *Okay, now she's done.*

*

Matthew's first day on the job was a mixed bag. He had a good grasp on the physiology of Morgan's issues, but not the reality of them. Sure, he knew why her lower extremities were in a scissor position—hypertonia in the legs, hips, and pelvis, tight adductors—but not how to put her leg braces on, with their layers of sock and batting to stop pain and chafing. He had done it on a fellow student and a rescue mannikin, but never a fragile human. Everything Willow taught him that day required more than he knew. She was exacting. "Every method has a madness," she said to him, clearly softening an admonishment with a joke.

Willow explained how food aspiration was the leading cause of pneumonia in children with cerebral palsy. The texture of Morgan's food was extremely important so she could swallow without aspirating, though she didn't swallow anything at his first attempt.

"It's on the back of her tongue," Willow instructed, pulling his arm down to stop him from giving her the next bite. "You have to watch her throat for the swallow—and get yourself and the spoon lower so she doesn't lift her head so high." Of course. The chin tuck technique. He had read these things but never experienced them. Everything Matthew knew was in theory only.

*

"I'm going into the box for an hour, leave you two to your own devices," Willow declared, after a forty-five-minute lunch session and cleanup. *I must not be screwing up too badly*, Matthew decided.

"Do you have a stroller? It's beautiful out. Maybe I could take Morgan for a walk." The look of panic on Willow's face couldn't be mistaken for anything else. "We won't go far and I'll have my cellphone," he assured.

“Morgan has never been out of this house with anyone other than me,” Willow said. “And I have rarely left without her. Let’s not push things.”

“Sounds good,” he said, hiding his disappointment that she didn’t trust him. “How ‘bout if I run out to my car and get my guitar? I promise not to be too loud.” The guitar wasn’t something he always carried with him. It was in the back of his old Ford Explorer with just about everything else he owned. The sublet wouldn’t be out until the next week, so Matthew had been commuting from his parent’s house, an hour and a half away. He told his mother Faith’s co-worker had tested positive so he was staying away to be on the safe side. She, too, had been rooting for a ring instead of a necklace. Matthew was becoming adept at disappointing the women in his life, a thought that made not failing Morgan and Willow take on greater meaning.

*

By his third visit, Matthew was on his own with Morgan, with Willow beginning a recording session a half-hour after he arrived. Because even the smallest interruption would ruin a fifteen-minute block of audio, they developed an alert system in case he needed her. It was two signs. One said WHEN YOU HAVE A MINUTE. The other simply said I NEED YOU. Thankfully, Matthew managed to figure things out on his own that morning. He did Morgan’s physical therapy, then a corny guitar/speech therapy session. Though it was obvious Morgan was an easy laugher, Matthew was duly impressed by his previously hidden clown talent. They were laughing so hard that neither noticed Willow.

“I need a break,” she said. “Let’s take a walk.”

*

“You’re a natural with her,” Willow said.

"No one is more surprised than me," admitted Matthew. "I'm usually better with books than people."

"I might be too," she said.

"Tell me about the book you're narrating." Morgan had fallen asleep, effectively removing herself from their conversation.

'It's a complicated story—and yet, the oldest story in the world," she started. "A love triangle between a woman who loves her husband very deeply and the man she's drawn to beyond her control."

"Ah, a romance."

"More than a romance," she said. "It involves generations of decisions that all factor into the collision of these two people. She is Greek. Her husband is an American. Her lover is an Italian immigrant. That's why the author chose me as narrator—Greek, Italian, and English, I am fluent in them all."

"Were you born in Italy or Greece?" Matthew asked.

"Italy. I left when I was twenty—a man."

"Morgan's father?" Since when do I ask personal questions?

"No, a different man." She didn't seem to find that embarrassing. Matthew was alarmed to realize he somehow thought she should—a totally chauvinistic reaction. Being with Willow made him analyze his shortcomings, whereas Faith readily pointed out his failings, forcing Matthew to defend himself and then believe his own defense.

"And you?" she asked, breaking into his thoughts.

"I was born here," he answered. Her laugh was unexpected and loud.

"I meant do you have a girlfriend—or, um, a boyfriend?"

"An ex-girlfriend." His quick response reeked of a masculinity statement. Why was he suddenly analyzing everything? "We broke up two weeks ago." *Stop talking, fool.* "She's a respiratory therapist at Mass General. I couldn't take care of Morgan if we lived together …"

"I don't know how to feel about that," Willow responded.

"Me neither." Matthew suddenly felt … wrong. *Oh, Jesus! What is the matter with me?* The rest of their walk continued in silence, broken only by the end of Morgan's nap.

*

After moving back into his apartment, Matthew saw how much more free time he had. No commute or evenings spent pleasing a girlfriend had left him with tons of hours for research on his thesis. One night, he texted Willow and offered her a third workday. She declined and he over-analyzed his disappointment. Then he analyzed his over-analyzing. In the middle of his analysis, Matthew got a call from Faith. He let it go to voicemail but listened to it the minute it went through.

"Hey. I canceled our cable, which was in your name. I'm just gonna stick with Hulu and Netflix. Then I worried that I might have canceled your apartment cable too. Just a head's up. I hope all is good."

Was a casual call normal three weeks after a huge breakup? Was this an attempt at reconciliation? Matthew had no idea. He and Faith had never broken up before. They hadn't had to, his master's degree and her stint as a traveling therapist had given them plenty of breaks over the years. For the first time since their fight, Matthew let himself wonder if he missed her. He couldn't decide, so he went to bed—the only place where he was certain the answer was yes.

*

Every shift included some time with Willow. Their conversations became relaxed and personal.

"So why did you and Kevin break up?" he asked when the subject of her husband came up.

"I didn't love him enough. It became obvious after I transferred his meager amount to the volume of love I felt for Morgan. I wanted to make it about his lack of commitment to our daughter, but we both knew better. After the malpractice suit, she and I were all set, so he moved back to England. How long were you and Faith together?"

"Five years."

"She didn't want to marry you?" Matthew marveled at Willow's ability to cut to the chase.

"I didn't ask her," he answered. "I have a hard time with change."

Without warning, she laughed in his face.

"That is a load of bullshit! What was your first career choice?"

"Orthopedic surgeon."

"How many times have you moved since college?"

"Four." Five if I count moving back to my apartment.

"How many jobs have you had?"

"I don't know. Ten? Where are you going with this?" Matthew was getting aggravated.

"You don't have a problem with change, Matthew. You have a problem with commitment. Why did you take this job?"

"Because—"

"Because you knew it would blow up your relationship," Willow answered for him—something Faith did all the time. His mother did it too.

Matthew didn't know what to say.

"You know I'm not attracted to you, right?"

"Of course," he said, indignantly. *But don't worry about hurting my feelings ...*

"People don't stay with someone for five years without a reason," she continued.

"You did," he retorted.

"It was three years, and I knew my reason. I wanted a baby." *Again, with the honesty.*

"You need to figure out if it was lack of love or fear of commitment that made you break up with her." She said it like a command, then reached inside the tapestry purse slung across her chest and handed Matthew a small drawstring pouch.

"Take this and figure out what you really want. I won't have you using Morgan as an excuse to not have a life. I already tried that, and it doesn't work."

*

The fear of her demanding to know how it went was what impelled Matthew to use the mala beads that night. The whole thing was so strange. In three short weeks, Willow had replaced Faith as the demanding woman in his life. True to his analytical, second-guessing nature, Matthew made a list of possible asks then threw the whole thing out in favor of Willow's insistence he figure out what he really wanted. *Help me figure out what I really want.* Seven slow breaths. "Help me figure out what I really want …"

*

Saying the mantra turned out to be extremely satisfying. Matthew felt a little let down when it was finished, wishing he could have chanted for another hour. Of course, he was going to analyze the mala bead process, beginning with how he felt. His pen and paper sat right beside him on the floor. Matthew picked up the pen to write the word *satisfying*. Instead, his hand wrote, *I want to be Craig's best friend.* "Well that's crazy," he said aloud, feeling a tingling sensation from head to toe, and a cold deep fear in his belly. He tried to record these new sensations. The words *I want to be Craig's best friend* again wrote themselves on the paper. "Oh fuck," he said, dropping the pen and jumping up from the towel he had placed on the floor. The mala beads were still in his hand. He flung them like they were on fire.

"I must be having a stroke," he said to the empty room and ran to the bathroom to check his face in the mirror—no lopsided drooping, even with the test smile. He opened the medicine cabinet and grabbed the Advil—at that point, he would have taken whatever was in there—and choked down two capsules by drinking water straight from the faucet. He envisioned Morgan swallowing. "What the fuck is going on?" Unable to calm himself, Matthew laid down on his bed and covered his eyes with crossed arms. *Just breathe, it'll pass,* his mind instructed. Everything was swirling in a kaleidoscope of color. When it settled, he was at his high school hockey game. His best friend, Craig, had the puck and an open net, with a defenseman from the other team bearing down on him. Matthew pushed hard, hoping to intercept the defenseman before he got to Craig. A final thrust and a dive, but he missed him by inches. From his belly slide across the ice, Matthew experienced the scene at the same angle as his friend. A low last-minute check sent Craig soaring head-first into the goalpost, and forever out of the life he had known.

*

Matthew was covered in sweat and hyperventilating. It had taken years to erase that scene from his mind. He didn't want it back. It was only after he had stopped visiting Craig regularly that the nightmares went away. He grabbed his phone and texted Willow: *"What the fuck?"*

She texted back immediately: "I know it's hard, but stay with it, Matthew."

Stay with it? He couldn't get out of it! He sat at the kitchen counter with a different pen and paper and tried to collect his thoughts. He would write something normal. A grocery list. Five minutes later every line was filled with just two words: *Love hurts*, written over and over again, the full length of the legal pad. It didn't take an emotional genius to see where this was going, but how could he make it stop?

Think it through. Think it through. Think it through. He suddenly had control over his words, and began writing:

> *Craig was my best friend.*
>
> *I feel responsible for Craig's accident.*
>
> *It was too painful to keep loving him, so I made myself detach.*
>
> *Loving Faith makes me responsible for her happiness.*
>
> *What if I ruin her life too?*
>
> *It is less painful to detach than to take the risk of hurting someone I love.*

Matthew felt his heart rate return to normal. His head cleared, and his surroundings leveled back to their familiar 3D dimension. Just when he thought he was on the other side of this madness, he became overwrought with despair. "I miss you, Faith," he blubbered, laying his head on the counter and dissolving in tears. Matthew couldn't judge how long that state lasted before he was suddenly filled with hope and resolve. "I can fix this! She still loves me!" He raised his head. The microwave clock said eleven-thirty. Six hours had passed since he began the mala bead journey. Faith would be just walking through her apartment door, finished with her three to eleven shift. He picked up his phone and called her. She answered on the first ring.

"How was work?" he asked.

"Matthew—"

"Faith. If you can forgive me, I know beyond any earthly doubt that we are meant to be together. I've figured out what's really important to me, and it's you." Matthew wasn't an expert on love, but he guessed that the crying on the other end of the phone was a positive sign. *Thank you, Willow. Namaste.*

October 5, 2020

FINAL CHAPTER ~ CLAIRE

Cape Cod, Massachusetts

Claire suspected her husband was still in the house, or at least she hoped that was the case since she had been speaking to him non-stop all morning.

"Joe, I'm gonna wear this gray dress even though you didn't love it—and don't say that you did, because we both know it was never your favorite. I think 'drab' was the word you used. But I can't wear the black and tan one because it bunches up when I hug people and I'm not gonna keep fussing with it all day." The problem was Claire had already given the funeral director Joe's black and tan tie. It was one of their things—matching his tie to her outfit, a little quirk that had created quite a tie collection for her husband over the years. No matter how wild the print of her dress, a tie for Joe was part of the project. Claire had become so adept at tie-making that she could whip one up in thirty minutes. *I could probably make one to match this gray dress before heading to the funeral home.* The thought relapsed her into tears. *Why would I make a tie for a dress my husband hated?* She ripped the drab gray dress over her head with reckless consequences to her hair and changed back into the black and tan dress. "Okay, Joe. You win."

*

Claire stood in the doorway of the large funeral home where everyone would be spaced apart and encouraged to wear a mask. "Maybe all funerals should be this way—put on a mask and stay the hell away from the crazy widow," Claire muttered under her black and tan mask to her best friend, Susi, who hadn't left her side since Joe's death. Susi squeezed her arm and pointed to Matthew and Faith, who were heading toward them.

"You made it!" Claire said brightly to her eldest son and his fiancé.

"Mom, we slept at your house last night. We had breakfast together this morning. We pulled out of the driveway right behind you." Matthew looked worried.

"She's just kidding," Faith said, providing the first test hug for Claire's dress. "How are you doing, Claire?"

"Oh, you know. Just another day in paradise!"

The good part about a devoted, thirty-five-year marriage was you didn't have to act morose when your spouse died. Everyone knew you were hanging on by a thread, so any behavior was acceptable. Pointless really, since being married to Joe had already given Claire license to be herself. "As if I could stop you," was Joe's well-used line about how she behaved. Or sometimes he said, "Go for it—I'll sit back and enjoy the show." Joe was the straight guy in their wedded vaudeville act. The guy who found her keys, reminded her to charge her phone, and switched to Shirley Temples whenever Claire ordered a third glass of wine. "You should stop babysitting me," she would say. "What am I gonna do if you're not here to follow me around?" *Well, it looks like we're gonna find that out now, huh Joe?*

Matthew was repeating something that Claire was not understanding. His mask was a good excuse for her confusion, but not the reason. He pointed to the door where his sister and brother-in-law were entering the funeral home. Melanie had the baby with her.

"I thought you weren't bringing the baby?" Claire's voice sounded loud in the empty room. Not empty—a coffin sat at one end.

"I couldn't bring myself to leave him." Melanie immediately handed the baby over to Claire, as was expected. Claire pulled off one ear of her mask and buried her face in his smell, leaving a make-up stain in her wake. “Here comes Joey,” Melanie said.

Joey was the afterthought in the family lineup—a decision made late one night, a week after Melanie began first grade. “I don’t think I’m done having babies, Joe,” was what Claire said to get the ball rolling. “You sure we need another one?” he had asked. She nodded her head and got naked. “Alrighty then,” he said. “As if I could stop you.” They named him Joseph Junior, “Joey”—an honor normally reserved for the firstborn. “I don’t want him to feel like an afterthought,” she remembered saying.

“Joey. How you doin', baby?” He had been Joe’s little shadow.

“Good, Ma. How ‘bout you?”

“Another day in paradise,” she answered. The mortician appeared out of nowhere.

“Is the family ready for the final viewing?” he asked.

“Is the family ever ready for the final viewing?” Claire asked in response.

“Please follow me,” he said, as he turned, with elegance and grace, to lead them toward Joe’s dead body.

*

Autumn on Cape Cod was Claire’s favorite time of year, perfect for so many things—weddings, that last-chance clam bake—a tented after-funeral gathering. Today was breathtaking. Clear and sunny, with temperatures in the high sixties. *If only Joe were here to enjoy it.*

“Joe would have loved this,” Claire endlessly repeated in her ‘thanks for coming’ moment with each guest. She surmised she wasn’t the first widow to make this observation. When you gather all a dead man’s favorite people together in one room—or in this case, one tent—the only thing missing is the dead man.

The service had been sweet, if a bit impersonal. A Catholic church short-coming, as far as Claire was concerned. The pamphlet in the burial packet was pretty clear on the dos and don'ts. *"The funeral liturgy is a celebration of salvation and mercy, of grace and eternal life. It is not meant to be a commemoration (much less a canonization) of the person who has died."* Joe was not much on religion, anyway. "I think the big picture is a little bigger than a bunch of rules and rituals," he would say. Joe was a deep thinker with a simple persona. "Just give me a decent open mic night," was the request he made, years before he died. *Okay, Joe. Here it is.* With Joey's old karaoke microphone in her hand as a prop, Claire entered the tent and stood in front of the dessert table to address their friends and family. The conversation tapered to a murmur as she braced herself to speak.

"Hello, everyone. Thanks for coming today. Joe would have loved this. Years ago, when we talked about what we'd like for our funerals, he accused me of trying to control things from the grave because I knew exactly which flattering portrait I wanted on my closed casket, what hymns I wanted sung, who my pallbearers would be—although I secretly hoped they would all be too old to carry a casket by the time I died." Claire got the laugh she knew she would. *Definitely not a sympathy laugh.* She continued. "I had a plan for everything. But not Joe. He didn't care what we did for his funeral. 'I'll take an open mic night,' he said. 'Don't even bother with the obituary, just let my family and friends tell my story."

"So without further ado, if anyone wants to come up and share some thoughts or a story about Joe, now is your chance to be part of Joe's Open Mic Event." Claire barely made it to her front-row seat before someone came forward and took the plastic mic from where she had placed it next to Joe's favorite dessert, Boston Cream Pie. *Let the show begin ...*

*

Claire was exhausted like she had just attended a week-long cocktail party. She couldn't imagine what deranged things she may have said to people. Someone should have been filming. It would make a great reality TV show—*Crazy Grieving Widows Say the Darndest Things!* Or maybe they could just call it *Funeral Follies.* The producers would encourage family members to pick fights and wrestle in the church aisles. Family fun at its best. *Not our family.* Either way, the whole day was a blur.

As soon as the last mourner left, she changed out of her inconvenient dress and into her sweatpants, then headed straight for the sunroom. At the beginning of the summer, she and Joe had added the three-season room to the back of their house. "We're gonna live in this thing until it's too cold to be out here," Joe had declared, totally in love with the space. "Then we'll get a fake fireplace. Screw the electric bill!" Now, sitting in his oversized comfortable chair, Claire watched as the caterers folded up the tables and stacked the chairs. Joey was out there saying nice things to the staff. He was just like Joe, who would unobtrusively oversee things without ever giving an order. They were all more like Joe than they were her. Even Melanie had his sneaky sense of humor and steady personality. Joe had genetically watered down her family's nut-case traits. Claire shut her eyes and tried to imagine filling Joe's shoes with this growing brood of theirs. *No chance.* She would never be enough. Her half of their dynamic duo was the weak half. She didn't have a clue how to even *be* herself without Joe. Most of her schtick was predicated on Joe's expected response. He was the mechanical governor of her speed-demon personality. Who would be there to legitimize her and make certain she didn't make a complete fool of herself? Claire wanted to give in to the despair of these thoughts, except that every couple of minutes a family member would drift in to check on her, forcing her to buck up. She couldn't decide if she wanted to be alone. *Of course, I don't want to be alone. I want my husband!* Matthew came in, shutting the glass doors behind him.

"How you doing, Mom?" It was the same question everyone asked, but so much sweeter coming from the lips of her Matty—a nickname he abandoned, but she hadn't.

"I'm hanging in there, kiddo. Everything going okay out there?"

"Yup. Melanie and Scott are getting ready to leave. The baby's starting to lose it."

"He's been an angel. Is Faith pregnant?" Like the daughter's wedding scene in *The Godfather*, Claire had free reign to ask anything on this funeral day.

"No. Why would you think that?" She almost laughed at his look of panic.

"Last week when you guys told me and Dad about the engagement, it seemed kinda sudden—"

"Mom, we've been dating for five years." Matthew sounded annoyed.

"That's what Dad said."

Matthew took a seat on the ottoman in front of her. He held something in his hands.

"This is gonna sound crazy, but I have this *thing* for you—like spiritual magic. I know it's too late for a miracle for Dad, but there's gonna be something you need—maybe something you don't even know about yet—"

"Matty, what are you talking about?" He sounded a little unbalanced—*maybe he really is my kid.*

Matthew opened his hand, holding out a little bag. "These are mala beads—"

Claire felt light-headed and blinked hard to regain her focus.

"Where did you get those?" Her voice was a whisper, disbelief sucking the air from her throat.

"The woman I work for in New Hampshire. You don't have to take them—"

Claire pulled the bag from his open hand, the swirling in her head making her feel faint.

*

The spaghetti stain on the pouch was barely visible. She had thrown the beads in the trash the day Susi had given them to her, angrily scraping a Weight Watcher's frozen dinner on top of them. Her husband was in the hospital with Covid. His oxygen levels were sinking fast and the doctors were getting ready to put him on a ventilator. Claire remembered exactly how she felt, like her best friend was an idiot if she believed a necklace could save Joe.

"If prayers and magic could stop this virus, no one would be dying," she had said to Susi but took the bag anyway.

Later that night, Claire crept out of bed and went to the kitchen, afraid to challenge fate by throwing the mala beads away. While the gauze bag was drying from her attempt to clean it, she read the directions and did the mantra. "Give me more time with my Joe," she begged of the magic. The next morning her husband's condition turned around and continued to improve until, eventually, he was released from the hospital.

In the months that followed, she and Joe would watch their youngest son graduate from college, welcome their first grandchild just days after burying Claire's mother, and later rejoice in the engagement of their oldest son. Claire would have traded her soul to keep her husband by her side for those moments. It was seven months of pulling tighter the bonds that glued their family together—seven magical months.

*

Claire closed her eyes. A vision of a desperate young man holding a gun rolled over the movie screen in her mind. She hadn't told anyone about the robbery at the beach, instead adding the man, like a fourth child, to her nightly prayers. *Dear God, please keep my children safe, and let every stumble lead them to greater happiness.*

Claire pulled the strand of beads from its worn bag and held them to her heart. She took seven deep breaths. A vibration hummed in her chest as the power of the beads connected her to the oneness of everything. "*You're not alone.*" The voice was Joe's. Joy and gratitude filled her being. Claire finally knew, without question, that her husband would walk by her side every day for the rest of her life.

*

"Mom, are you okay?" Matthew's worried voice broke through her vision.

Claire slipped the beads into their bag and handed them back to her son.

"Thank you, my sweet Matty, but you can give this to somebody else—I've already had my miracle."

I love you, Joe.

~Namaste

Charities near and dear to the characters of
THE MALA BEADS

(Page)

CLAIRE (9) **American Heart Association** ~ For nearly 100 years, the American Heart Association has been fighting heart disease and stroke, helping families and communities thrive.
www.heart.org

NATE (15) **Mashpee Wampanoag Tribe** ~ The Mashpee Wampanoag Tribe, also known as the People of the First Light, oversee 150 acres of land in Mashpee and support the Mashpee Wampanoag Tribe and its many programs, services, and efforts to preserve the Wampanoag Peoples way of life.
www.mashpeewampanoagtribe-nsn.gov

LORI (23) **Independence House, Inc.** ~ Cape Cod's leading domestic and sexual violence emergency housing resource, counseling, and advocacy center to address and prevent domestic and sexual violence. www.independencehouse.org

DEBBIE (27) **Beauty Changes Lives** ~ Scholarships Mentorships Inspiration. www.beautychangeslives.org

TONY (33) **Area 23/Southern Indiana** Alcoholics Anonymous. www.area23aa.org

JAIMIE (36) **Memphis Area Prevention Coalition** ~ Promoting community safety by educating youth and adults about substance abuse and prevention. www.memphisprevention.org

ANGEL (41) **Give 365 Memphis** ~ Community Foundation of Greater Memphis Scholarship Fund ~ Inspired, collective giving makes an impact on our members and grantees—bringing those two together in a meaningful way that creates more intentional philanthropists and builds a Greater Memphis. www.give365memphis.org

KHAN (46) PAM **The Pakistan Association of Memphis** is the home to Pakistani Americans based in Memphis TN. PAM is a non-governmental, non-profit organization. www.pakmem.com

DANI (50) **Mid-South Food Bank Mobile Pantry** ~ A Mobile Pantry is a method of direct client distribution in partnership with an organization that acts as a host site. The Mobile Pantry utilizes refrigerated vehicles to provide nutritious food in a drive-thru setup. www.midsouthfoodbank.org

BARBARA (55) **Aging Commission of The Mid-South Memphis** ~ We offer programs that make a difference in the lives of all older adults and adults living with disabilities. From the older person who can remain at home if they receive the right services to those who are healthy and can benefit from the activities and socialization provided by our community-based programs, such as senior centers, we´re here to help. www.shelbycountytn.gov/3433/Aging-Commission-of-the-mid-South

KALIE (60) **The Bee Conservancy** ~ Protecting Bees, Building Habitat, and Strengthening Communities Together. www.thebeeconservancy.org

AARON (65) **The American Kidney Fund** ~ From prevention and research to treatments and transplants, The American Kidney Fund takes a comprehensive approach to working on behalf of 37 million Americans with kidney disease. www.kidneyfund.org

JOHN (69) **NEDS New England Donor Services** ~ To be a leader in the development and implementation of strategies to increase the life-saving and life-enhancing gifts of organ and tissue donation through effective relationships with our clinical partners, donor families, and communities we serve. www.neds.org

CHARLOTTE (75) **Friends Who Stutter** ~ The National Association of Young People Who Stutter. www.friendswhostutter.org

MARIANNE (79) **Christopher and Dana Reeve Foundation** ~ Today's Care. Tomorrow's Cure ~ We are dedicated to curing spinal cord injury by advancing innovative research and improving the quality of life for individuals and families impacted by paralysis. www.christopherreeve.org

SANURA (85) **Give Back Yoga Foundation** ~ Our mission is to bring the benefits of yoga to all people, especially those facing mental and physical hardship (e.g. addiction, incarceration, poverty, military service, and eating disorders).
www.givebackyoga.org

BARRY (95) **Orchid Project** ~ Orchid Project is a UK-based NGO that is catalyzing the global movement to end female genital cutting (FGC). FGC is a human rights violation that harms the lives of girls, women, and their communities. Together, we can create a world free from Female Genital Cutting. www.orchidproject.org

ROBERT (99) **Breast Cancer Research Foundation** ~ When you give to BCRF, you're funding critical hours in the lab. More time for research means more progress towards ending breast cancer—and longer, healthier lives for the ones we love. Every moment matters for people who have breast cancer, so please do all you can to help right away. www.bcrf.org

VANESSA (105) **American Pregnancy Association** ~ From conception through birth and all the wonderful in-betweens, our nurses and pregnancy educators are here to provide the resources and information you need for the healthiest possible pregnancy. www.americanpregnancy.org

KATRINA (110) **Saint John's Program for Real Change** ~ Saint John's Program for Real Change, located in Sacramento, California, supports women in crisis and their children through a comprehensive 12-18 month residential program developed to help them build a successful new life for themselves and their families. www.saintjohnsprogram.org

JUAN (117) **The Muwekma Ohlone Preservation Foundation** ~ Partnering for a Brighter Future for the Muwekma Ohlone People
www.muwekma.org/muwekma-ohlone-preservation-foundation.html

FRANK (126) **Solano Community Animal Response Team** ~ working toward animal safety during natural disasters.
www.greatnonprofits.org/org/solano-community-animal-response-team

JESS (133) **Solano Pride Center** ~ Celebrating 25 years of inclusivity ~ 1234 Empire Street Fairfield, CA 94533 707-207-3430

SETH (145) **The Wilderness Society** ~ An environmental organization working with local communities and heeding both rigorous science and traditional Indigenous knowledge to build a network of lands and waters that will sustain people and nature for generations to come. www.wilderness.org

BELLA (155) **Alzheimer Society of Canada** ~ Whether you want to learn more about the programs and services we offer, or find dementia-related information specific to your needs, the Alzheimer Society has the education and resources to help. www.alzheimer.ca

AMELIA (163) **MOSAIC** ~ Improving communities by welcoming and supporting immigrants and refugees to settle and start a new life in Vancouver British Columbia, CA www.mosaicbc.org

DIANE (178) **Lower Mainland Grief Recovery Society (LMGRS)** ~ To support the bereaved in the greater Vancouver, BC area to rebuild their lives by helping them understand their grief in a safe and confidential environment. www.lmgr.ca

JANELLE (182) **Adler Centre** ~ Cultivating Belonging with Affordable counseling services for Individuals, relationships, and families in Greater Vancouver, BC. www.adlercentre.ca

SELMA (190) **Catherine White Holman Wellness Centre** ~ We provide low-barrier wellness and legal services to Two-Spirit, transgender, and gender non-conforming people in a way that is respectful and celebratory of clients' identity and self-expression. www.cwhwc.com

CHILI (202) **Vancouver Community College Scholarship Fund for Nursing Program** provides scholarships for nursing education within the Greater Vancouver BC area. www.vcc.ca

PETER (214) **The Treehouse Vancouver Child and Youth Advocacy Centre** ~ focuses on getting Vancouver's children and youth who have experienced abuse back to feeling like kids again. www.treehousevancouver.ca

DAPHNE (219) **The Trauma Foundation** ~ The Trauma Foundation's mission is to support the healing of unresolved trauma for individuals, families, and communities.
www.thetraumafoundation.org

BETTY (227) **Clean Trails** ~ Step by step, and little by little, we aim to eliminate waste on all the trails that grace our public lands. www.cleantrails.org

CHERYL (236) **Asthma and Allergy Foundation of America** ~ The Asthma and Allergy Foundation of America, a not-for-profit organization founded in 1953, is the leading patient organization for people with asthma and allergies, and the oldest asthma and allergy patient group in the world. www.aafa.org

WILLOW (251) **Cerebral Palsy Research Network** ~ focuses on optimizing the lifelong health and wellness of people with cerebral palsy and their families through high-quality research, education, and community programming. www.cprn.org

MATTHEW (264) **Granite State Independent Living (GSIL)** ~ With the help of our local New Hampshire communities, we assist people with tools for living life independently, so they can change their lives for the better. www.gsil.org

SUSI (Claire's best friend and the one who gave her the mala beads)

~ **Oneness Golden Age Movement United States & Canada** ~
Sri Amma Bhagavan's worldwide humanitarian mission to end world suffering by transforming humanity's inner state into one of peace and higher consciousness in order to create a world that works for everyone.

The Golden Age Movement USA—Canada is one of many communities around the globe supporting this grand vision for humanity. Be a powerful force of love and compassion in the world. www.74kgoldenage.com

Printed in the USA
CPSIA information can be obtained
at www.ICGtesting.com
CBHW032330011224
18292CB00010B/537